ACCLAIM
DEN

MW00779299

THE OATH

<u>2016 BAIPA BOOK AWARD FOR BEST FICTION</u>

"Dennis Koller's mystery-thriller debut is a strong one. The novel has it all; intrigue, politics, murder and romance. Combined with characters and dialogue that are ultimately believable, *The Oath* is a real page-turner."

—The Irish Herald Book Review

"A dying former POW, four dead women, a world-weary homicide cop and the Vietnam War are expertly woven together by Dennis Koller in a masterful piece of storytelling that will leave you guessing right until the last few pages of 'The Oath.' An excellent book with just the right amount of social commentary woven into its pages to make it not just another murder mystery."

—Mike Billington
Author of 'Corpus Delectable'

"This is the book today's sailors, soldiers, marines and airmen want to take on their long deployments for those short moments they can get away and unload their minds on an entertaining novel."

—CAPT Kris Carlock, USN (Retired)

"An exciting and well written story with a plot that could have been the real life biography, or dream, of many Vietnam Veterans during and since Jane Fonda's visit to Hanoi. I think this book should be in the Mid-Shipman's store and in every Exchange in the world."

—*LCDR Richard Pariseau, USN (Retired), USNA '60, PhD.*

KISSED BY THE SNOW

"Driven by a clever plot to bring down a drug lord, in fact, the entire economy of destructive drugs, this thriller spirals the reader through a satisfying slash and burn journey up the ascending echelons of international narco-traffic. The story is smooth (one is tempted to say smooth as 50-year-old Scotch, but these days it might be more like a well-balanced chardonnay), fast-paced, and seasoned with just enough techno-thriller hardware to add guy-spice."

—*Rob Swigart*
Author of 'The Delphi Agenda'

"If you thought Fast and Furious was an ill-thought out scheme by the government to track illegal gun sales among the Mexican cartels, wait until you read what it does to end the War on Drugs in Kissed By The Snow."

—*CAPT Michele Lockwood, USN (Retired)*

THE CUSTER CONSPIRACY

BOOKS BY DENNIS KOLLER

The Oath

Kissed By The Snow

The Custer Conspiracy

THE
OATH

Mike,
Thank you for your
service aboard submarines.
You guys were (+ are) my
Dennis Koller *heroes!*

Dennis

PEN
BOOKS

California

Pen Books
A Division of Pen Communication
Pleasant Hill, CA

This book is a work of fiction. Names, characters, places and incidents either are products of the author's imagination or are used fictitiously. Any resemblance to persons living or dead is entirely coincidental.

Second Pen Books paperback edition February 2018

Edited by: David Almeida and Rosemary Cook

Cover Design: Will Jackson at wdjacksoncovers@gmail.com

Manufactured in the United States of America

ISBN-13: 9780692656730
ISBN-10: 0692656731

Thank you for purchasing this Pen Books paperback.
Please remember to leave a Review
at your favorite retailer.

This book is dedicated to the
566 POWs
held in the infamous Hoa Lo prison
(better known as The Hanoi Hilton)
between 1964 and 1973.

Their sacrifice, courage, endurance
and, in the end, their forgiveness,
reflects all that is good and noble in the
American soul.

"The Oath is one of those books difficult to put down once
you start it! If you are one of us who did not appreciate
Jane Fonda giving aid and comfort to the North
Vietnamese during her visit to Hanoi in July 1972, you
will appreciate this book. Very entertaining."

RADM Thomas F. Brown III
Naval Aviator and veteran of three
deployments to the Gulf of Tonkin
in support of the War.

Friday, July 2nd

Ruth Wasserman had been a news reporter and syndicated columnist for various San Francisco newspapers for the past twenty-five years. Today she would generate the biggest story of her career. Too bad she had to die to do it.

The man in the beret stood in the gathering twilight watching her approach. He had his story ready, though the groceries she carried were an unexpected bonus. He would offer to carry them for her as he waited for "Bobby." If she refused, well, then he would be forced to show the gun. He felt a tingle of anticipation as she waddled toward him. He hadn't been this close to her since 1969 – thirty-one years ago. And yet her memory still haunted his dreams. He felt for the reassurance of the silenced .22 semi-automatic tucked securely in his waistband. The wait was finally over. It was payback time!

2

November 1966

His last day of freedom for seven years dawned cold, crisp and cloudless over the South China Sea. A beautiful day for flying, the young lieutenant thought as he came up on the flight deck of the USS Ticonderoga. His mission, as explained to him in the just-concluded flight briefing, was to bomb a truck staging area between Vinh and Thanh Hoa on the coast of North Vietnam.

An honor student, he had graduated eighth out of 692 in the U.S. Naval Academy class of 1964. This was his sixteenth mission over North Vietnam, and he was beginning to feel invincible.

That feeling, along with his F8E Crusader, was shattered by a Russian made S-A2 surface-to-air missile about 10:32 a.m. that same day – November 28, 1966, two days after Thanksgiving and exactly two months shy of his twenty-fifth birthday.

He parachuted into a small village that seemed overpopulated with exceptionally hostile people. The soldiers who captured him stood idly by as the villagers beat him senseless – jarring loose five teeth and breaking his right leg.

If he thought this was to be an isolated incidence of random cruelty, he was sadly mistaken. He reached the Hoa Lo prison – dubbed the Hanoi Hilton by those who passed through her horrors – on December 2nd. It was to be his home for the next seven years.

By the time he reached Hanoi that December, the Communists already knew they could never win the military battle raging in the South. In the fall of 1966, they conceived a new strategy for winning the war – make it one of attrition. By doing so, they hoped to undermine the American people's will to fight. In this strategy, the prisoners of war were to play an integral part.

On Christmas Day 1966, the young pilot was dragged into an interrogation cell in the south wing of the Hoa Lo prison and made to sit on a low stool in the middle of the room. The leg broken by the villagers had never been set, and it stuck out at a grotesque angle. He was asked to write down the information on his ship, airplane, the ordinance it was carrying and his bombing mission.

Even though the lieutenant knew the North Vietnamese had this information already and were asking simply to compromise him, he invoked the Geneva Accords and politely refused to answer. In response, the guard stationed behind him struck the side of his head with the butt of his AK 47. The blow opened a two-inch gash on his skull and sent him crashing to the floor like a rag doll. The interrogator, a Vietnamese major who would be christened Pigeye by the prisoners because of the way his eyes protruded from his face, screamed, "You will answer. You will answer" – and stomped on his broken leg.

Immediately, four guards appeared and pulled him back to his cell. Throwing him on the stone floor, *they proceeded to beat him with their fists and boots. Forcing him onto his stomach, they tied his arms together from shoulders to wrists. The pain coursed through him unlike anything he'd ever experienced before. He was certain his breastbone would break through his skin. His right shoulder was pulled from its socket. The agony was so great, he lost control of his bowels.*

This can't be happening, his mind told him. Humans don't do this to other humans. His whole body, every fiber of his being, was consumed in pain. They abandoned him in the middle of the tiny cell. Struggling to his feet, the smell of his own feces sharp in his nostrils, he tried to rub off the ropes on the granite walls. His efforts only increased the pain. Drenched in sweat, he started to scream. He screamed and cried until he had no voice left, and then he cried and screamed noiselessly.

Early the next morning, they came for him. Without relieving the pressure from the ropes, they dragged him back to the interrogation room. Pigeye asked him again to sign a confession. The young pilot –the toughest kid in his neighborhood, the guy who once played a whole half of a high school football game with a broken wrist, the lieutenant who thought he could and would withstand any pain, even pain unto death, before he betrayed his country and his Military Code of Conduct – sobbed noiselessly his assent. It had taken less than one day to break him.

The torture continued intermittently for the next four years. Every time the North Vietnamese wanted to manipulate the American public, they trotted out a supposed confession from some downed pilot. The American press always ran the story. Consequently, the enemy began winning the war for public opinion.

In an attempt to break any residual will to resist on the part of the POWs, the North Vietnamese began broadcasting statements over the camp loudspeakers by American journalists and dissidents opposed to the war. In 1969, Americans started arriving in North Vietnam, not to help seek the prisoners' release, but to use them for propaganda purposes. Selected prisoners were chosen to meet with the visiting Americans. It was all a staged show, properly rehearsed and managed for the television cameras. The prisoner was supposed to bow to his captors, look apologetic in front of the visitors, and ask them to help end the war so they could all go home.

"Excuse me," the man in the beret said as Ruth put down her groceries and rummaged through her purse for her keys.

Startled, she watched him limp up the stairs toward her. "I was supposed to meet Bobby at seven thirty but got here early. I'm in from Los Angeles, and he told me if I arrived early to see his landlady. That she was a nice person and a friend and probably would let me wait for him in his flat. I know this is an imposition, and I'm embarrassed to ask, but I saw you coming and – well, here I am."

Just like Bobby, Ruth thought. His way of showing off his newest boyfriend. Nice looking, too, in an older, hippie sort of way. If he wasn't gay, she might have been interested herself. She smiled at the thought. "I don't think it would be a good idea for me to let you in Bobby's place without him telling me it was okay," she said, "but you're welcome to come up to my place and wait, if you want. You'll know when he comes home. You can hear him coming up the front steps from my living room."

"Well, the least I can do is carry your groceries for you. Here, let me take those." She unlocked the door, and together they walked up the interior stairs to her flat.

Ruth's Victorian had been turned into a duplex. She lived upstairs, Bobby below. "You can put the bags on the counter there, if you like," she said, putting her purse on the kitchen table. The man did as he was asked and then slipped off his backpack, putting it on the table next to her purse. "How long have you known Bobby?" she asked, conversationally.

"Never met him before in my life," the man answered casually.

"But, I thought you said ..." It was when she turned toward him that she first saw the gun.

"I lied." He pointed the gun at her. "Please, no hysterics," he said calmly.

Fear chilled her spine. She steadied herself on the kitchen counter. He took off his hat and was in the process of taking off his jacket.

"Ruth? You and me? We're going to have a little chat. Please sit down."

"Why me? What do you want from me?" she stammered. "I don't have much. If it's money you want, I have about five hundred dollars in the top drawer of my dresser. Please – take it and go. I won't say a word to anyone. I promise."

"I'm not here for your money, Ruth. I'm here for you. Look at me." He came closer, bending to her eye-level. "Take a good look. Try to remember. Go way back. We've met before. A long time ago."

He knew something was up. For the past two weeks he'd been fed like a visiting dignitary. Three, maybe four, times a day a guard would come in and place roasted rabbit, duck, pork and lots of rice in front of him. The only thing missing was silver and a napkin. From an emaciated one hundred twenty pounds, he started to gain weight. He was allowed out in the yard to get some sun and exercise an hour a day. He still couldn't talk to the other prisoners, but what the hell. This was great. He felt better than he had in four years. It was early October. The boards were taken off his windows and his cell was given a fresh coat of whitewash. He even received a new waste bucket. Luxury.

All this turned out to be in preparation for a meeting with an American Delegation. He was sure he'd been selected because he'd been broken and they owned him. Since the prisoners weren't allowed to speak with one another, he was unaware that every prisoner had broken under the torture. But the food gave him his strength back. Like Samson's hair in the Bible. His will to resist returned. When the day came, he was led into a room where four women were seated on couches in front of television cameras. They represented an organization called Women Against Imperialistic War. *Introductions were made. Jennifer Tower, Rebecca Steele, Heidi Schmidt, and their leader, Ruth Wasserman.*

"Think back, Ruth. Thirty-one years ago this October. You sat in a small room in Hanoi with three other women – and a prisoner. Me."

"My God," she gasped, her hand trailing down her cheek in disbelief.

"You wrote about our little meeting. In fact, thanks to me, you won a Pulitzer Prize."

Wasserman stared numbly at him, swaying like a metronome in her chair.

"Do you know what happened to me the day after you left? Of course you don't. You didn't see the ugly things they did to me. To all of us. Blinded as you were by your righteousness. I suspect that even if you did know, you wouldn't have cared much one way or another."

They seated him on a sofa across from the women. No one spoke for a minute, sizing each other up. The television cameras were turned on. The women, speaking into the cameras, started the interview by telling their audience how evil it was for America to deliberately target innocent women and children. They then introduced him as an apologetic American pilot who, because he'd been so humanely treated by his captors, had seen the error of his ways. They asked him his name and hometown. Did he have anything to say to his family? What hospital was he assigned to bomb on his run over North Vietnam? He simply looked at them for a few moments and quietly asked, "Why are you here? Do you hate your country that much?" The two questions hung there in space, like ominous soap bubbles. The women were silent.

They looked searchingly at one another for help. This was not how the interview was supposed to go. "Are you Communists?" the pilot asked.

"No," one of the four replied, looking nervously at the camera. For the next two hours, the women verbally attacked him on America's illegal and immoral war policy. After they left, he was led back to his cell. An hour later, they came for him. Pigeye was furious.

"They fed me my toes, Ruth. Because you told them I was 'impudent.'"

"I don't remember saying that. You're making this up."

"Well, believe me, I remember. I was tied up in ropes. You have no idea how much that hurts. Like a son-of-a-bitch! I was tied in positions the human body was not meant to be in. They left me that way for ten straight days. In one way, I owe you my life. If I hadn't hated you so much and dreamed about what I'd do to you, if and when I got out of there, I probably would've died. You kept me going, believe it or not." He reached into his backpack and took out a cassette recorder. "Sorry, I don't have a video camera to film you like your friends did me. Just this humble audiotape. But now I get the pleasure of interrogating *you*." He placed the recorder on the table. "Maybe I can write an article about our time together and become famous like you did with me. And, Ruth – please don't lie to me. I pretty much have the story from the other three women who were there that day."

9

"You've talked to them?" she asked incredulously.

"All within the last year," he said. "Doing my own research paper, so to speak. But before I begin, Ruth, I'd like you to open the backpack and empty the contents on the table." He leveled the gun at her for emphasis.

She pulled it over and undid the straps. Cautiously putting her hand into the opening, she froze. Then, starting to shake uncontrollably, her hands pulled out a long length of rope.

3

Saturday, July 3rd

It was my first weekend off in a month. Planned on getting in a round of golf with a fireman buddy from Santiago Station at Harding Park at nine. Be home about three. Work in the backyard building that damn retaining wall I'd been trying to get to for the past two months, and then listen to the Giants game after dinner. Is this a great country, or what?

The best laid plans! The call came at 7:30 a.m. I was just sitting down to my morning ritual of coffee, the Chronicle Sporting Green, bite-sized Mini-Wheats, unfrosted, and non-fat milk. Well, the Mini-Wheats and non-fat milk had never been part of the ritual. The *real* ritual, the one with staying power, was doughnuts or a Thomas English muffin slathered with butter and Smucker's apricot jam. But since I decided a month ago to go on a diet, Mini-Wheats and non-fat milk took the place of the doughnuts and muffins.

I'd been on these diet kicks before, so I knew it wouldn't last long enough to become its own ritual. Especially the non-fat milk. Funny how things change. When I was a kid it was called "skim" milk. To make it more palatable to our modern culture, the marketing gurus renamed it "non-fat" milk. Guess what? It was still skim milk as far as I was concerned.

I'm one of twelve kids from an Irish-Catholic family. My dad never made much money, so my mom was always looking for ways to cut costs. One of the ways she did this was periodically buy what had to be a fifty-pound box of powdered milk. The operative word here was *powdered*. It had to be mixed with water. God, it was awful. When none of the kids would drink it, mom thought she'd fool us by mixing that watery mess with whole milk. Who would've thought that my sainted mother, God rest her soul, invented "low-fat" milk? But what goes around comes around. She must be smiling down on me this very minute. Here I was, forty-five years later, drinking skim milk again. And, because of the thirty calories I was saving, feeling damn righteous about it, too.

"McGuire?" I recognized Carberry's voice and groaned. Carberry was the duty sergeant at SFPD Operations. "This is Carberry." I didn't say, *well who the hell but you would be calling me at seven thirty in the morning on my day off?* but thought about it for more than just a fleeting moment. "We've got a *187* out on Steiner. The ME's already there. Bristow told me to have you check it out."

"Timmy," I said. I knew he hated to be called Timmy. He was fifty-two years old – my age – and he thought it demeaning to call anyone Timmy or Tommy (that's me) or Mikey or Denny after their thirtieth birthday. Hell, I liked it when somebody called me Tommy. Made me feel younger.

"Timmy – tell Bristow he can kiss my ass. It's the 4th of July weekend, for God's sake. My first weekend off in a month. I've got a tee time in a little over an hour. I'm just sitting down to read the paper. Finding out what's going on in the world. Sucking up a little culture. The Giants won again last night, in case you didn't know. They're six up on the Dodgers, and I just want to sit here and be dumb and read about the game. In other words, I want to have a nice weekend. Know what I'm talking about?" I wasn't going to let him guess. "So by the time I get to the office on Tuesday, I'll be a happy camper and a much better team player." Carberry knew the reference and chuckled. Bristow was constantly having meetings about how everyone should get along and be a *team player*. I knew he really didn't believe any of that shit. To him, *teamwork* meant a whole bunch of guys doing what he said.

"Can't he get Kaufman or Mayhew?" I whined, feeling incredibly sorry for myself and knowing there was no way out.

"They're already out, Mac. Sorry."

"Damn it." A lost cause. "Okay. Let me shower and dress and I'll get over there. Give me the address."

I took a few more spoonfuls of my cereal, dumped the rest down the disposal, and padded back to the bedroom. Catching sight of myself in the mirror, I stopped to admire the image. Instinctively, I sucked in my stomach. Actually, I didn't look too bad. Two months ago I had a thirty-eight-inch waist on my five-eleven frame. Now it was down to thirty-five. But I worked hard for it. God, I'd done more crunches this past month than in my whole military career. The catalyst for this *let's get back into shape* thing was a street punk.

A little over two months ago I was driving through the Mission District on my way to the dentist when some young punk grabbed a woman's purse and took off. I debated whether I should get involved. But I thought, What the hell – if this was my mother, what would I do? And I was always the first one to bitch about citizens not getting involved in helping stop street crime.

So I jumped out of the car and started yelling for someone to stop the kid. Yelling that I'm a police officer. Nobody paid any attention, of course. Especially the kid. He couldn't have been more than fourteen, but he was fast. He was running, and I was running. But he was running a hell of a lot faster than me. I was winded after a block. So much for being in shape. After two blocks, my lungs were exploding in my chest, and I was on the edge of blacking out. As luck would have it, some good citizen actually ran by me and caught the kid. Held him down until I came wheezing up. I stood over him with my hands on my knees trying to catch my breath. At the same time, my stomach started feeling queasy from the overexertion. I actually got sick and lost my lunch. Hurled all over the kid. Truth be told, I could've turned my head and missed him completely, but I was so pissed at him for making me run all that way, I aimed right for his face. Got him real good, too.

The next week – thanks to some good citizen complaining to the Department that I abused this poor child – I was suspended, with pay, while Internal

Affairs looked into the matter. Bottom line was I got slapped on the wrist and the punk walked – and all because I was in such pitiful shape. Hence my desire to lose weight and get back to where I could at least run two lousy blocks without puking.

4

There was a lot of police activity around the Steiner Street address by the time I arrived a little after eight thirty. The morning fog clung to me like plastic wrap, wet and uncomfortable. As I got out of my car, I thought of my topcoat hanging uselessly at home in my front closet.

My partner, Mike Irvine, was standing out front talking to a young patrolman. "God, Mike, they must have called you before this even happened. How the hell you get here so quick? What are you – like, a doctor? Always on call?"

"Thanks, Mac," he smiled. "Just what I need. I'm a hard-working street cop and get stuck with a shanty Mick like you. What a way to start the weekend." Irvine was a thick-necked old Irishman with bushy eyebrows and a nose that had taken more than its fair share of hits from street fights when he was a kid. He'd been on the force for nearly twenty-five years. Definitely wasn't just any old street cop. Knowing the City in all its myriad rhythms, he and I teamed up as partners in Homicide over a year ago after working a drive-by in Butchertown. A good cop!

"Becker here," Irvine nodded toward the patrolman, "gets dispatched at sometime around five thirty this morning after Operations receives an anonymous call saying someone's been whacked at this address. Is that right, lad?"

"My partner, Gil Eckels – you know him Inspector?" He asked. I shook my head.

Becker was a smooth faced young man with an Adam's apple that bobbed crazily when he spoke. I felt sorry for him. It was almost a physical deformity. He obviously was aware of it because his hand kept nervously pecking at the flesh under his chin. Unfortunately for him, the movement only served to draw more attention to the area.

"Well, we were up on Sutter and Webster cruising the Western Addition," he continued, "when Phyllis at Dispatch called. About five thirty. I can check my log to get the official time, if you want." Again I shook my head. "We rolled up about ten minutes later and parked over there." He pointed across the street and down one house. "I called in to get the owner's name. Both flats owned by a woman named Ruth Wasserman."

"You're kidding," I exclaimed. "Ruth Wasserman? The columnist for the Chronicle? *That* Ruth Wasserman?" Just the mention of her name made my shoulders ache. Like twins separated at birth who swear they can feel each other's pain even though a continent apart, I began to feel the beginnings of tingling in my wrists and ankles where the circulation had been cut off by those metal cuffs thirty-some years ago.

"Well, Inspector, we didn't know that then. Neither of us ever heard of her," he responded, the Adam's apple bobbing like a float in choppy water

"In fact, you and the M.E. are the only ones here who ever heard of her."

"That's because no one in the department reads anything but comic books," I said, looking over at Irvine and winking. "Actually, though, I knew her by reputation many years ago." I moved my shoulders back and forth, trying to relieve the strain I felt in them. "How did she buy it?"

"It was hard to tell at first. Want you to know, Inspector, Gil and I followed strict procedure. We rang the bell, and when no one answered, we tried the door. It was unlocked, so we went in. Had gloves on of course, so we wouldn't spoil prints."

"You did well, Officer," I praised him. Cops, especially the younger ones, had been so marginalized by the various commissions looking into their conduct that they'd become paranoid about procedure.

"Didn't disturb a thing, Inspector. We walked up the stairs. The door was open. We walked in and there she was. In a chair. Arms all twisted in back of her. Trussed up. Like you would a rodeo steer. I'd say we're looking for one sick puppy."

"Trussed up? Like, with a rope?"

"Yes sir, Inspector. A rope. Arms tied in back of her from shoulder to wrist. It was obvious she was dead, so we didn't get too close to the body. Didn't want to disturb evidence."

"You okay, pardner?" Irvine asked as he noticed how I was rotating my shoulders.

"Fine," I said. "Just a little early morning ache in my shoulders. Must be age." I smiled. "Continue," I told Becker.

"Well, we didn't notice much blood. We couldn't see her face from where we were, so we walked to the other side of the table and saw a bullet wound right on top of her nose. No exit wound we could see. Must have been a small-caliber weapon. I'd never seen anything like that before. Literally shot between the eyes." He gave a little smile and pulled at his neck. "We both came downstairs. I called the ambulance and they called the Coroner's office. Gil got out the police tape and started to secure the area. That's really all I can tell you, Inspector. The Coroner's still up there."

"Good job, Becker. Tell your partner I appreciate the professionalism." Ever since the O.J. debacle in Los Angeles a number of years ago, cops became extraordinarily careful about contaminating a crime scene. The difference between the procedures in Los Angeles and S.F. was here we called the coroner first. Homicides were his cases. In L.A., murders were looked on first-and-foremost as a police matter. They secured the area and looked for clues. In S.F., we weren't even allowed into the crime scene until the medical examiner had done his thing. That meant, theoretically, no evidence could be tampered with because everything has been photographed, bagged, dusted and examined before we were even allowed in.

Irvine and I walked up the stairs. The medical examiner was a guy named Fastbein. I'd known him for years. He'd been deputy coroner when I first made inspector over ten years ago. Odd little fellow, but competent. He was standing by the body directing his staff when he looked up and saw us enter the room.

"What've you got, Ed?" I asked with an exaggerated sigh.

Fastbein looked down at the mess that was Ruth Wasserman and shook his head. "What do you think I've got? It's what I've always got. Human tragedy. In this case, a good old-fashioned murder. But with an unusual twist, if you'll forgive my pun." He chuckled mirthlessly.

"You're a sick fellow, Ed." I was constantly teasing him about his profession. Having to hang out with dead bodies all day was not my idea of a healthy environment or fun time. I kidded him about what the conversations he had with his wife when he got home at night must be like. "Hi, honey. Boy, you should've seen this corpse today. The blood spatters. *Really* interesting, sweetheart. Let's eat while I tell you all about it."

We put on the plastic booties Fastbein's aide gave us and walked slowly around the body. Wasserman's arms were figuratively sewn together, wrist to shoulder. I was immediately uncomfortable again. I'd seen this kind of handiwork before. In fact, I'd been the recipient of it on many occasions. I could feel beads of sweat forming on my forehead. If Fastbein or Irvine noticed, they didn't show it. I mentally thanked them.

"As you can see, Inspector, it looks like our lady here was tortured prior to being killed with a gunshot wound to the forehead. At least that's what you'd expect, right? A rather gruesome way to spend your last minutes on this earth. Both shoulders were pulled from their sockets. The human form was not meant to be torqued in such a fashion."

How well I knew. The tingling sensations sparking downward from my biceps and out through my fingertips gave me the same message.

"You need a glass of water?" Fastbein asked. "You don't look so good. Probably the stairs."

"And the diet," Irvine interjected.

Again, I silently thanked them for covering for me. I swallowed hard, then said, "So what are you telling us, Ed?"

"Look at this." He walked behind the body and pointed out with his pen how deeply the ropes had cut into the flesh on her upper arms. "The rope was so tight it split her skin. It would've stopped all circulation. The blood would've congealed in the hands, bloating them and turning them black. But do you see that here?"

"Ed, you're a genius, I know. But tell me in English what you're trying to say, okay? That Ms. Wasserman was dead when she was tied up?"

"Exactly. I still have some more tests to run, but I think it's pretty clear. Strange, don't you think? Maybe we're dealing with a new breed of murderer here. A humane psychopath."

5

By the time we got back to ground level a small crowd had gathered beyond the protective yellow tape securing the scene. Pajamas peeking out beneath bathrobes. Primarily neighbors at this time of day. Talking excitedly amongst themselves. Death relieving boredom. What a society!

A single sea gull wheeled high above me. A gray ghost against the leaden sky. Curious about what was happening below. Like the neighbors.

We noticed a group of blue-clad police officers off to our left and walked over.

"Got anything for us?" Irvine asked. They all looked at the ranking officer, a sergeant named McNally. I'd worked with him before. A good cop. He came over.

"Awfully damn early, guys. Not many people up. Went door-to-door. We only got one hit." His head jerked left to indicate the house across the street. "She happened to be standing on the porch there …" he pointed, "…when she saw some guy come out of Wasserman's place. I told her to wait. That you'd be over to talk."

The house McNally pointed out was a canary yellow Victorian. Happy colors for a sad block, I thought. I couldn't see the front door because a colonnaded porch enclosed it. The stairs ran parallel to the sidewalk. Someone standing on the porch would be virtually invisible to anyone leaving Wasserman's house.

"Can you debrief the first officers on the scene one more time?" I asked Irvine, as I stepped off the curb. "Let's meet back at the station about eleven, okay?"

"You got it."

Walking toward the house, I could tell someone was on the porch by the smoke wisping around one of the columns. The scene reminded me of a song – *Smoke Gets in Your Eyes* – which I started to hum. Don't ask me why. Sometimes I just do that sort of thing. Okay – so it's not something you'd expect from a guy fifty-two years old. But I never let that stop me before. And didn't now. I was already on the second stanza and the third stair when I looked up and saw her.

She was one of those rare women you meet every once in a while, who know they are beautiful and know *you* know they are beautiful. Caught unaware, I didn't quite know what to say, but knew I should say something rather than just stand and stare. Or worse, stand but not stare. Just shift my eyes around so she wouldn't think I was staring.

I did the "or worse." I let my eyes dance around her edges, not willing to confront her head-on.

"High across we fly, something here inside, cannot be denied," she intoned.

"Pardon me?" I wasn't too quick on the trigger today.

"The Platters! *Smoke Gets in Your Eyes*. That's what you were humming, right?"

She was sitting on the shelf between two columns, a half-smoked cigarette dangling precariously from her left hand.

"I think you got it. But the caller before you won the prize."

She smiled, rewarding me for my quick wit. She had on a terry robe with some kind of insignia embroidered on the pocket above her right breast. Her feet were crossed at the ankles, which allowed the robe to part just above her knee. Casually, she reached down and pulled it closed when she saw my gaze linger there.

"You're not one of those people who's going to lecture me on the evils of smoking are you? Something endearing, like, *those things will kill you*? Because if you are, better turn around right now. I won't be talking to you." She took another drag, defiantly. The smoke curled over her shoulder before being sucked into the gray fog.

She had a remarkable combination of gray-blue eyes, dark brown hair and translucent skin. Even in the muted backlight in which she was framed, it was that striking combination of dark and light that caught ... and held ... my eyes.

"No, ma'am." What else could I say?

"Good! I get enough of that from my mother." She jerked her head toward the door. "She's not doing too well, so I come over here on weekends. Stay overnight. Every time I want a cigarette, I have to come outside. Sneak it. Like a criminal."

I nodded and continued my climb up the stairs.

"Michele," she said. "One *L*."

"Ma'am?" I asked quizzically. I was beginning to sound like some fake TV cop. She definitely had me off balance.

"*Ma'am*? Is that all you can say? Who do you think you are, Joe Friday? Or do I remind you of your mother?" She smiled, then said, "Just kidding. Michele. That's my name. Michele. But with one *L*, not two. I thought you'd be writing it down and wanted it spelled correctly." With her forefinger and thumb, she flicked the cigarette out between the columns and into the cool morning air.

"Well, Michele with one *L*, what's your last name?" By this time, I'd extracted the notebook from my back pocket.

"Sullivan."

I reached out to shake her hand. Soft. Confident. "I'm Inspector McGuire. One *G*."

She studied me a moment with an odd look, then said, "I knew you looked familiar. Tom McGuire, right?"

I stood up a little straighter and took half a step backward while my mind raced over the possibilities. A bar? God, I hope not. Somebody I went to school with? Nah! She was much younger than me. A case I worked on? The girlfriend of somebody I rousted? I thought about saying something cute, like, she was so beautiful that I certainly would've remembered meeting her. Instead, I just thought it.

"From Saint Anne's grammar school," she continued when I didn't respond. "Sullivan is my married name. Well, my *ex*-married name even though I still go by it. My maiden name was Doherty."

The synapses in my brain were sparking, trying to remember "Doherty." I just stood there dumbly.

"Mike Doherty," she said. "You were a friend of my brother Mike."

Mike Doherty! A name out of the past. My family had moved from one side of the park to the other just as I was starting third grade. Mike was the first friend I had. We lived within a block of one another. Went to Saint Anne's together. I went to a different high school, but even then we still palled around together. After graduation I went off to Annapolis. Mike wasn't exactly a brain surgeon. But hey, in those days it wasn't considered a crime if you didn't go to college – so Mike got a job at Rudy's, the neighborhood grocery store. We corresponded off and on for a few years, and then Mike got drafted. We lost track of each other, but one of the first things I did after I returned home from the war in '73 was go over to his house. His mom told me he'd been killed in Vietnam. A waste, I thought then, and still think today. As were they all.

"Jesus," I said. "Mike's little sister. I remember you. When we graduated from high school, you were – what? Eight or nine?"

"Something like that. Around there, anyway. I remember you because I had this big crush on you. I was just heartbroken when you went away to college."

"The Naval Academy," I responded, feeling for some reason a correction was in order. Maybe a touch of bragging. "I was really sorry to hear about Mike."

"Thanks. It was a tremendous blow to the whole family. The oldest boy and all, you know. My dad never recovered. Died less than a year later."

"Too many good people were lost in that damn war," I said. There was a pause as we both lingered on things past. Breaking the silence, I said "Tell me about you. You obviously got married."

"Yeah. To John Sullivan. Do you remember his family? They all went through Saint Anne's. Lived up on Kirkham. No – you probably wouldn't. He had an older sister, but she would have been after your time, too. John and I were what you'd call 'childhood sweethearts.' He was a year older than me. I went to high school at Saint Rose, and he ended up at Commerce. You know, the continuation school. A bad boy. But I was always attracted to the wicked ones." She arched an eyebrow my way, and the sides of her mouth turned up in a smile. "Got married when I was twenty-one. Divorced when I was thirty. No kids." She paused, then said, "Well – that's my sad tale. How 'bout you?"

I leaned against the wall opposite her and shrugged my shoulders. "As I said, I went to Annapolis. Became a Navy pilot. In July of '68, was sent to 'Nam where I flew off carriers. In late '68, on my fifty-sixth mission, I got shot down and spent the rest of the war as a guest of Ho Chi Minh."

"I remember that. I read about you in, what, Time Magazine? I guess you had it pretty rough, huh?"

I shrugged, like it was no big thing. "Hey, I came back. Better than what happened to a lot of guys. Like Mike. Anyway, I got back in '73. Bummed around for about a year. Traveled the States, mostly. Settled back in San Francisco in '75. Joined SFPD in early '76. Been at it ever since."

"Married?"

"Married and divorced," I said. "Paula and I married in '67. Right after I graduated from the Academy. Divorced in '88."

"You or her?"

She could tell I didn't understand her question.

"Did you divorce her, or did she divorce you?"

"It was a mutual thing, really. She was a good lady. We had a baby. A boy. Named him Tom. But called him LT, for *Little Tom*. Never called him Junior, even though he was." She smiled. "He's thirty-two now. Lives over in Berkeley. Teaches high school. Coaches football. Has a boy himself, also named Tom."

"You're a grandpa?"

"Yeah," I replied, all of a sudden feeling old.

"Young to be a grandpa," she said.

"It's what happens when you get pregnant on your honeymoon."

"You've been divorced how long?"

"Twelve years."

"Seeing anyone?"

"No." I laughed. "I've found that being celibate has its advantages. At the very least, I wake up every morning with someone I like."

"I can relate to that," she said with a smile.

There was a pause in the conversation while Michele fished around in her robe pocket for another cigarette. I would've much rather have stayed and conversed with her, but had to get going. Irvine would be wondering. He'd give me a bad time for a week. I pushed myself away from the wall and said, "I've got to ask you a few questions about what you saw this morning, if you don't mind. But I would like to continue *this* conversation sometime, too. If that's all right?"

She gave me that Mona Lisa look, knowing, as all women do, when interest has been piqued.

"I'm going to need your phone number and address anyway. Maybe I can give you a call and we could get together for coffee or something, okay?"

"I'll look forward to it."

"You're on." I paused, then gestured with my head toward Wasserman's house. "My partner says you actually saw someone leaving Ms. Wasserman's house early this morning?"

"I did," she replied. "About five. I'd been up with mom and couldn't get back to sleep, so I came out here for a cigarette. It was awfully cold. I was standing about where you are and heard a door open and close across the street. I was curious, thinking it was either a lover leaving early or another dumb person like me, out sneaking a cigarette. I looked through these columns." She moved a little forward and to the left to show me where she'd stood. The robe gaped open and it was all I could do not to stare. But I did anyway. She looked over at me, smiled, and pulled the robe closed. I moved over next to her and saw the clear line of sight she had to Wasserman's front door.

"Now, you have to know – it was foggy as hell, so I didn't get a really good look. It was a guy. Older. Probably about your age." When she noticed my head twitch backward, she said, "Not that you're old. I didn't mean it that way." I didn't say a word. Interested to see how she was going to get out of this. "I should've just let it go at *older*. Oh, hell, you know what I mean. Anyway, I say that just because of the way he walked. Real slow. Had a limp. Let's see ..." She tested limps on both her legs. "His right leg. A limp in his right leg."

"White? Black? Asian?"

"Again, it was hard to see clearly. I can definitely say he was not African-American. But he could have been Hispanic. Or Anglo. Hard to tell."

"Did he have a car?"

"Not that I saw. He just walked, limped actually, all the way up the block and turned the corner on McAllister. I didn't think much about it. I don't live in the neighborhood, so I don't know who lives here. I do remember one thing, though. He had long hair. Wore it in a ponytail. Long. It came out from underneath his hat."

"His hat?"

"A beret. Like that guy Che-whoever wore back in the Sixties. I couldn't see what color it was. Everything was gray this morning. Oh – and he wore a backpack."

I was writing furiously. "Okay. Let's go through one thing at a time. He had long hair, right?"

"Right."

"In a ponytail. Black? Red? Blond?"

"You mean the color of his hair? I don't know. As I said, it was still pretty dark. And misty. Only got a look at him under the street light. But if I had to guess, I'd say it was gray."

"Okay. That's good. Now what about the backpack?"

"It was just an ordinary backpack. Like the ones kids wear to school. Nothing special. But this guy wasn't a student. A teacher, maybe – but not a student. Too old."

"How big was he? Could you tell? Even approximately? Was he tall? Short? Fat? Slim?"

She moved back a few steps and lit another cigarette. Cupping her right elbow in her left hand, she looked me up and down. I quickly sucked in my gut. "I'd say he was about your size. Medium height. Not fat. Not skinny." Her eyes squinted as the smoke wafted up around her. Either that or she winked at me. I hoped it was a wink.

I stopped writing and put the notebook away. "Well, that'll get us started. For now, at least. Thanks for the help. It was great meeting you. Would your mom remember me? I'd like to go up and say 'Hi.'"

"I don't think it would do any good. She's suffering from Alzheimer's. Has it pretty bad. Sometimes she doesn't even recognize me."

"I'm sorry," I said, meaning it. She nodded. "I'm going to ask you to come downtown and work with our sketch artist. We have a computer that can draw any face you describe. Maybe we can get a good resemblance of the guy. It's Saturday. How 'bout

Monday? Wait, I forgot. Monday's a holiday. Tuesday okay?"

She nodded. "I'm off all this week."

"I'll contact you. Here's my card. If you happen to think of anything else that might be helpful, let me know."

"And you have my number!" It wasn't a question.

"Yes." I retrieved my notebook and flipped through a number of pages until I found it and read it back to her.

"Use it." The smile she flashed left little doubt in my mind that calling her would be right up there on my priority list.

Walking down the steps, I started humming again. This time, though, it was another song from my youth. From the movie Gigi. *Thank heaven for little girls. They grow up in the most delightful way.*

6

The Ford Taurus pulled into the rental car lot at San Francisco International a little after nine in the morning. The man's flight to LAX was booked for 11:30 a.m.

After phoning the police about Wasserman, he knew the airports and bus stations would come under surveillance. It didn't particularly worry him, not only because it would take them time to mobilize, but also because the police wouldn't have a useful description of him. After discarding the fake wig and the backpack in two south-of-Market dumpsters, he gave the beret to the first homeless person he saw.

The man arrived in San Francisco three days ago to make the final preparations. He'd kill Wasserman, then go back home for a few days before coming north again to kill Bill Schaeffer, the last person on his list. Schaeffer was the current governor of California. Curiously, when the man undertook his journey of retribution, Schaeffer wasn't even on his radar screen. He was just one of hundreds of people who, back in the day, had made a name for themselves protesting the Vietnam War. But unlike most of his contemporaries, Schaeffer had used his notoriety to carve out a successful political career.

Having conquered the California political landscape, rumors had him about to announce his intention of running for the presidency.

As the man sat waiting for the shuttle bus to take him to the airport, he patted the briefcase on his lap. Inside were the cassettes. On those cassettes were the interviews with the four women he killed. Their implication of Bill Schaeffer as the driving force behind their visits to North Vietnam. And while the man believed the women's actions classified them as traitors to their country, their flat out assertions about Schaeffer's involvement now placed him on the man's radar screen.

While in the City the past three days shadowing Wasserman, the man learned that Schaeffer had a planned fund raising event at the San Francisco Marriott this coming Thursday evening. He canvassed area realtors about renting office space near the hotel. One found him the perfect spot. They showed him a fifth floor office suite one block away, with a direct line of sight to the hotel's entrance. He had no doubt he could make a killing shot from there. He immediately filled out the rental agreement. The application had been approved yesterday morning.

"No chance of you becoming president, Governor," the man muttered to himself as he boarded the shuttle. "By next Thursday evening you'll be dead."

The bus dropped him off at Terminal Two. The man had an hour to wait for his flight. He hadn't eaten in over fourteen hours. His stomach alternately ached and growled, but the thought of food made him queasy. The doctor told him this would happen. The pancreatic cancer was literally eating him alive. Food for him was food for it. And so he figured the less he ate, the more time he bought himself. He lost sixteen pounds in just the last three weeks. The doctor told him he had six months to live. That would take him to November, but it was clear he didn't have that long. In fact, with what he was about to do, it was doubtful he would live beyond next Thursday. He fully expected to meet Schaeffer in hell that night.

Mortality. It was such a fickle thing. He looked at two pretty girls as they walked past, giggling at something or other. In their early twenties. Wide-eyed in the face of their future. Whatever lay in front of them, it had to be good. The optimism of youth.

One returned his glance, caught his eye, and looked away, continuing her conversation. When he was a younger man those same eyes would've locked onto his and held, filling him with life. Now they just looked through him. He was part of the ever-changing landscape, like the chairs and ticket counters that outlined the gate area. He was old. The world was young and belonged to the young. They knew it just as surely as he had when he was their age.

A crushing sadness enveloped him. He was so utterly and acutely alone, even in this place teeming with people. Time passing. His time.

He knew he was an anachronism. Most people had long ago made their peace with what happened in Vietnam and moved on. Most would consider what he was doing to be murder. Not him. In his estimation, the people he targeted were traitors to the country.

Domestic enemies. And the Oath he had taken so long ago justified their deaths. But he wasn't fooling himself. It was first and foremost revenge that motivated his bitterness. Revenge for the intense and brutal torture that was inflicted upon him and his comrades every time an American war protestor visited North Vietnam. He had no problem with the anti-war sentiment that swept the country back then. That was democracy at work, and it was democracy his Oath required him to protect.

My quarrel, he thought as he lined up for his flight, is with the traitors. The ones who visited North Vietnam during the conflict. The ones who caused me so much agony. He gave his ticket to the attendant and walked down the gangway. Now it's their turn, he thought with a satisfied smile. Indeed, revenge *is* a dish best served cold.

7

Irvine was still at the scene. After asking him to put out an APB on an older guy with a limp and a ponytail, I walked down the street and around the corner to my car. It was parked next to a fire hydrant on Grove Street. It's virtually impossible to park in any of San Francisco's neighborhoods. Garages in these old homes were so narrow that even a motorcycle barely fit. And if the motorcycle sported a side mirror, forget about it. As a consequence, curbs long enough to accommodate regular size cars were more closely guarded than the Pope in Northern Ireland. There's an apocryphal story San Franciscans tell about the guy who lost his job and his wife, and now he was broke. But the realization that his luck had definitely turned south came when he found that perfect parking spot – but wasn't driving.

Over fifty cars a day are purloined on the streets of San Francisco. As I came around the corner, I was once again delighted to see that my blue 1967 Mustang convertible wasn't one of them. My pride and joy. I bought it used in '75. You know the proverbial story about the used car for sale? One owner, low mileage, not a mark on it except, of course, for the lipstick stains on the tail pipe? In my case, that's pretty much what happened. A sixty-eight-year-old woman closed her garage door one day, ran a hose from the exhaust into the back seat, closed the windows and started the engine. Neighbors found her two days later. No next-of-kin. The police put the Mustang up for auction. I got it for $700. Only 26,000 miles on her. Course, I had to keep the top down for the first two weeks to get rid of the smell, but what the hell. It was worth it.

My kid loved it, too. Thought it was cool his old man owned such a hot car. Wanted to put stickers all over the windows and bumpers. You know, things like "Skate-Boarding is Not a Crime", "Billabong", "O'Neill", "Quicksilver", "Sex Wax." Surfer stuff. Not a chance! Hell, I never even allowed him to drive the damn car. Only person who was going to get behind the wheel of that beauty was yours truly. I told him if he wanted the car for a date, he'd have to take his old man along as the chauffeur. That didn't go over too well. To my parental way of thinking, having the Mustang taught him a valuable lesson – life was all about trade-offs.

I drove down Oak to Van Ness, crossed Market and pulled into the Hall of Justice lot at 850 Bryant. Try as I might, I couldn't get Michele out of my mind. Part of it had to do with memories of her brother, but I didn't want to kid myself. She had me interested. Moved me off center. It was a pleasant feeling, but scary. I'd purposely stayed away from women since the divorce. Simply hadn't allowed them in my life. Actually, I was distrustful of them. Of getting involved. Sure, I'd dated. Gone out a number of times. Had some good times, too. But finally it became just too much trouble. Dating. The whole dance you had to go through. And I knew, as sure as I was sitting here, that if I pursued this rather vague, agreeable feeling, I'd be putting myself back in the game.

The Hall of Justice was a decrepit, seven story building that housed various courts on the first three floors; Homicide, Robbery, Drugs and a few other departments were on the 4th floor; administrative offices on the 5th floor, and jail cells on the 6th and 7th floors. All in all, not really a pleasant place. The crooks simply referred to it as "850" – as in

"Where you been, homey?"

"Oh, I been 850'd."

Crooks and cops. We were all in the same business. To all of us it became known as "850."

I took the elevator to the 4th floor, turned right, walked past Robbery and entered room 405 – Homicide. Lt. Bristow occupied the corner office on the left. I felt a wave of relief wash over me when I saw he wasn't there. He made me feel like a teenager sneaking in the house past curfew. Hoping the old man wasn't waiting up. Feeling pure pleasure when you opened the door and saw no light peeking out from beneath your parents' bedroom door. Safe again! A shitty way to live your life, especially when you're my age.

I told Irvine to meet me at eleven, so I had half an hour to kill. I sat at my desk and thought about the Wasserman murder. The ropes. The god-damned ropes. The way her arms were tied. I'd been tied up just like that. Identical. My shoulders ached even now just remembering. A hell of a way to go. But Fastbein said the ropes were post-mortem. What the hell was that all about?

I put my feet on the desk. Thoughts of Vietnam pierced my consciousness like thorns from a rose bush. Unbidden. Unsolicited. Unwanted. Unwelcome. So many good people. Society's fabric ripped asunder, and even after so long a time, the threads of peoples' lives still dangled from its frazzled end. I thought of Mike Doherty.

"The hell with this," I yelled into the empty room. Kicking back from the desk, I jerked myself upright. Mad for allowing the past to intrude on the present. I promised myself a long time ago that I wouldn't beat myself up with the horrific memories. And now some asshole had come along and resurrected the whole sorry mess. I took a deep breath, and then another. Think about it tomorrow, I told myself. Tomorrow is another day. My Scarlet O'Hara routine. One that I've kept alive these past thirty or so years.

The phone on my desk rang. A welcome intrusion on my thoughts.

"McGuire here."

"Inspector McGuire? This is Bob Cummins over at the Chronicle. I understand you bagged the body of Ruth Wasserman this morning."

I hesitated, hating talking to reporters. They were generally rude, arrogant and managed to make you look like a prick no matter how cooperative you were. "We have some reason to believe it was her," I demurred. "But we won't know for sure until the forensics come in." That bullshit line usually held them for a while, I thought. With Cummins, unfortunately, it didn't.

"She worked at the Chronicle, you know."

"I knew that. How long she been there?"

"I asked one of the older guys. He thought she'd been here since the Eighties. Around there, anyway. Before my time. She was one of the older writers. I didn't know her well. Probably because she was a columnist. Not regular staff. Had an office away from the newsroom. Lot of the older guys thought she was hot shit. Mostly those who were around in the Sixties and Seventies. She apparently won a Pulitzer or something back in the day. Sorry I can't give you more. Anyway ... can I ask you a few questions, Inspector?"

"On or off the record?"

"What would you prefer?"

"Neither."

"I could call your supervisor."

"You'd get less out of him than me, pal." But then I started feeling sorry for the guy. This kid. Probably just a few years older than my own son. I softened up. "Okay, ask away. I'll answer the best I can."

"What time was the body discovered?"

"What did you say your name was?"

"Bob Cummins."

"Bob, tell you what. I'll make a deal with you. I'll answer all your questions, at least as much as I can divulge, if you promise to use all your resources to get me everything you can on Ms. Wasserman."

"What, like a bio?"

"Everything you can. A bio. Articles she wrote. Everything."

"Deal. What's your fax number?"

I gave it to him and proceeded to answer all his questions, leaving out only the part about the ropes. But I did tell him we had several leads. A lie, but it would sound good in the morning paper.

After I hung up and was punching out a Diet Coke from the machine on the back wall, Irvine walked in. "Jesus. This place is like a morgue," he said surveying the empty room. "I guess crime does take a holiday, at least over the 4th. And crime *fighters,* too, from the look of things. What's up?"

"You scheduled to be on the rest of the day?" I asked.

"I guess. Tomorrow, too, by the looks of it. Got to write up the Wasserman report. See if numb-nuts over there," he gestured toward Bristow's office, "wants to set up a team on this one. Depends on how it plays out in the press, I guess. No matter what, though, it's still our case."

"I got tickets to the ball game at AT&T tomorrow. Hofmann sent them over since he'll be out of town. Tahoe, I think. Anyway, if you can cover for me today and tomorrow, I owe you."

"Sure. I can do that. You authorizing OT?" He laughed. We had this running joke about the ton of guys scamming the overtime system. With a little imagination, you could double your salary. Some cops did. "Got any ideas on this?"

"Nothing right off the bat. You?"

He shook his head.

"Well, shit," I said. "Looks like we're just going to have to actually work this one."

"Damn. I was afraid of that," he said with mock seriousness. "Where do you want to start?"

"Usual way. Let's see if we have any similars on the books. Maybe you could spend the day looking, okay? Go back two years. If nothing there, forget it. Also, because of the rope business, it probably wouldn't hurt to contact the Feds and get them to check VICAP. See if they have any similars. You know, tied up post-mortem. I asked the guy at the Chronicle to get me all the info he could on our late Ms. Wasserman. That should keep us busy for a while."

"Keep *me* busy, you mean."

"Aw, poor Mikey. I'll be thinking of you at the game tomorrow. Have a nice day." I got up to leave.

Mike gave me the finger as I walked behind his desk. "This is for you, pardner," he said. I grabbed at it as I went by, but missed. "And if I get any hits over the weekend, while you're out having fun, I'll leave them on your desk."

"Mike. You're a gem. Really, I appreciate it."

8

I pulled into the garage of my modest three-bedroom a little after two. I purchased this house after my divorce. Nothing fancy, but comfortable. The three bedrooms were perfect. I had visions of LT coming home from the Academy during the summer with friends and staying with me. Never happened. He spent his summers on the east coast with his Academy buddies honing his craft. I was sad he never made it home in all those years, but now that he came back and was living just across the Bay in Berkeley, I'm a happy camper. Like I used to tell him when he was a kid, life is just a series of trade-offs.

I slung my coat over the sofa, threw the mail on the kitchen table, picked up the phone and dialed.

"Hi, LT. what's going on?"

"Hey, Dad. Nothing much," he said. "What's happenin' with you?"

"Scored some tickets to the Giant's game tomorrow night. Was wonderin' if you'd like to go with me. Should be a good game. Atlanta's in town. Seein' as how it's the 4th, big fireworks display afterwards."

There was a pause on the line. "Damn, Dad. You know I'd love to, but it's the 4th, as you said. A holiday. And you know Maureen. She'd have a cat-fit if I left her alone with Tommy."

I knew that he and his wife were going through a rough patch in their marriage, so it didn't surprise me that she'd be resistant. "Then how 'bout the little guy? I'd love to take him."

"I don't think that would work either, Dad. Sorry. And not to unburden myself to you or anything, but I don't think Maureen would go for that. She's not a big sport's fan, and she's already pissed at me for spending so much time coaching my football team. Says I'm never home." He paused. "Besides, the little man is barely six. He'd be asleep by the third inning."

"Hey, that's okay. I understand. Some other time. Give the little guy a big hug for me." I hung up and went back to my room.

Changing into my sweats, I turned on the radio to see how the Giants were doing. Down five to three going into the bottom of the eighth. Dodgers already won their game with the Cardinals. Shit!

I hadn't eaten since breakfast and my stomach was starting to let me know. I rummaged around the kitchen for something low-cal. I settled on two pieces of lite bread and a banana. Mealtime really wasn't much fun anymore. Paying for past sins, I guess. I grabbed a handful of flesh around my middle. *Less there than a month ago*, I thought. Looking at the banana, I felt better.

~~~~

Feeling better or not, I still had those two damn Giants tickets staring at me from the counter near the sink. I knew whom I wanted to take. Would she go? Did she like baseball? Is it too soon to call? She said to call, didn't she? God, she had me off-center. Who did she think she was insinuating herself into my orderly, predictable life? And in just twenty minutes. Screw it! I picked up the phone. She answered on the second ring.

"Michele? This is Tom McGuire."

"Inspector McGuire. What a pleasant surprise." Her voice – different from this morning. Like tinkling crystal. Girlish. Flirty. Confident. Like, why did it take you so long to call me? I visualized her leg where it parted company with her robe. Remembering the knowing half-smile when she caught me looking. I felt my heart pounding.

"Ah, yeah, I know it's kind of soon. But, uhhh – I've got tickets to the Giants game tomorrow night at AT&T. Should be a great game. Fireworks afterwards." The words just spewed out. Trying to convince her without sounding like I really cared. Trying to get this over with. "And I was wondering – you know – like, if you'd want to go." This was a hell of a lot harder than I thought. The very reason why I took myself off the dating track years ago.

"Well, Inspector, I'm flattered. Is this like a date or something?" She was playing with me. "Or is this official business? Am I going to be expensed?"

"Not expensed."

"Good. I'd be embarrassed if you asked the hot dog vendor for a receipt."

"I know this is kind of soon. My son told me once if you get a lady's digits and call within, like two days? She won't go out with you because she'll think you're desperate."

"A*re* you desperate?"

"No. But then again, if I waited two days, the damn tickets wouldn't be any good." A solid comeback. Felt more in control now. Give and take. The dance had begun.

"Well, Inspector McGuire, I haven't been to a baseball game in years. But, yes, I'd like to go. What time?"

"It's a night game. Due to the fireworks. Starts at seven. What say I pick you up at five? Get to the park at six or so, have a few dogs and beers first. How's that sound?"

"Like a real date almost. I'll look forward to it. You have my address obviously. We're not going in one of those awful police cars are we?"

"With lights flashing and sirens. To get us through the traffic."

"What is appropriate dress for a baseball game nowadays? Formal?"

"Semi. Jeans, sweatshirt and heels. See 'ya at five."

9

Riverside, California

After negotiating the interchange between I-10 and the Golden State freeway, the man set the cruise control and opened the briefcase sitting next to him on the seat. Removing the tape marked *Jennifer,* he inserted it into the vehicle's tape deck.

"Jennifer, do you know who I am?" The voice was tinny, metallic sounding as it came through the car speakers. The man turned up the sound. He'd already listened to one of the tapes in its entirety. Still had two to go. This would be the last one before he got home. He'd listen to the rest on his six-hour car trip back to Northern California two days from now.

"Yes. You told me." Jennifer's voice. High pitched. Midwestern inflection. Quavering. Intimidated.

"And why am I here?"

"You're some guy we interviewed in Vietnam."

"Some guy?"

"A prisoner."

"In Vietnam. Could you be more specific, Jennifer?"

"North Vietnam. Hanoi. Okay?" Scared, but with a slight hint of sarcasm.

"And when would this have been? Approximately."

"I don't know." A catch in the voice. A sob? "What is this, an interview? What do you want from me? I don't understand. God, this is a nightmare. It was so long ago. I haven't thought about this stuff in years."

"Where are we now, Jennifer?" The man's voice was smooth. Calming. "Describe what we are doing." Setting the place. Proof of authenticity.

"You're in my house, you bastard. You broke in here and ... and ... kidnapped me."

"Kidnapped?"

"Well, what then? Holding me prisoner?" Voice louder. Her mouth closer to the microphone. Anger having replaced fear. "We're sitting at my kitchen table. You've got that *gun*, and we're having a conversation. God, I don't believe this. Something that happened, what, thirty or so years ago? I think you're probably out of your mind is what I think." Her voice softened. "I'm sorry, okay? Whatever happened to you, I'm sorry. Please – just go away and leave me alone." Her sobbing audible now.

"Jennifer, tell us the date."

"It's March 11th. Why?"

"Just wanted to make sure everyone knows, that's all. Now, I want you to tell me why you went to Vietnam in the first place. I want to know everything. We were at war. Didn't it dawn on you that you were committing treason?"

"Oh, please. Come on. It was a long time ago. I was a student at Columbia. We all were. No – that's not right. Ruth wasn't. She was already a writer for the Voice by that time."

"The Village Voice, right?"

"Yes. She'd already graduated. I knew her from the protests. All kinds of things were going on then, especially at Columbia. The radicals were there in force. I mean, hell, they shut down the damn university. Students rioting all over the place. Cops. Jesus, there were a lot of cops. Tear gas raining down on us. We were all radicalized in those days. And if we weren't, the tear gas soon made us. It was really a lot of fun, tell you the truth."

"So, how did you get involved with that group?" His voice again. Syrupy. Like Dan Rather on Valium. "What was it called? Women's something-or-other."

"*Women Against Imperialistic Wars.* It wasn't a big group or anything. Hell, I think there were only four or five of us. Four of us got to go to Vietnam."

"And how was it formed, this group?"

"Honestly, I can't remember. I think it was Heidi who asked me to meet a friend of hers. It turned out to be Ruth Wasserman. As I said, I'd met her before. I already knew who she was. We were doing drugs and experimenting with just about everything in those years. Really messed up, you know? It just seemed like the thing to do."

"So Ruth was the ringleader as far as you know? She founded the group?" A regular conversation going on. Chummy. Intimate. Friends talking.

"I think that's what happened. Yeah! Ruth invited us all to come to her apartment. Damn nice digs, too. Up on East 68th and Lexington. It was *really* nice, now that I think about it. Anyway, four of us were there. Betsy couldn't make it. She was kind of out of the group by then, anyway. Well, Ruth had us up, and we are all talking about unity. You know – solidarity. All for one, one for all. That kind of thing."

"Unite behind what?" he asked.

"Anti-war. Anti-establishment. Being anti-*anything* was so popular then." She laughed. "We were all so smug. Getting on television. That was the thing. Television. Bring the *cause* to the masses through the media."

"What *cause*? That's what I want to know about. You talk about the *cause*. What was that all about?"

"Hell, I don't know. In terms of political persuasion? We were all on the left, if that's what you mean? We got it in the classroom. Everywhere. Hey, when I came to Columbia, I was a naive Midwestern girl from Springfield, Illinois. A Republican, for God's sake. Land of Lincoln. You know – God, Family, Country. That sort of thing."

"What happened to change you?"

"It wasn't just one thing. The whole atmosphere was charged. You were supposed to question everything. The whole civil rights thing was going on. The three kids had been killed in Mississippi a few years before. We could see there were some serious problems in this country. In the classroom, though – that's where it all started. When I came to Columbia, I wanted to talk about the things I'd grown up with. You know … my values. Test my WASP values. Test them against what was going on in the world at the time. But my professors? They wouldn't argue with me. They wouldn't even discuss them with me. Instead, they laughed at them. Laughed at me. I don't know about you, but I didn't want to be laughed at. By the time I was a sophomore those values had pretty much been ripped out of me. They embarrassed me. I was empty. A bucket waiting to be filled. The fervor of the anti-war, anti-establishment thing was what filled the vacuum."

"Okay." The man's voice. Pausing. A gap in the tape. Then, "How well did you know Schaeffer?"

"Schaeffer? Why? What's he got to do with this?" Her voice challenging. "He ..." A phone rang in the background. Silence. Another ring. Chair scraping back.

"Don't." The man's voice commanded. Another ring. "We'll just let it ring, okay?"

The call went to voice mail. A man's voice. "Hi. You've reached 555-1793. Sorry we're not here to receive your call. You know what to do." The beep, but then only silence. The caller had already hung up.

"Jennifer, tell me about Schaeffer," the voice on the tape said, sounding tired now.

"I only met him a few times. Mostly over at Ruth's. We were all impressed she knew him. He was a big star. Kind of cute, too. I remember wanting to get together with him. Kind of like a groupie, you know? But he and Ruth were living together by then. Later I heard he and Heidi shacked-up. Ruth was really pissed about that. He probably could've had any of us. But looking back, I think he was just using us. I still read about him in the papers. He's governor of California now, isn't he? Thinking about running for president?"

"That's the word, yes."

"What a sellout. Government! I'm surprised he's so into it. Though I suspect he's good at it. He could really get people fired up. Personally, I think it's all a bunch of horse manure. I don't even vote."

"Given up the fight, huh?"

"It doesn't do any good. Voting just perpetuates the *status quo*. Protecting the rich and the corporations. Nothing changes."

"Schaeffer thinks he can make a difference."

"Maybe he can. Who knows? But he's probably become establishment by now."

"Hmmm. Maybe." A pause. "Perhaps." Another pause. "That's why I'm asking you about him. Was he the provider for your group?" The man was back to his conversational tone. Not wanting anything to seem coerced.

"Provider? What do you mean?"

"I mean did he give you the money to operate?"

"To tell you the truth, we all thought it was Ruth who had the funds. At first we thought it came from her salary. From the newspaper. But when we started traveling across the country to various demonstrations, and all the bail money that we required, we knew Ruth couldn't be funding us. And when we went to Hanoi? Well, Ruth actually wrote the checks, but we knew she had to get that money from someone. And Schaeffer was the one who actually urged us to go."

"Good. I wanted to talk about that, too. How did you actually get over there? Obviously you just couldn't hop a plane at JFK."

"No, I guess not." A chuckle. "When we got word we were going ..."

"From whom?" the man interrupted.

"From Ruth. We were in the quad at school, as I remember. In the middle of some demonstration. Ruth told us Schaeffer thinks we should go to Hanoi. Make a big media splash. Maybe interview a few of the prisoners. That he thought it could be arranged.

"We weren't the first, you know," she continued. "All kinds of people, mostly celebrities, were going over there. I thought it would be a blast. You know – little ol' us. *Women Against Imperialistic Wars.* We'd made the big time. Ruth told us we'd leave the following Tuesday. That was it. And we ended up in Vietnam twice. Did you know that? A year apart."

"No. I didn't know. Did you ever wonder how all this was paid for? I mean it obviously cost a lot of money. And Schaeffer wasn't a rich guy." His voice more deliberate now.

"No. And I still don't. There were plenty of rich people against that war. It was popular in those years to be against the war. But there are plenty of rich people even now who really don't like the way America is going. I read about them all the time."

"I have no doubt that is true, Jennifer. Sadly."

"But I'll tell you about what I thought was strange then and still wonder about even today. I had my passport. We all did except Rebecca. She didn't have one. You should've heard her bitch. *Why so soon? Why can't we wait?* Well, normally it took months to get a passport. Guess what? Becky had her passport the next Saturday."

"Well connected, huh?"

"I guess so. Somebody high up had to pass on that one. We felt pretty special. A part of something much larger. Anyway, we flew out of JFK to Paris. Stayed overnight and then flew to Moscow."

"I've seen some of the news footage. Weren't you met in Paris by the North Vietnamese delegation?"

"Yeah. Our first real TV exposure. Heady stuff. That's what we were there for. Get on television. Reuters interviewed us. Got picked up by all the media in the States."

"So you didn't set that up? Your group, I mean? You got off the plane and not only were the North Vietnamese waiting for you, but reporters as well. Is that what you're telling me?"

"As far as I know we had nothing to do with it." A pause. Then, "Are we through here? I'm getting tired – and hungry."

"Almost." A scratchiness on the tape. The sound of it being moved. Repositioned.

"Okay. So now you're in Moscow. How long did you stay there? Did anyone meet you there?"

"I can't remember how long we were there. A day or two, max. Guarded day and night. Kept away from everyone. Only contact we had was with each other. Could hardly go take a pee." She laughed.

"You left Moscow how?" The man, back to serious conversation.

"On some Chinese airplane. God, it was so old. A DC-1 or something. A prop job. Do you believe it? Older than dirt."

"It couldn't have flown you directly to Hanoi. We effectively shut down all air traffic in and out of Hanoi and Haiphong."

"You're right. We landed at some little airport in south China. Took the train to Hanoi. Had to stop three or four times after we crossed the border because you guys were bombing rail lines. We came close to getting hit once. I was scared shitless."

"Do you remember our interview?"

"I'm sorry! I said I was sorry. Look. It was a long time ago. I was just a kid. Hell, I've got grandkids older than I was then." Her voice singsong. Scared.

"What do you remember about it?"

"The thing I remember most about Vietnam was the horrible food. It could give you major stomach cramps if you weren't careful. About the interview? I don't remember yours specifically. As I said, we were there twice. We did a group thing the first time. I think there were four or five prisoners all together then. The second time, we interviewed four or five individually. I remember there were TV cameras everywhere. Japanese cameramen, I think. Maybe Chinese. Some kind of Oriental, anyway. The four of us sat on couches. The prisoners were brought in through a door on the side of the room."

"Were the questions prepared for you?"

"Some. We didn't need much prompting. We wanted to make the country and the administration look bad. That they were bombing hospitals and schools and things. Killing indiscriminately. Come on, we thought you guys were devils, doing the work as part of an imperialist land grab. America's modus operandi."

"And?"

"Most of you were real smart-asses. That's what we thought, anyway. How did you get off talking to us like that?"

"Do you want to see what they did to me after you left?" The metallic sound of the tape running, then a chair being pushed back. "Look Jennifer."

A gasp, barely audible. "Oh, God. I'm sorry." Crying now. "Please, I'm sorry."

"Too late," came the reply as the tape clicked off sharply, like a miniature guillotine.

10

Sunday, July 4th

I woke up about ten and glanced out the window. It was cold, wet and thoroughly miserable. Another typical summer day in San Francisco. I retrieved the Chronicle from the front porch. This was the middle of the summer for God's sake, and the paper was wrapped in plastic so it wouldn't get wet. For all of San Francisco's fabled beauty, God sure didn't bless it with good weather.

Wasserman's murder was the headline. I scanned it quickly to see what details the department released. Not much, thank goodness. Bristow was quoted about what a tragedy it was, and how the SFPD was on top of it and had several leads. Usual bullshit. There were other stories, features really, about Wasserman, her life and times. I didn't even bother. I'd more important things on my mind that day. I found the sports page, hunkered down in bed, and read every inch, front to back.

Went to noon Mass at Saint Cecilia's. My parents are looking down from somewhere smiling. I'd gone years without going to church. Been a regular since my divorce. Strange how that works.

I was looking forward to the game and Michele, and, I realized, not necessarily in that order. I was undeniably nervous. She'd been right. I couldn't hide the fact that this *was* a real date. My first in about five years. It's not that I haven't been out with women. Shortly after my divorce, wives of my friends tried to fix me up with their single girlfriends. But I was clearly not interested in getting involved with anyone, and, over time, they picked up on that. But it was really my relationship with Tracy that stopped any matchmaking those wives might have had in mind. Ah, Tracy. Even after so many years, the thought of her gives my ego a burst of adrenalin. She was a medical technician I met in a bar one night. An extraordinarily pretty girl. Long blonde hair. Blue eyes to die for. A tight little body. But that's what she was – a girl. Twenty-four. I was forty-seven. Old enough to be her father. And she was married. We started talking and the drinks were flowing and she ended up that night in my bed. I should've just left it at that, but, no, my vanity got the better of me. I called her at work the next day and asked her out for dinner. She accepted. I took her to my house afterward and we made it again.

The relationship lasted for the better part of three months, a relatively short time considering the coming long-term consequences. Once it became known that I was banging a twenty-four-year-old, my friends' wives stopped trying to hook up their single girlfriends with me. Since then, I've been pretty much alone. Told myself that I was at an age where it didn't matter. That I didn't need female companionship. What a crock!!

~~~~

59

Michele lived in a white bungalow on Jackson Court, on the east side of Twin Peaks. Living on one of the higher hills in San Francisco definitely had its perks. For one, if the fog layer that usually blanketed the City wasn't too thick, it would burn off at the higher elevations. Today was such a day. I hit sunshine about two blocks from her house. The sensation is much like breaking through clouds when you're in an airplane. Looking down, I could see the ashen carpet that still covered the rest of the City.

I parked and walked up her front steps. Taking a deep breath, followed quickly by another to quiet the butterflies flapping their wings in my stomach, I rang the bell. Her beauty again stunned me as she opened the door. Some women get better looking with age. She was certainly one of them. While I'm sure she was pretty at twenty, at forty-something Michele was way beyond *pretty*.

She wore a fuzzy purple turtleneck sweater over jeans. Neither did much to hide her figure. Her hair was swept back and held in place by one of those clippie things women wear. Not much make-up, or at least not that you'd notice. Dark rose lipstick framed the smile that greeted me. I thought of the old real estate adage ... it's all about curb appeal. The one thing I could say about this lady was she definitely had curb appeal.

The house was sparsely furnished, but definitely feminine. A large white Haitian cotton sofa sat under the window. Crimson throw pillows formed geometric patterns across the back. In one corner was an overstuffed chair of the same material as the couch. Beside it was a small table with three or four carelessly stacked *Architectural Digest* magazines. My eyes were drawn to a large wooden pedestal in the opposite corner, atop which sat a small figurine of a ballet dancer. Offset track lights from the ceiling illuminated this delicate alabaster statue, throwing overlapping shadows on the wall behind.

Following my gaze, Michele asked, "Do you like it?"

"Very much." I walked closer. "Degas?"

"Good knowledge. You surprise me."

"Whadda ya think? I got no class or sumpin'?"

"Sorry. It's just not the impression I had of you. Well, maybe not you, but cops in general, I guess."

I laughed. "Reminds me of advice I got from an old southern gentleman in a bar one night in South Carolina. We were talking about women." Michele gave me a crooked grin. "I know. I know. What else do guys talk about, right? Anyway, he leaned close to me and said 'You gotta remember, son. You hafta treat women differently. They ain't like ordinary people.'" I looked at her and winked. "I guess you could substitute cops for women. But some of us cops *are* ordinary. Like me. I took some art classes at the Academy of Art five or six years ago. This is really beautiful."

"I got it in Paris last year. I'm personally not too fond of the Impressionists, but I've always liked Degas. His work is so – so sensuous. I paid way too much for her. Wouldn't let them ship it. I wrapped her carefully and held her in my lap the entire trip home."

"Like your child."

"Yes. Like my child." She finished putting on her boots, stood up and grabbed her purse.

"Before we go, want a tour?"

"Normally, I'd love to but we really have to get going. The traffic can be a bear, and I left the squad car home."

"Okay. Some other time."

She took my arm as we headed down the stairs. The shock of the unexpected intimacy took me by surprise. "Wow," she exclaimed. "Cool car. You're full of surprises." She took a step back, appraising me. I sucked in my stomach. Reflex. "I would've expected a Lexus. Something like that. More ... stuffy." She smiled. "You're going to be fun, Inspector. Can we put the top down?"

"Honestly, I don't think that would be a good idea. One of the scams the bad guys are running these days is waiting for traffic to back up and stop. While you're stuck, they come over, reach through the window and make off with your purse. If we put the top down, we'd just make their job easier. Can't chase them because you're stuck in traffic. Happened to a friend of mine and his wife. They were coming home from a Niner game last year. At Candlestick Park. Driving up Third Street. Late afternoon. Cars everywhere. A regular parking lot. Some jerk sees the window down, runs across two lanes of traffic, and reaches through the window for the purse he thinks is on her lap. It's not. It's on the floor. While the guy is feeling around for the purse, she grabs his arm. The guy gets pissed, pulls his arm back and cold-cocks her right through the open window. She saved her purse at the expense of six stitches inside her mouth."

"Well, I wouldn't have to worry because I'd have you to protect me. Isn't that right, Inspector?"

I glanced at her sideways. She was leaning against the car door looking at me. That half smile on her face. Flirting. And damn good at it, too.

"What the hell do you do for a living?"

"I'm a stewardess. Oops, sorry. Flight attendant. Why?"

"I'll bet you have the men on those planes eating out of your hand. You're really good at this stuff."

"And what *stuff* might that be?"

"This interaction stuff. Flirting. I'm not all that good at it anymore. Used to be, but not anymore."

"Out of practice?"

"Yeah. Out of practice."

"Good. Stick around. I'll help you get it back."

I smiled. "Deal. But do me a favor, okay? Do we know each other well enough yet for you to call me Mac or Tom? This 'Inspector' stuff is just a bit too formal."

"Maybe when I get to know you better."

I looked over at her, not knowing if she was serious or not. That half smile, again. She wasn't.

"So, since you won't put the top down, and I can't put the window down, what you're really telling me is I can't smoke, huh?"

"That's exactly what I'm telling you."

"Then I take back what I said before. You are *no* fun," she said, a practiced pout on her lips. "Next time we'll take my car."

11

We got to the park about an hour and a half before game time. Not too many people in the stands yet. AT&T Park opened this spring. The first privately funded ball park since Dodger stadium in 1962. It was a throwback – built along the lines of the old Forbes Field in Pittsburgh. Small and cozy. A far cry from Candlestick. The fans registered their appreciation by immediately selling out the place for the season. If you weren't one of the lucky 40,290 who bought Giants season tickets and wanted to see a game, you had to know somebody. Luckily, I knew "somebody." Actually, a bunch of "somebody's." In the four months the Park has been open, I've been to sixteen games. Being a cop had its rewards. We grabbed a couple of hot dogs and two beers and made our way to the seats.

"You know ... I really love this game. Where else can you get this?" I made a sweeping gesture across the field. "Look at all those kids down there with their moms and dads getting autographs. See that little kid right in front? The one with his hat on sideways? The one on his dad's shoulders? What is he, maybe three? Four? He'll never forget this. I sure as hell never did."

"I haven't been to a game in years and years. When I was a child I went a few times with my dad. About all I remember about it was how cold it was."

"That's because you went to Candlestick. Not a weather friendly place."

She nodded. "But mostly he took Mike," she continued. "So I'm glad you asked me. Even if you don't let me smoke in your car, you *are* fun." She squeezed my hand.

We spent the next hour or so eating and drinking while she asked me about particular players from both teams. Who was that? Was he good? Can he hit? Pitch? I was in my element. Loved showing off. But then, there was more to it than that. I knew it, and I think she knew it. The dance. It was in full swing. The music was deafening. We were surrendering to its rhythm.

I asked her about herself. Not like most times you ask people. Just to be polite. Could give a good shit. But with her? I was really interested.

I started gently prying. "You got out of Saint Anne's about, what, ten years after I did? Was my sister in your class?"

"I think she was a year ahead of me. Didn't you have a brother about that age, too?"

"Yeah, Jeff. He'd probably be about your class. I've forgotten all their ages. When I left for the Academy I was eighteen. My family's individual ages all froze in time."

"I remember your brother. The reason I do is because he wasn't as cute as you. What are they doing now? Your brothers and sisters. As I remember, you had a bunch."

"Yeah. Eleven. They're scattered all over the country. We get together once a year at Christmas. Those that can make it, anyway. We rent a hall somewhere. All the nieces and nephews come. God, it's like an orphanage. How 'bout you? You get together with your brothers and sisters?"

"We didn't have as big a family as yours," she laughed. "More normal-sized. I have one other brother and two sisters. We don't see each other much. Even at Christmas."

"What about the ex's family. Do you keep in contact with them?"

"Not since he died."

Now that was a revelation I didn't expect. "Died? He *died*? I thought you said you were divorced."

"We were. Well, almost, anyway. He died before it was finalized."

"Was he sick?"

"No. He was shot dead. In Ireland."

This was going down a road I wasn't sure I wanted to travel. But curiosity was stronger than common sense. "God. I'm sorry. What happened?"

"By the police. He was shot by the police in Northern Ireland."

I was silent for a moment. Thinking of the possibilities. It wasn't too hard to put together a scenario where Northern Ireland was involved. I ticked off the years in my mind. Probably talking about the mid-Eighties, maybe a little later. Northern Ireland. The heart of "The Troubles," the Irish euphemism for the war waged between the IRA and the British in Northern Ireland.

"John was Irish, obviously, with a name like Sullivan," she continued through my silence. "Grew up like every other Irish kid in this City. A united Ireland. It was in all the songs their parents sang to them while growing up. That the British stole their country and then treated the Catholics like dirt. Well – you know what I mean."

I nodded. I knew exactly. That cultural and religious identity shit was powerful stuff. My upbringing was the same. Hell, I remember hating the British. Thinking they were all devils. Until the first time I visited England. Found out they were just plain folks like me. But it took the visit to bring about the change.

"When John got out of school he worked on the waterfront unloading freight. Belonged to a union, of course. As you know, in those years most of the San Francisco unions were controlled by either the Irish or Italians. Same was true of you civil service types. The police. Firemen. Most of the city government. Well, anyway, in the late Seventies, the Irish Republican Army came to town to raise money for the *lads*, as they called them. Primarily money, but volunteers, too."

"I remember those times," I said. "I'd been on the force for two or three years by then. Was supposed to be on the lookout for those IRA types. They were classified as terrorists. Generally had rap sheets in Ireland as long as your arm. Trouble was, half the force was Irish, me included. No way any of us were going to curtail their activities. Most of the cops I knew – and I must admit I was one of them – thought those guys were freaking heroes. Liberating the people from oppressive foreign domination and all that. Were you working at the time?"

"Actually, John got me a job at his union. As a secretary."

"Did you like it?"

"It was a job. What can I say? Got me out of the house and was a good supplement to our income. Being around the guys was kind of fun, too." She raised her eyebrows and gave me a coquettish smile.

"I'll bet. You probably drove the boys wild. Imagine it was the best thing to happen to them in a long time, too."

Her face acknowledged the compliment. I was making points. "John got heavily involved in NORAID. You remember that?"

"Don't know what the acronym stands for. Had to do with aiding the Catholics in Northern Ireland, as I remember. Or something like that. It was an IRA front. We monitored their meetings."

"Well, John started helping them raise money. Through the union guys. I mean, come on. I'm not stupid. I knew the money was going to buy guns. But he never said a word to me about it. Pretended it was all legit. And he started hanging out with a lot of unsavory characters." She finished her beer and put the bottle in the cup holder attached to the seat in front of her. "Our marriage started to suffer from it, too. He never talked about anything but *The Troubles.* God, I got so tired hearing about it. It all seemed so stupid to me. So unnecessary. It's the only thing all the union guys talked about, too. I got it at home and at work.

"I don't know about you, but I grew up with that romantic notion about marriage. That you were supposed to grow together into old age. Mine wasn't happening like that. Oh, John and I were growing all right. He in one direction, me in another."

"That's how it is with everybody, I think."

"Maybe you're right. But with me, John was living a secret life. He might as well have had a bimbo. It was the same thing. Either he couldn't, or wouldn't, share with me. Put a huge strain on our relationship. By the time he left, it was all but over. We both could tell."

"By the time he left?"

"Yes. He went to Ireland. 'To lend a hand,' as he put it. That was a couple years after that prisoner starved himself to death."

"Yeah. Bobby Sands. And nine of his friends."

"Caused a big ruckus over here. All the union guys were outraged. He may have died, but his death was the best thing that ever happened to the IRA. Over here, anyway. God – guys started coming out of the woodwork. Wanting to give money. Whoever the English politician was that let those fellows die made one big mistake."

"I think it was Thatcher," I said, trying to remember my history.

"Well, whoever. I know from just our own union, the money was pouring in. The IRA made a windfall. And some, like John, were so angry that they volunteered to go fight the Brits. And that's what he did. Just left me. One day I got up and he was gone. A note. That's all I got."

I marveled at the calmness with which she told her story. If it were me, I'd still be pissed. "Did he ever come back? You know, like, for a visit or something?"

"No. I told you he died over there. But I knew from the beginning he wasn't coming back. Even if he had, it really wouldn't have mattered. Not for me, anyway. A week after he left, I filed for divorce. Two weeks before it became final I got a notice that he'd been shot dead by the police. In a little town just south of Derry. He was planting a bomb. The police got a tip. Apparently he tried to escape, and they shot him."

"Jesus, Michele. I'm sorry." What else could I say?

"Don't feel sorry for me. It was for the best, really. I felt bad for his family, though. They took it really hard. For me? I know this sounds awful, but because the divorce wasn't yet finalized, I got his insurance money. Wasn't a whole lot, but it sure as hell helped."

"What did you do then? Stay on with the union?"

"No, I quit immediately. But a strange thing happened. I got a call shortly after John was killed. A man named Pat something or other. Said because I was the wife of one of the 'lads,' if there was anything I needed, *anything*, just call him. I still have his number. In fact, someone from his group calls me every year on the anniversary of John's death. Asking if I'm all right and if I need anything. Kind of like my own protection agency. One thing you have to say for those guys, they take care of their own."

"Damn. I guess I'd better be careful around you. Don't want some goon knocking on my door in the middle of the night."

"You're damn right," she said with a laugh. "But, I think I can take care of you myself, seeing as how you're such a pussycat." She snuggled up against me. "But if I can't, I have my own private army to call on. Don't you forget it."

I started to put my arm around her but changed my mind. Maybe a little too intimate. I was still learning. "So what did you do then?" I wanted to know everything about her.

"Well, I didn't know what to do at first. I hadn't gone to college, no skills to speak of. I moved back home with my mom. Dad was dead by then. I was like the black sheep of the family. First one to be divorced. It was terrible."

We both stood when they played *The Star Spangled Banner*. "I know what you were going through," I whispered, thinking myself unpatriotic for talking during the Anthem. "I've thought a lot about that whole divorce thing. I don't know about you, but when I was growing up I didn't know one person who was divorced. Talk about an insulated life." The crowd roared as the Anthem neared its end, and we sat down. "So you got a job as a stewardess, slash, flight attendant?"

"Not right away. After the divorce, I didn't know what to do. A girlfriend worked for United Airlines. Told me I should apply. I did and got a job. Started on the milk run like everybody did but gradually got seniority, and now I can virtually dictate my schedule."

She touched my hand. "I'm off this week. Have the Chicago run starting next Monday."

"How does that work? Do you stay overnight and then fly back?"

"Uh huh. I have the 11:30 a.m. flight out of SFO. Gets to O'Hare at six in the evening. We stay overnight and then work the 7:30 a.m. flight back. It's a good schedule. I do it four days, and then I'm off three."

"Let me ask you – I've often wondered. Is there much hanky-panky going on between you guys and the pilots? Everybody teased me that instead of going into police work, I should've become a commercial pilot and spent the nights with the Stews. Oops. Sorry. Flight attendants. True?"

"Well, you might have, Inspector, but in my experience it doesn't happen that often. And I can tell you that it won't happen on this trip to Chicago." She looked up at me, her eyes gleaming in the stadium lights.

"Gee," I said, "that's comforting."

By now it was the bottom of the third. Bonds ripped one out off Glavine. The wind picked up. Hot dog wrappers started whipping around home plate before swirling off into the night. If I didn't know better, I'd have thought we were still at Candlestick instead of AT&T.

"Is it always like this here?" She put her arm through mine and burrowed closer. Snuggling. "You don't mind, do you?" I couldn't see her face, but I knew she was teasing. The warmth of her touch radiated through me. Made the night suddenly warmer.

"I should've told you to bring a coat." Glad that I didn't. "This is actually pretty mild. You remember Candlestick? Probably not too much, huh? I used to go to games there where you'd swear you were getting frostbite." She pulled the sweater down over her hands and drew her knees up to her chest. Rolled up like a ball. Her face pressed against my shoulder. Shivering like a frightened animal. I couldn't resist. I put my arm around Michele and pulled her close.

"You know, I'm curious." She was talking into my shoulder. "I don't know if I should even bring this up, because maybe you're not supposed to tell. But what happened with that lady across the street that got killed. Did you catch the guy?"

"No."

"Was it a robbery?"

"No. At least as far as we know. It wasn't a robbery."

"God. This city. It's becoming worse than New York. If it wasn't a robbery, what was it? Just a random thing?"

"Well, we really don't know yet. I'll work on it tomorrow,"

"You have to work tomorrow? Too bad. I have it off." She sounded disappointed.

I laughed. "The law never sleeps. But then, you're not going to be able to, either. You have to come down to 850 and work with our sketch artist."

"Wait! I thought you said I could come in on Tuesday."

"That was before I remembered that I had to work tomorrow."

"I don't think it will do much good, do you? I didn't see him clearly."

"No, I don't think it will do any good. But it will give me a chance to see you."

We actually lasted longer than I thought. By the middle of the seventh inning Michele wanted to go home. Or at least somewhere warm. By that time the Braves had gone ahead two to one. We would miss the fireworks, but what the hell.

I got to listen to the rest of the game driving her home. The score never changed. Dodgers were now within four.

We drove up in front of her house. I kept the car running so the heater would work. We hadn't said much on the way back. She spent most of her time rubbing her hands together under the heat vent. This was such an awkward situation. When I was dating it was the worst part of the evening. Just one of the many reasons why I was glad I didn't do this anymore. Do I kiss her goodnight? Is it expected? I'd been out of the game for so long I'd forgotten the rules. What was she thinking? Does she want me to kiss her? If I don't will she think I'm a wimp? That I don't find her attractive? What if I try and she turns away? How embarrassing would that be? As if sensing my discomfort, Michele leaned over and kissed me on the cheek. She lingered just long enough for the hairs on the back of my neck to salute. "Want to come in for a minute? Have some coffee?"

"Uh ... no thanks. I have to get to work early tomorrow and should be getting home." Saved another embarrassing situation in her living room.

"Well, okay. Thanks for the nice time." She reached for the door handle.

"I'll see you tomorrow at the station," I quickly said. Not wanting her to leave. "Want to have dinner after that? I could pick you up about seven if that works for you. I promise to take you somewhere warm."

She leaned close and fixed me with those remarkable eyes. The corners of her mouth tilted upward into a smile. "I'd love to, Mac. See you at the office."

12

Monday, July 5th

As I looked out my front window at the gray, dreary mist enveloping the neighborhood, I thought, What a beautiful day. I was eager to get going. Even the skim milk on my Cheerios tasted good. Michele was having a salubrious effect on my mental outlook.

I took my time getting to 850. Wasn't supposed to be working today, so what the hell, right? I walked in and saw Bristow already behind his desk. Damn!

"Hey, Matt, what brings you down here today?" I already knew, of course. The Wasserman killing had his well-honed political antenna all-aflutter. I just knew he'd gotten here early and been pacing, waiting for me to arrive. He wouldn't say anything to me directly, but I knew it would show up on my evaluation next spring. I'd have forgotten all about it, but these are the kinds of things *he* never forgot. I could be caught with my pants down getting a blowjob in some public restroom and my evaluation would only reflect I was late on July 5th. He was a strange dude.

"Just checking on a few things," he said nonchalantly and then added offhandedly, "Oh, I was wondering about the Wasserman case. Anything new?" God, he was so transparent. "By the way," he said before I could reply, "thanks for coming in today. I know you weren't scheduled. The Department owes you." He and I both laughed at that one. There was an official policy regarding comp time. You were owed it, but no one ever put in for it. Especially in Homicide. Last guy who did was Tarantino. He found himself transferred to Domestic Violence within the month. A warning to us all. Ask not what the Department can do for you, but what you can do for the Department.

But it was a good trade-off. Being a homicide inspector in San Francisco, like most major cities, was a plum job. Only fourteen cops in the whole damn unit. Fourteen for all the murders committed in the City. A routine part of the political landscape every four years was mayoral candidates promising to add more inspectors to Homicide. Beef up the department. But they were just blowing smoke. The realities of the budget process in this city were such that every social agency in creation got funded before the police department. But, hey, we didn't mind a bit. We saw ourselves as an elite group in an elite situation. We'd gladly work a few extra days for that trade-off.

I sat down at my desk with Bristow sitting at Irvine's facing me. This configuration was one of his ideas. SFPD's Homicide Department was broken into teams. Two inspectors comprised a team. Seven teams in all. The partners' desks butted up facing one another. Seven pair of desks front-to-front dotted the large room. Efficient. Sometimes Bristow's anal side came up with workable concepts.

"So, what you got?" he asked, getting down to business.

"Not much, Matt. It's early though. We've snagged a witness. She'll be in later today to work with Harry. Come up with a composite. I don't expect much. It was still dark and foggy when the perp left Wasserman's house. She only saw him from the side as he walked under a street light."

"I read Irvine's report. What's with the rope business? Got any ideas?"

"Some. But nothing for public consumption. I want to go through Irvine's report to see if he got some of the crap I asked him to get." I gestured with my head at the pile of papers stacked irreverently on the side of my desk.

"Okay," he said sliding out of Irvine's chair. "Keep me up-to-date. We have the beginning of a real media circus on this one."

"Yeah. I saw you quoted yesterday."

He turned to me and grinned. "And today, too, if you'd read your paper. I was even better."

13

I bellied up to the gunmetal gray desk, pulled Irvine's stack of reports over in front of me, and quickly leafed through them. Autopsy summaries. Forensic reports. A record of all the personal items in Wasserman's house, including ten pages of book titles. I moved it all to the side and opened the note Irvine left.

Went through our own records going back two years. There were no similars to Wasserman. I wired VICAP. Sent them pictures of the knot just in case it might be a factor. Also, Fastbein called. As a favor, he did the autopsy yesterday. On his day off. He just wanted you to know and told me to say you owed him. Summary copy is in the pile. Ropes were done post-mortem as he suspected. I included that in my VICAP request. Decided I couldn't let you handle this all by your lonesome, so I'll be in today sometime after lunch. Mike.

As if on cue, Kathy from the reception desk downstairs came through the door loaded with two big manila envelopes she deposited on my desk. "This came for you, Mac. Faxed from the Feds."

I had to admit the FBI was efficient. Inside the envelopes were about three hundred pages of VICAP reports. The ones Irvine requested yesterday. The only thing I could think of as I glanced around the empty room was the enormous payroll they must have to staff up on a holiday.

VICAP is an acronym for Violent Crime Apprehension Program. The FBI started it in the mid-Eighties. A national crime clearinghouse. It's been extremely useful, and a long time coming. However, it did have its limitations – the biggest one being it was only as good as the guys who used it. Lots of cops I knew didn't like to share information on a case they were working. Especially with the Feds. It's stupid, I know. A pride thing. They felt they could solve it themselves. Consequently, a lot of crime profiles never made it to VICAP. The reports in front of me could be a huge waste of time. Irvine asked only for open cases. It was conceivable that in each of these cases the criminal could already have been caught, tried and convicted. You never knew. The only way to find out was to call the investigating officer. Even with all the downsides, though, VICAP was a giant leap forward in cooperative law-enforcement. Give it any unusual aspect of a case, and it would spit back all similar cases nationwide, most of the time with the actual crime photos.

I didn't want to start plowing through all of it just yet. First things first. Any good homicide investigation began with a cup of coffee. I want to say a *good* cup of coffee, but you never knew. I went down the hall to the kitchen and made a fresh pot. It was either that or microwave the sludge left from yesterday. At least somebody turned off the machine. There were times I'd arrive in the morning and find just a thick black stain on the bottom of the glass pot. I could've used the coin operated coffee machine around the corner, but that crap tasted like shampoo. I waited for the water to drip through, cleaned out a mug, filled it, opened the door to the hall … and ran right into Michele.

My heart thumped and I jerked back, almost spilling the hot liquid down the front of my shirt. "Hey," she said, "I won't hurt you, honest." She smiled. "I was looking for you. I went to where they said your office was, and the man there said to look down here. And *here* you are."

She looked spectacular. Short black skirt, black tights and black boots. A clingy beige silk blouse opened to the third button. No cleavage showing, but that damned blouse gapped just enough to make you want to get a good look.

She noticed me appraising her. "Do I look all right? I didn't want to embarrass you at your place of work." That knowing smile on her face. God, she was good at this shit.

"You look ..." I wanted to say "beautiful" or wonderful, or luscious, or sexy, or incredible, or good enough to eat, or hot ... or a hundred other descriptors that floated through my brain. But not knowing how far I should commit myself, I simply said "real nice." Not your most sophisticated answer, I know. Actually, it sounded pretty dumb. And to add nuance to my appraisal, I said, "You're early."

"I know. I thought about calling first but then decided to surprise you. I guess I was successful, huh?"

"And how."

"Really, I was hoping, if you weren't too busy, we could go to lunch after I finished with the artist."

"Yeah. You can see how busy I am," I lied, thinking about the pile of papers awaiting me at my desk. "Why don't I take you downstairs to Harry's office, and when you're finished, have him call me and I'll come down and get you. In the meantime, I'll think of someplace nice we can go." I took her hand and started back toward the elevators. "You like doughnuts?"

14

Riverside, California
Monday, July 5th

One of the things you learn in the military is that no matter how meticulously an operation is planned, something will always get screwed up. More often than not, the outcome of a battle is determined more through dumb luck than clever planning.

These were the thoughts circulating through the man's head as he sat in the Jeep Cherokee two blocks from his house, watching two men walk up his front stairs. He'd noticed them because they'd circled the block twice before parking just fifty feet in front of him. Well dressed. Oriental. Given Schaeffer's associations, he thought, probably Vietnamese or Chinese.

Today was move day. He'd planned this part of his operation as carefully as he'd planned anything in his life. He just hoped all the contingencies were covered. And they were. Except one. And that one had nearly proved fatal.

The first thing he did when he got home from the airport Saturday afternoon was to make the copies of the tapes he'd recorded, package them up and send them via overnight mail to Schaeffer. He wanted to make the son-of-a-bitch squirm. The enclosed note read: "I know all your dirty little secrets. Listen to the tapes. Run for president? Your soul will be rotting in hell before the first primary. I've done the others – now I'm coming for you." And then he thought, *what the hell*, and signed his name, rank and serial number. He knew it was probably stupid, but he calculated the risk and decided it might spook Schaeffer just enough for him to do something foolish. After all, he couldn't go to the police with the threat. It would mean exposing who he was. The real Bill Schaeffer. Which meant he would use hired guns. And the man sitting in the Jeep Cherokee was ready for the hired guns.

What he hadn't factored into the equation, however, was how quickly Schaeffer could mobilize to protect himself from the threat he posed. By the man's timetable, Schaeffer would've received the package sometime between nine and ten this morning. Another hour or so listening to them. A few hours to round up a hit squad. Everything being equal, I should've had at least until early afternoon before I started north, he thought.

Good planning, good fortune, and dumb luck. It was a mixture of all three that placed him in the Cherokee that morning, watching the destruction that was about to unfold.

Good planning had him pack everything he would need for the next week, including his 12-speed mountain bike, the night before. It was equally good planning that had him set the C-4 plastic explosive charge at the back door of his house, also the night before. He knew Schaeffer would send people, he just didn't know when. He knew they'd knock politely on the front door and, not receiving an answer, go to the back of the house and break in. He molded the C-4 into 2 one-half pound cubes and placed the cubes on either side of the kitchen door. He ran wires from the twenty-volt battery he purchased at RadioShack to each cube. He then attached a circuit breaker to an infrared beam, also purchased at RadioShack, and ran the beam past the door. When the door was opened, the beam would be interrupted, the circuit would close, and electricity would flow into the detonators inserted into each cube causing the C-4 to explode. To enhance the effect, and cause confusion to those first responders, he turned on the gas to the stove before leaving the house that morning. The resulting blast would not only blow the intruders into the next county, it would also cause a firestorm that would engulf the entire residence. It would take hours to put out the blaze and days to sift through the rubble before evidence of an explosive device and body parts would be found. At least that's how he'd planned it. He hoped it worked.

It was good fortune that his neighbors, the Elliots, gave him the keys to their Jeep and asked him to make sure the battery didn't go dead while they vacationed in Europe for the month of July. Perfect! That bit of good luck allowed him to leave his car in the garage. Responders would initially believe that he'd been in the house and engulfed in the firestorm.

It was dumb luck that he'd arisen early this particular morning, and instead of eating his breakfast at home, had gone to the corner 7-11 for coffee. It was there he purchased a copy the L.A. Times with the Wasserman murder emblazoned across the front page. He took it home and plopped on his couch to read it. His muscles jerked involuntarily when he saw that Inspector Thomas McGuire was in charge of the investigation. God, what were the chances of that, he thought. A cellmate at the Hanoi Hilton. Someone who'd understand the demons driving him. Maybe!

Dumb luck. The article so absorbed him that he was an hour later than usual leaving the house for the office. It was during that hour that he received the phone call. Nothing big. Just a phone call. But when he answered, no one was on the other end. A warning siren screamed in his brain. He just knew it was them, and he knew they were coming.

Dumb luck! His original plan had him going to the office at eight thirty. Just like always. Nothing unusual. Leave for lunch and never come back. The explosion and body parts at his house would lead most people to conclude that he'd died in an unfortunate accident. At least for a while. It would buy him time. But the phone call meant he had to change plans, and in a hurry. It was nine thirty when he called his office to tell his secretary he was running late because of what he thought was a gas leak in his kitchen and wanted to check it out before coming in. That would fit the story line that was just about to play itself out.

~~~~

The pain started two inches to the left of his belly button and arced across his whole abdomen, bending him double. He gasped. It felt like someone had taken a hot dagger, inserted it above his rib cage and cut diagonally across his stomach. Sweating profusely, he reached in his pocket for the bottle of Vicodin. It would be his third today. The doctor told him this would happen. The process of dying. Pancreatic cancer advances quickly. As it devoured him from the inside, the pain would become unbearable and unending. Vicodin helped in the early stages, but it was getting close to morphine time. He wouldn't allow himself the luxury of morphine, preferring pain to the trance-like side effect of the more potent drug. He grimaced as he dry-swallowed the capsule. He lifted his head so he could see his house. The two men, having tried the front door, were now walking down his driveway to the back of the house. It would be another ten minutes before the Vicodin kicked in.

His condition reminded him of a joke he'd heard recently, where the guy goes for a checkup and the doctor tells him he has some bad news.

"Bad news?" the patient asks. "What's the bad news?"

"You're terminally ill," the doctor tells him.

"Jeez, Doc," he asks. "Terminally ill? How long have I got?"

The doctor answers, "10".

"10?" the patient asks. "10 what? 10 years? 10 months? 10 weeks? What?"

The doctor replies, "10 ...9 ...8 ...7..."

The man, clenching his teeth against the pain, was only asking for ten days.

~~~~

The back of the house blew out with a deafening roar, followed by a second sound, a *whomp*, that signaled the gas igniting. Even though he expected it, the fury of the scene stunned him. The inside of the house lit up for one brief instant. Like lightening – it was there and then it wasn't. Simultaneously, all the windows in the house blew out and the house turned orange with flames.

It all happened in the blink of an eye. The next moment the concussion hit the car, rocking it violently on its suspension.

While saddened by the loss of his house, he was elated in a perverse sort of way that, with all the effort he put into making the bomb, the damn thing worked. Better, his mission was still operational.

Time to saddle up, he thought, as he started the car's engine. He had some things to do in San Francisco before the close of the business day. Going the speed limit, he knew he could make it to the City by five. He had a place further up the coast where he planned to stay the night. He entertained the idea of calling McGuire while passing through. The thought amused him. By the time the Jeep entered the on-ramp to Interstate 10, the beginning of another plan began to hatch in his brain.

15

San Francisco

I had about an hour before Michele got back from Harry's office. Not enough time to get through all the VICAP reports, and I wanted to do that in one sitting. Instead, I swiveled my chair around to face the freeway running past our fourth floor window – the first leg of Highway 80 before it disappeared into the mouth of the Bay Bridge's lower deck. Traffic was light that holiday Monday.

This was the part of homicide investigation I loved. Trying to piece the thing together. Checking out theories, leads, and dead-ends. This was the painstaking, unglamorous aspect of the job that most of my peers hated. To me it was like doing a puzzle. Or playing *Clue*. The adrenalin rush when you could confidently say, "I accuse Mr. White, with the lead pipe, in the conservatory."

I swung back to the desk and took out a piece of paper. I wanted to tally what I had. Leafing through the initial report from Officers Becker and Echols, two things immediately struck me. The first was no forced entry, meaning she must have either known the guy or he came up on her while she was opening the door. Since the report stated that no neighbors heard any loud shouting or screams, I made a note to check out her friends and acquaintances. I looked through the stack and silently cursed Bob Cummins from the Chronicle for not sending over her bio. Made a note to call the son-of-a-bitch.

The other peculiar thing was, of course, the ropes. I put that on the list and put a star next to it. The killer was telling us something. His signature. I felt that nagging dread again at the base of my skull. Like seeing a rock on a trail and knowing that something evil lurked beneath it. Not wanting to turn it over but knowing I must. Well, VICAP might help with that one.

I took out another piece of paper and made a quick grid, putting "motive" on the horizontal axis and "suspects" on the vertical. People kill for a reason. Some of those reasons can be pretty obscure. A guy may simply like the power it gives him over life and death. Another might be answering the call of the Lord Jesus Himself to off some poor, dumb son-of-a-bitch. A drive-by is usually about somebody's place in the hierarchy of a gang. But all-in-all, there are three basic human appetites at work in most homicides. The first had to do with wealth. I killed so-and-so because I can inherit a lot of money. That's why one of the first things we do is check insurance policies. I made a note to look at Wasserman's beneficiaries. The second had to do with some form of sexual manifestation, like jealousy. "This guy was doin' my ol' lady." Or, "She was cheatin' on me." The third had to do with revenge. Somebody did something to somebody and was being paid back.

Lots of permutations among the three, of course, but if you can establish motive, the other two become clear soon after.

Under suspects I wrote "Family," "Friends," and "Co-Workers." Now all that remained was to start filling in the blanks. If only it were that easy.

~~~~

"Bob Cummins, please. Yes! This is Inspector Tom McGuire of the SFPD calling." I decided I couldn't wait for him to send me Wasserman's bio. "Bob? This is Inspector McGuire. I spoke to you on Saturday about the Ruth Wasserman murder, remember? Good! You promised to send me everything you could on Ms. Wasserman. I was wondering where it is." I put a real tone of exasperation in that final sentence.

"Inspector, I'm sorry. I was going to call you. Really." *Sure*, I thought to myself. Who'd this guy think he was talking to? Feeding me this crap. "I have a lot of stuff here. I ran a LexisNexis on her, and you wouldn't believe all the stuff that came back." He was hurrying through. Apologetically. "I had to get permission to even run it off, there was so much. Must be six hundred pages of articles alone. And it's still spitting out paper."

"Okay, Bob. I understand." I didn't, but what the hell. Be nice to the press. "Can you at least send me over a one or two-pager on her life? You must have something there. Get it from her application. Anything. I need to start figuring this out, and I'm blind if I don't know anything about her. I could have done it myself, but I was counting on you." Make him feel bad, I thought. Beholden to me. "You can messenger the rest when you're finished printing. Our department will pay for the service. That okay with you?"

"Sure." He sounded relieved. I know I shouldn't feel this way, but the power you have as a cop is a real rush sometimes.

"Okay, Bob. And I need you to do something else for me if you would – I need a list of everyone Ruth worked with at the Chronicle. Can you do that? I need a list going back two years or so."

"Jesus, Inspector. I don't know if I can do that. There are privacy rules, you know."

"I know. I could get a subpoena, but that takes time. You just go ask. I'm sure they'll give it to you."

"Let me get this straight," he said. "I'm doing all this for just that crappy information you gave me last Saturday?" He was becoming aggressive. The beginning of a good newsman.

"Tell you what, Bob. You do this for me and I'll call you the minute I know anything on the case. You'll be the first to know."

"Your word?"

"My word." What a fool. I wondered how young this guy was. "And, Bob, I need that bio ASAP."

"You got it," he replied, and hung up.

I called down to Evidence and asked if everything of a personal nature from Wasserman's place had been bagged and tagged. It hadn't. And further, it wasn't even scheduled until tomorrow morning. Oh, well. Tomorrow's another day, as they say.

I'd just started feeling sorry for myself when Michele poked her head through the door and announced she was ravenously hungry.

16

I returned from lunch about two. Mike called and left a message that he wouldn't be in after all. Had to take his wife to the doctor. Just as well, I thought. I should start plowing through the VICAP reports.

Michele and I had eaten Chinese over at Mike Lee's place on Brannan. While the food wasn't all that good, a lot of cops from 850 ate at Lee's, and I wanted to show her off. Mission accomplished. We got our share of looks. I knew I'd be fielding questions about her for weeks.

We mostly talked about her session with Harry. She didn't think the image of the perp she helped produce would be of much use. I assured her it would and then drove her back to her car, thinking all the while about the mound of paperwork that awaited me back at the office.

First thing I did when I got to my desk was to open the VICAP folder and read the cover page.

GLCX1790947005

13:52 EST
Fm: Violent Crime Apprehension Program
To: Inspector Michael Irvine, SFPD. Request verification 22xr4

Specified: Unsolved murders with the following aspects:

Gender: M/F

Age of Victim: 44 to 75 and all unspecified

Weapon: unspecified

Parameters of Search:

1. Use of Rope
2. Rope not murder weapon
3. Tie was possible post-mortem
4. No special knots
5. POB - hands, legs, neck
6. Affixed tight enough to cut circulation

RESULTS

Eight hits - all parameters

Twenty-seven hits - 5 parameters

Fifty-two hits - 4 parameters

Thirty-seven hits - 3 parameters

Police Reports and Photos enclosed. Good Luck!

I separated the stacks and began with the eight that fulfilled all parameters. I first looked at the pictures. As a policeman you get accustomed to the gore surrounding a murder scene. Probably as a defense mechanism. You train yourself to look at the details. The minutia. You're checking angles of entrance and exit wounds. Trying to put yourself in the victim's place. What did he see? Did he try to defend himself? Then you put yourself in the shooter's shoes. Ask the same questions. Motive. Always motive. And that's how you make out your report. By definition it's a sterile document that doesn't begin to describe the horrific scene in front of you. But the photos are a different story. Just the cold, stark reality of violent death. Human waste forever frozen in their indecent departure. On the back of each photo was a short analysis of how the victim died.

Theron Campbell. Age 46. Black male. Arms tied behind him and hung from a beam in an abandoned Detroit warehouse. Feet dangling three feet from the floor. It didn't feel right to me. When you've been in the business as long as I have, you get the feel. This was most likely a drug hit, but more study would be needed. I started my "keep" pile with Theron.

Jennifer Tower. Age 52. White female. Curled up in a fetal position on what looked in the photo to be her dining room floor. Arms bound from shoulder to wrist. I turned the photo over to look at how she was found. Unmistakable. Just like Wasserman. I'd found another victim of our killer. The adrenalin rush made my heart convulse in spasms of silent thunderclaps.

Harvey Ellenbaugh. Age 58. White male. His naked body was face down on the kitchen table. Legs and arms tied spread-eagled to the table legs. Looking at the photo, it just wasn't right. An obvious sex crime. Harvey became file number one in my reject pile.

Heidi Monroe. Age 50. White female. Arms stitched together from elbow to shoulder. It was all I could do to stop from letting out a whoop. Whoever did Wasserman, did Tower and Monroe for sure.

Tracey Gilligan. Age 45. White female. Lying on her living room floor. Arms tied conventionally behind her back. Another rope was tied to both her ankles and pulled up so tight around her neck that the soles of her feet almost touched her head. It didn't look or feel right, but I put it in my keep file anyway for further review.

Roy Bell. Age 47. White male. Arms tied to a chair, head hanging listlessly to one side. Too conventional. Not right. I put Roy in my reject pile.

Angela Zahn. Age 49. White female. Hands tied to the headboard of her four-poster bed. Legs drawn up over her head and also tied to the headboard. Her mutilated, naked body open obscenely to the camera. Again, not right. Angela was number three in my reject pile.

Rebecca Steele. Age 52. White female. The photo drove a cold shiver right down my spine. The way she was tied. How many times was I tied like that? Whoever did these women was purposely leaving a trail and daring someone to recognize it for what it was. Rebecca's ankles were tied together in front of her. Her arms were tied in back of her at the wrist and elbows. Then her arms had been drawn up over her head, and a loop of rope connected her wrists and ankles. Body was bent forward in the most unnatural position. So far forward her forehead touched the ground in front. I silently prayed she was dead before this happened to her. If not, she was wishing she were dead. I knew. The agony is indescribable.

Eight reports with five possibles, I thought to myself as I stacked the pictures together at the top of my desk. I knew I was onto something, but I pushed the obvious conclusion to the far recesses of my mind. I knew I'd have to confront those demons sooner or later. I opted for later. Picking out the written reports that corresponded to the keep file, I started reading them.

VICAP reports look like all those damn credit forms you hate to fill out. Another reason why some cops shy away from using the system.

I scanned down the body of the first report. Theron Campbell was found hanging from a beam in an abandoned warehouse. He was shot twice in the back of the head with a .38 caliber handgun. No latents were found. First bullet entered at the base of the neck, traveled upward and exited the right frontal lobe. Death was instantaneous. Second bullet was post-mortem. Entered left temple, deflected off right temple and exited under the chin. Evidence of torture. All fingernails of left hand ripped off by a tool, probably some sort of pliers. Victim's hands tied behind his back. Also post-mortem. No suspects as of the date of the report. It went on to describe what I'd seen in the accompanying photographs.

Theron was a bad, but unlucky, dude. Had six priors. Two weapons possessions. Beat one and served six months on the other. Served a total of eight years on three drug charges and beat a pimping charge. Investigating officers suspected this to be a drug hit.

I was pretty sure there was no connection to my case, but decided I should call Detroit PD anyway to make sure. I put the dossier near the phone and picked up Jennifer Tower's report.

Ms. Tower died from a single .22 caliber bullet that entered below her right ear. No exit wound.

Twenty some years ago, I reflected, only fools, or kids who couldn't get their hands on a heavier weapon, used .22s. That was before someone started passing the word around that the Israeli Mossad used the .22 Long Rifle as its favorite assassination cartridge. Instant popularity. Besides being fairly quiet, it's the non-exit feature that made the .22 such an effective assassination cartridge. Since it's not powerful enough to punch through the skull twice, once it penetrated the head, the bullet kept ricocheting off the inner skull, pulverizing the brain.

Jennifer had been found in her apartment two days after her murder. A phone tip. Just like Wasserman. No forced entry. Just like Wasserman. No witnesses. No fingerprints. Just like Wasserman. Time of death was put at anywhere from seven thirty to midnight. As nothing seemed to be missing from her apartment, robbery was ruled out as a motive. She was divorced twice. Two daughters by her first husband, who was now deceased. Daughters were investigated and cleared. Second husband lived in Germany with his current wife and three stepchildren. He'd also been cleared as a suspect. Investigation was still open, though I knew from experience that her death would be on the back burner as newer cases superseded hers.

Under the heading: *For Eyes Only* - the section the investigators withhold from the public so they'd be able to distinguish between the real murderer who would know the details and some crazy who wanted to become famous for a day by confessing to a crime he didn't commit. It focused on the unusual use of the ropes. Things I'd noticed in the photographs. It also contained one final piece of information – the one that convinced me I was on the right track. The ropes were applied after her death.

Heidi Monroe was murdered in Orlando, Florida. I quickly looked over her report. Besides noting she was a housewife, I didn't find anything I didn't already know. My guy had done her, too. The same was true for Rebecca Steele, a retired stockbroker from Flushing, New York.

I leaned forward in my chair, stretching my back that was beginning to hurt from being in one position so long. I checked my watch. Four fifteen. I'd been sitting there two hours. I knew I should stay and try to find the connection between Wasserman and the others, but I was tired and had to go home and change. Even so, I was going to be late to Michele's. I picked up the phone and dialed her number. It rang and rang.

I was about to hang up when she answered.

"Hello."

"Hi. Remember me?" Just enough of a pause to insert "I'm the one who took you to that fantastic Chinese place today."

"Oh, the handsome policeman who paid the $6.95 for the Mandarin Beef special?"

"$8.50 with tax and tip, don't forget. Yes, that's me. I'm glad you're home. I wanted to tell you I'm going to be about twenty minutes late. Didn't want you sitting around in your finery wondering if I was going to show."

"How thoughtful you are, Inspector. I'm glad you called now. Any earlier and I wouldn't have been here. I've been out running. That's why I sound a little breathless. I was just coming up the steps when I heard the phone ring."

"The heavy breathing is cool. Keep it in the act. Very sexy. Hoped it was for me." Usually I wouldn't make a comment like that, but I was feeling extraordinarily comfortable with this woman. A good sign? A bad sign? I wasn't sure. I was half-hoping she'd say it *was* for me. She didn't.

"Are you still at the office?"

"Yeah. Just rolling out of here now. That's why I called."

"Have you picked out a warm place for us tonight? At least warmer than the ball park?"

I wanted to say something like "in your arms," but thought it too corny. "Have you been to Allegro's? It's a little Italian place on Nob Hill."

"Never. I've read about it, though. What time will you be here?"

"I made reservations for eight. What if I pick you up about seven fifteen? We'll have dinner and then go to someplace like Harry Denton's."

"Sounds delightful." Her voice low and sexy. "I'll be wearing a black dress, so you dress accordingly. Don't want to outclass you on our first, oops, scratch that, second date."

"I guess I'd better get home then and take my one-and-only suit to the cleaners. Get the mustard stains out of it."

"Good idea. In the meantime, I'll get out of my wet clothes and slip into something more ..." She paused so I could fill in the blank.

"Comfortable," I said with just a moment's hesitation. I was getting back in the game, slowly but surely.

"Exactly. How did you know?" She was playing with me again. "And warm bubble bath where I'll fantasize about what a wonderful evening I'm going to have."

"God. You're really putting the pressure on me."

"I know you're big enough to handle it, Inspector," she breathed into the phone.

The double entendre was so blatant I didn't quite know how to respond. All I could say was "Sure."

"Bye, Mac," she said.

"Bye. See ya soon." I hung up. A satisfying feeling started to pulsate through my groin. And I thought I was too old for this shit.

17

I'd noticed this for a while now – as soon as I pulled up to my house at night I became overwhelmingly tired. I asked a shrink about it once and was told it was an offshoot of the "nesting" syndrome. The home, or *nest*, was a symbol of peace and relaxation, she said. As one approached the nest, the body started producing *endomorphines* – or *extomorphines,* or some kind of *morphines* – in order to shut it down. Natural melatonin, she said. Scientists observed the same thing in the animal kingdom. Some primordial sense from when we were still walking on four legs, she said. Our natural survival instinct released chemicals into our system that kept us alert for predators during the day. As we approached our safe haven at night, the glands secreting those chemicals stopped, and those whose job it was to secrete *morphines* took over, leaving all our mental and physical faculties tired from being on edge all day. She said it got worse as we got older.

I thought she was full of shit. Except the part about it becoming worse when you got older. She had that part exactly right.

Most nights I could hardly make it up the front stairs. But tonight was different. I was flying high.

Even thought to stop by Greta's to buy flowers. I'd known Greta for years. She owned a flower shop over on 30th and Rivera. Friend of my brother Billy. I was sure she could tell I was nervous. You should've seen her eyebrows arch when I asked her for a bunch of violets. Not in season, she said. And besides, they were so old-fashioned. I told her so was I. Didn't help. She didn't have them in stock.

Greta suggested that a nice bouquet of roses was still the standard. But she said that, for her personally, one long-stemmed red rose was the most romantic gift for that someone special. Her "I thought so" smile accompanied my one red-rose purchase. As I left the store, I could imagine her running to the phone calling my brother. "Tommy's got a girlfriend. Tommy's got a girlfriend." Eighth grade all over again.

When I opened my door it was five forty-five. I had an hour and a half. Stripping off my clothes, I checked my physique in the mirror before heading to the shower. It wouldn't be long before I won't have to suck in the ol' gut. It was in the middle of shampooing my head when I remembered I hadn't made reservations for dinner. Drying off quickly, I found the phone number for Allegro's and called. Got a recording. They're closed Mondays. Shit! I wracked my brain trying to remember what good restaurant I'd gone to in the past year besides McDonald's, Burger King, and Denny's. I jerked open the yellow pages. Restaurants. Started to run my finger down the page. Found just the place. *Boulevard*. Off the Embarcadero. The ad read – Fine Dining. Sophisticated – Intimate – Romantic. What the ad conveniently forgot to say was *Pricey*. I remember having been there before. Once. Had to put in for OT just to pay the damn bill. But tonight I was willing to pay the freight. Wanted Michele to know I wasn't just a chili-cheese dog and beer kinda guy. At least for one night. I called for reservations. Eight o'clock. For two.

I dressed and checked myself in the mirror again. Starched shirt – yellow. Red-patterned silk tie. Gray suit. Shoes shined. I hardly recognized myself. "God, McGuire. You are *so* money," I said to my reflection. With a final tug on my tie, I checked to see if I had my wallet and keys, made sure the front door was locked, and vaulted down the stairs to my car.

Rose in hand, I rang Michele's doorbell at precisely ten minutes after seven. The anticipation of seeing her heightened as the sound of high heels clicked across the floor.

The door opened.

She stood there framed in the doorway by the soft light that spilled out from behind. It filtered through a wayward strand of hair which she absentmindedly brushed back into place. She wore what Cosmo would refer to as her LBD – little black dress. I'd dated a number of women who wore little black dresses, but I can truthfully say none looked better than the woman standing in front of me. Black lace, short and form-fitting. Sparkly hoop earrings and spiky black heels completed the look. I smiled and started humming a song from my teenage years, hoping she'd remember it. She didn't disappoint.

"*Just One Look*?" she asked.

"*Was all it took*," I replied with a nod. "Glad you recognized it."

"You're sweet," she said with a feathery smile. "But better come in before I freeze in this dress." She took my hand.

"Sorry. It's hard not to stare. You look beautiful." She pecked me on the cheek as I walked by her into the living room. "Here. This is for you." I handed her the rose.

"Ohhh, you're even *more* than sweet." She raised it to her nose. "I love roses. Thank you. Let me put it in a vase and we can go." I followed her into the kitchen. "Can you reach the vases up there?" she asked opening a cabinet and pointing to the highest shelf.

"Of course," I said, trying to impress her with my chivalry. I could feel myself falling down that rabbit hole. A warning voice sounded in my brain. *Do you want to become involved? Be careful. Relationships are a lot of work. This woman is uncharted emotional terrain.* I pulled down a small vase, refocused and said, "I made a reservation for eight. At Boulevard."

"I thought you said we were going to Allegro's?"

"I did. But, as fate would have it, they're closed on Mondays. Boulevard is a nice place."

"Don't I know it. I'll eat lightly, I promise. Don't want to put you in the poor-house." She smiled and took the vase from me. "Let me put this in the bedroom. So I can think of you at night."

I smiled inwardly as I watched her walk to the back of the house. She knew the game and played it damn well.

Coming out of the bedroom she took a final look at herself in the mirror. With a satisfied nod, she turned, grabbed my arm, and steered me to the door.

18

The man walked up to the FedEx counter on Montgomery Street right before closing time. He'd arrived in San Francisco three hours before and rented a safety deposit box at the Bank of America on Market Street. Inside he placed a set of tapes. Borrowing bank letterhead, he wrote the words – *The Greeks Give the Honors of the Gods to Those Who Slay Tyrants* - sealed it in an envelope, and placed it in the box as well. The quote was from Cicero. He knew it would mean something to McGuire.

The problem with his plan from the beginning was how to get the word out about Schaeffer. If he'd merely disclosed it to some reporter, he had little confidence the story would ever get published. Not with the many friends Schaeffer had in the media. Killing Schaeffer would be a dramatic statement, to be sure. But even then, the man had no illusions that once captured, or, more likely, killed, these stories from the women would ever see the light of day.

He churned all this over in his mind on the drive up from Southern California. Having McGuire heading the Wasserman investigation gave him an alternative. Give McGuire the key to the safety deposit box. While the man didn't expect McGuire to condone what he'd done – or was about to do – he was fairly confident that because of their shared experiences, McGuire would at least understand the magnitude of what he uncovered. And hopefully make an effort to see it publicized.

After finding the address for the Hall of Justice, the man put the key inside the FedEx envelope. Borrowing a piece of paper from the clerk, the man wrote a personal note to McGuire. He added the note to the package, sealed it, and paid for two-day delivery service.

19

Boulevard was everything their ad said it would be – sophisticated, intimate and romantic. After all, it was French. What else would you expect?

Even though the restaurant was crowded, they gave us a window table. No doubt because of Michele. Having a beautiful woman with you buys a lot of favors.

I ordered a bottle of wine, and we made small talk over a dinner of heirloom tomato salad and chateaubriand. Revealing just enough of our insecurities to invite the other into our life without completely stripping away our carefully constructed masks. Baby-steps. Intimate without being threatening. I told her about police work, and she told me about her dream to become a teacher. Second grade. We talked about our families, and growing up in the City. People we knew in common. Politics. Skirting the edges of each other. Probing for likes and dislikes. Filing them away for future reference.

When the meal was finished I suggested we go to the Starlight Room. Harry Denton's place at the top of the Sir Francis Drake Hotel. Quiet atmosphere. Soft music. She looked a little disappointed and said, "I was thinking – instead of the Starlight Room, how about J. Love's? It's over on Broadway. You ever been there?"

I confessed I hadn't. I knew of it, of course. A famous hangout for the twenty-something crowd. Made the police blotter regularly. "Won't we be a bit overdressed?" I asked.

"Come on, Mac. Don't be so old-fashioned. Nobody will even notice. You'll see."

Old-fashioned? I thought. That stung.

As we made our way out, furtive glances followed us. Followed Michele, actually. Didn't blame them. My eyes were all over her, too.

J. Love's was a real slice of San Francisco. Tables crammed together around a large bar and small dance floor. Making our way past the bouncer, we found a table in the corner. I looked around. No one there over twenty-five. At least that I could tell. And I was right about being overdressed. There wasn't a dude in the place who wore a coat but me. Muscle shirts, chains and leather chaps were de rigueur for the guys. The women were sexually fashionable. The only dress I could see, beside Michele's, was a short white number with a completely sheer back. The girl wearing it must have thought it tasteless to show her underwear so she left them home. On the dance floor, guys were dancing with guys, girls with girls, a few heteros were thrown into the mix.

The music drowned out all conversation. Michele leaned into my ear and yelled, "Isn't this great? Look at the girl on the bar." Someone had climbed on the bar and was dancing sensuously to the music. Only way I could tell it was a girl were the boobs spilling out from her half zippered leather vest. She was actually attractive, in an androgynous sort of way. I'll bet if I checked, I'd have found her arm punctured with needle marks.

Mercifully the music stopped long enough for us to order drinks without having to use sign language. "What the hell kind of music are they playing?" I asked. "I certainly know I'm not at the Starlight Room."

"Come on, McGuire. You never heard *Jimmy Eat World*?"

"Uhhh. You're kidding me, right? *Jimmy Eat World*?"

"Don't know what I'm going to do with you, McGuire. This is emo. And *Jimmy Eat World* is the best. You've got to get out more."

"Swell."

A slow song started, and I asked Michele if she wanted to dance. After I promised not to embarrass her, we bullied our way through bodies to the floor. I loved the feel of her body as it melted into mine. The music wrapped around us. I buried my face in her hair, inhaling its fresh, soapy, female scent. I was disappointed when the song ended. Wanting more. Wanting her. I felt myself on the edge of a large precipice, allowing myself to get closer and closer to the edge.

It was past midnight when we left. I was clammy with perspiration and welcomed the cold night air. I put my arm around Michele and held her close. She offered no resistance.

I drove her home.

"Have a drink before you go?" she asked as we walked up her stairs. "I have a complete liquor cabinet. Just for times like this." She unlocked the door and we walked in. "What can I get you?"

"You have wine?"

"Red or white?"

"Red would be great. Thanks."

I listened to her rattling around in the kitchen as I sat on the couch, glancing through one of her *Architectural Digests*. She came out carrying two glasses of red wine and sat beside me, tucking bare feet under her.

"Here's to an enjoyable evening," she said, clinking my glass.

"I'll drink to that," I replied, putting my arm around her shoulder. I then raised my glass again and said, "And here's hoping it's not over yet."

She smiled, clinking my glass again. "It's so awkward, isn't it? Maybe not for men, but for women? Coming home from the first date with a guy – especially one where you had a really good time – and not quite knowing what to do next? I'm a forty-something year old woman sitting here feeling like I'm in high school again."

"How so?"

"You know, like … should I kiss him? Will my dad come in and catch us?" She laughed and snuggled closer. The warmth of her radiating through me.

"I sure hope not," I said. "I'm enjoying this too much."

She laughed again. "I'm a Catholic school girl. You know … Saint Anne's and all. I remember Sister Mary Benigna – I think that was her name – lecturing us girls about what you boys were really after, and to be careful not to put ourselves in, what she called 'the near occasion of sin.' "

Now it was my turn to laugh. "And you think Sister what's-her-name would think sitting this close on a couch, late at night, drinking wine could be considered *the near occasion*?"

"I think so. For sure."

"So do I," I said, putting my glass down and pulling her to me. I put my free hand on her cheek, guiding her mouth to mine. She responded immediately. Her hand came around my neck and pulled me closer, crushing my lips against hers. She opened her mouth to me and our breath commingled, as did our tongues – exploring the soft inner surfaces. Positions changed without breaking contact. Her body twisted until it reclined fully on the couch. Mine slid off the couch until I was on my knees leaning over her. My free hand sliding to her back, feeling for the zipper of her dress.

The reverie was broken when she pushed me back and moved her lips away from mine. "I hate to do this, but maybe this is going a little too fast."

I pulled back and looked at her. I wasn't real happy about this turn of events, but I didn't want to look or act like the typical aggressive male wanting to get his cookies off. Trying my witty best I said, "What? Did you hear your father come home?" It fell flat.

"No, seriously." She sat up and playfully kissed the tip of my nose, tugging at the hem of her dress that climbed half way up her thighs. "I like you a lot. Maybe too much. Going to bed with you would be so easy right now. And I really want to. But I don't want to cheapen whatever it is we have going by jumping your bones on our first date. Okay, *second* date. Maybe even our third, but who's counting? You understand, don't you?"

I didn't, but said I did. Women's logic was unfathomable, but you learned over time that there was no choice but to accept it.

"Hey – no problem," I lied, trying to act like if she hadn't stopped us, I would have.

She walked me to the door and we kissed. "I had a great, great time, Mac. Honest. Call me tomorrow, okay?" Sweet. Almost pleading. I said I would.

As soon as I got into the car, I turned on the radio to catch the Giants score. Seven to five over the Braves. Dodgers, though, won again. But what the hell. We were still four up.

I'd just walked in the house when the phone rang.

"Hi. It's me. Sorry, couldn't wait for you to call. Wanted to say goodnight. Hold me close." And she hung up.

20

Tuesday, July 6th

I was in the middle of one of the most erotic dreams I'd had in years when I was awakened by the insistent ringing of the doorbell. The clock read five thirty.

I stumbled to the door wearing my boxers and opened it as far as the chain would allow.

It was Michele. Hair in a braid down her back, sweat pants and a lycra workout shirt with DKNY emblazoned on one of the sleeves. Behind her the fog curled low over the street lamps. For someone who'd complained about how cold it was at AT&T, I didn't know how she could be standing there and not shiver. I was freezing. And she looked so fresh, like she just awakened after ten hours of sleep. I felt like shit. Like I hadn't slept at all. And I knew I looked worse than I felt. "Come on, McGuire. Time to get in shape."

"You've got to be kidding. It's still dark outside. It's cold. I've only had two hours sleep." I tried to think of every excuse, but my mind was too fuzzy. Undoing the chain, I let her in. "Who's your friend?"

A large golden retriever followed her into the house. "Cooper, meet Inspector McGuire. He's the one I've been telling you about on the way over." The dog just sat by her side. Unimpressed. I could tell he didn't like me. "He's my neighbor's dog. I run him every day. In return, the neighbor keeps my hedges trimmed." She giggled. "God, that sounds awful, doesn't it?" Her laugh brought Cooper to attention by her side.

"I looked down at the dog, then back at her. "You shoulda warned me you'd be over."

"Didn't want you to not answer the door. Pissed off about last night. Hurry up. We'll do a few miles down at the beach. It'll do you good."

I groaned. "A few miles? I haven't run a few miles since I was in the service. And even then it was because they'd kick my ass if I didn't."

"And a cute ass it is, too." She patted me on the butt as I walked past her to the bedroom. Closing the door, I hurriedly cleaned up the clothes and other junk strewn across the floor and put on my sweats. The theme from *Rocky* going through my head.

The run wasn't as bad as I thought it would be. Well, wait a minute. Let's be honest. It was more a walk than a run. I'd trot about half a mile and then give out. We'd walk awhile as I recovered, and then go off trotting again. Cooper loped along beside us, annoyed every time I stopped. I was annoyed, too. But Michele was great. Didn't get on me when I slowed the pace. Kept encouraging me. A good coach. I wanted to work hard for her.

For all the huffing and puffing I did, we actually made it back to my house in less than forty-five minutes. It was light already, though it would take a few more hours before the sun burned off the fog that still hung low over the Sunset. The hazy light filtered through the front room window as we entered the house.

"Wait here a minute," Michele said. "I've got something for you." She took Cooper out the door. I watched as she put him in her car and returned with a large grocery bag. "Didn't know what you had to eat, so I brought breakfast." She looked in the bag like she was discovering its contents for the first time. "Let's see. Egg Beaters, no cholesterol. Turkey bacon, no fat. Orange juice. Coffee. You hungry?"

With that menu I wasn't sure. But being the gracious host I was, I took the bag and held out my arm. "You have a nice house here," she said looking down the hall as I escorted her into the kitchen. "Can't wait to see the rest of it."

"Well, I'd be happy to …"

She didn't let me finish. "Why don't you go shower and I'll get the food going," she said, pushing me toward the bedroom.

I showered and shaved, brushed my teeth, spritzed myself with *Eternity for Men*, put on a fresh pair of warm-ups and was back in the kitchen within ten minutes. A plate of those fake eggs, four slices of fake bacon and two slices of real toast, no butter, awaited me at the table. Michele sat across from me drinking coffee and looking lovely.

"You're not eating?"

"I'm not a big breakfast person. Would you mind if I freshened up while you ate?"

"Absolutely not. If you want to shower, there are fresh towels on the rack." I did remember something from my marriage.

I heard the faucet turn on a moment later, and envisioned the hot water streaming down her naked body. "Stop that, you horny bastard," I told myself and went back to eating.

The shower turned off, and I heard her walking around my room. A moment later she padded into the kitchen wearing my blue terry robe. Her head was tilted to one side as she tugged at her wet hair with a towel. She looked spectacular. I could wake up every morning next to her, and never get tired of it, I thought.

"That's the outfit you were wearing the first time I saw you."

"What, your robe?" she asked.

"No. Yours. Remember? On the porch at your mom's house. It fit a hell of a lot better than that does."

"But yours is so cozy. And I can smell you on it." She came around behind me, tilted my head back and kissed me. Wet, stringy hair tickled my cheek. "Come with me," she said, taking my hand and leading me into the bedroom.

Standing by the side of the bed, I unwrapped her from my robe. She closed her eyes, allowing me to admire her beauty in the privacy of my own arousal. I took off my top and drew her to me, our bodies blending together. For the next two hours the ebb and flow of our passion, alternating between tenderness and frenzy, consumed us.

We finished exhausted and wet. Looking down at her, I was filled with an overwhelming sense of awe. I hadn't felt this way in a long, long time. But I hadn't gotten any sex in a long, long time, either. Maybe that's what's causing these feelings. In either case, I was too tired to dwell on it. Just enjoy the moment, I thought to myself. Whatever happens, happens.

The *whatever happens* was a phone call from Irvine.

"Mac, getting busy here. You comin' in?"

"Of course. Just …" I looked down at Michele, "… just squeezing the enjoyment of this beautiful morning for as long as I could. I'll be down within the hour." I hung up and snuggled back next to her, burying my face in her hair. "Gotta go."

"I know, dammit." She stretched languidly, rubbing her body over mine. "You sure you can't call back and say you're sick or something?" she purred. I could feel myself becoming aroused again. So could she. Smiling, she pushed me away. "Okay, enough. I know you have to get to work." She got out of bed and stood over me, naked and beautiful. "But you also have to come over for dinner tonight. It'll be better than breakfast, I promise you." Her voice husky, teasing. All I could do was to nod dumbly. With that, she winked and walked into the bathroom.

At the front door we kissed and held each other tightly. "Bring over a change of clothes for tonight, okay?" she whispered in my ear. "You'll need them to get to work tomorrow morning." Giving me a quick kiss, she skipped down the stairs to Cooper and her car.

I strutted back to the bedroom. It smelled of Michele and sex. Not at all unpleasant. I knew I was going to have a difficult time concentrating today.

21

I made it to the office at half past ten. There was a note on my desk telling me Mike had gone to Robbery to check on the Wagner case.

Police work was schizophrenic. Always something new on your plate. Never enough time to do any of them justice. The Wagners were a case in point. A couple in their late sixties, they were murdered last week at their home in the Richmond District. Mike and I drew the case. The house was burglarized, so Robbery was also involved. The way it looked, the Wagners came home from the movies while the burglary was taking place and were killed. Bad luck for them. Good luck for us in that there was a ton of evidence at the scene. Amateurs. They left the premises in a big hurry. We had an inventory of the things taken and were just waiting for the perps to try and dispose of them. They would, and we'd get them. Amateurs. God bless 'em. Made our job a whole hell of a lot easier.

The office was busier than yesterday. Kaufman and Wilkins came in and were quietly talking over a cup of coffee. Curious, I walked over to Kaufman's desk. "Hey shooter, got something new?"

"Yeah. A shitty one." Joe Kaufman was about my age. Been in Homicide for six years. Came over from Fraud. He was tall with a shock of black hair that defied combing. Two splotch marks on his left cheek were reminders of the skin cancer removed last year. Kaufman's claim-to-fame was that he'd already killed four guys in the line of duty. Most of us had never even pulled our guns. Kaufman already tallied four notches on his. We called him "shooter."

"Three thirty this morning. Domestic."

"The worse kind," interrupted Wilkins.

"One of those flop houses over on Mason. Guy and his old lady are having an argument. She's a prostitute with a rap sheet that dwarfs War and Peace. He was her pimp. Near as we can figure, he starts belting her around for some reason or other. Probably for holding out some of the night's take. You know how pimps are. Anyway, the lady wakes up her kid and takes a hike. Little girl – two years old. The broad gets in her car and starts to drive away. Dude grabs a .357 magnum and chases them down the street. Starts blastin' away. First shot goes through the back window and out the front. Second one hits the little girl in the back of the head. What a mess. Jesus. All she's doing is sitting in the back seat. Probably sucking her thumb. A real mess. I got a little girl just about a year older. The pimp's lawyer is trying to cop a plea of involuntary manslaughter. For what he did! And knowing the way the courts are these days, he'll probably get it. Sometimes I wonder why I'm in this fucking business."

"Were they druggies?" I asked? Already knowing the answer.

"Aren't they all? Christ, the whole damn world is doing drugs."

"At least our world," Wilkins added.

"Shit. They're all over the place. I was at a party at some big-shot lawyer's place in Marin last weekend. Friend of my wife's. Hell, a group of 'em sittin' around doin' blow. In plain sight, for God's sake."

"You should've arrested them." I'm playing with him and he knows it.

"Tell you what I felt like doing, Mac. I felt like pulling out my piece and wasting the whole pack of 'em. Probably would've gotten a medal. Five lawyer notches? Are you kidding me? A fucking hero. A parade down Market Street."

We all had a good laugh at that one. But I knew where he was coming from. Ask any cop and they'll tell you that virtually every crime, especially violent crime, has its roots in dope. Either it made somebody crazy in the head, or it's the money involved in its commerce. The scourge of a generation.

They wanted to write their report, so I left. Had just put a dollar in the Coke machine when Mike came sauntering back from Robbery. Wagner's property hadn't yet shown up at the usual places. Odd. By now you'd have expected the stuff to be on the street. Robbery distributed a list of all the stolen items to every pawn shop in the City. Standard operating procedure. Pawn shop owners get probably ten of these lists a week. I suppose some just trash them, but you'd be surprised how many crooks we catch this way. On this one, so far, no luck.

"So, what have you got going on the Wasserman case, pardner?" he asked me. Where do we start?"

I told him I looked through VICAP and found three definite similars. All women. Plus, another woman and a guy who were possibles. If there was something definite these women had in common with Wasserman, we'd at least be able to cobble together a possible motive.

"And how do you propose we do that?" He saw my look and groaned. "A day on the phone, huh?"

"I don't know any other way, do you?" Mike hated the tedious part of this business, but he knew the drill. I picked up the files. "We got possibles in Ames, Iowa; Flushing, New York; Orlando; Detroit; and Billings, Montana. You know anybody in any of these places?" Cops go to a number of conferences and conventions and meet police officers from other cities. Sometimes get to be pretty good friends. Go out drinking, do the town – that sort of thing. Comes in handy because you can cut through the red-tape bullshit at the front end. I've received calls any number of times from cops I'd met at conferences.

Mike thought for a few minutes and said, "I know somebody from Orlando PD. Not well, but I think he'll remember me. I was down there for some conference a few years back and we went to a strip-joint together. Got absolutely hammered. We caused some shit so the manager calls the cops. Two friends of his come in and pretend to arrest us. Reads *Miranda* right there in front of everybody. Really putting on the show. Leads us out in handcuffs. On the way out one of the cops reaches over and pinches one of the strippers right on her nipple. You should've heard her squeal. I nearly died laughing. We get outside – they take the cuffs off and send us on our way. What's the vic's name? I'll take that one."

"Heidi Monroe." I passed him the file. "And I know a guy in Flushing. Met him a number of years ago in Omaha. We've kept in touch over the years. I'll take that one. Why don't you take Detroit and I'll take Ames and Billings."

My first call was to Bill O'Keefe in Flushing. They told me he just stepped away from his desk and did I want to leave a message. I told the receptionist my name and number and to ask Bill to call me back.

Irvine made a connection. He was sitting across from me, laughing and telling stories. Reliving the strip show. I got the number for Ames PD from the VICAP report and called.

"Ames Police Department. Officer Kerrigan speaking. How might we be of service?"

I get a kick out of the new public relations shtick we civil servants are using these days. When I first joined the force, if the duty officer ever answered, "how might we be of service" he'd been hooted out of the squad room. What you got in those days was some crusty old officer on the verge of retirement saying something like "this is the police. What the hell ya' want?" Now they have some sweet young thing like Officer Kerrigan wondering how "we" might be of service.

I told her who I was and asked for Officer Tisdale. She told me he was off duty but would be back in the morning. I left my name and phone number and requested he call me back about the

Jennifer Tower case he handled last March. Zero for two. Irvine was over his case of the giggles and was writing furiously on his note pad.

I was pretty sure Tracey Gilligan was a dead end, but just to be on the safe side I called Officer Cruz in Billings.

"Billings Police," the voice said. No cutesy stuff. Just "Billings Police." The silence that followed implied *what the hell ya' want?*

I identified myself and asked for Officer Cruz, not expecting him to be there. Surprise. I was *talking* to Officer Cruz.

After explaining who I was and giving my I.D. number, I told him I needed any information he might have on the Gilligan case.

"Tracey Gilligan? Sure, I remember. Strange one. She was a chemist in town. Worked over at American General. Big employer here. Big here, of course, is not big by your standards. But more companies are relocating here. That's because people here work hard. Don't have all those freaks like down where you are. That's why companies are comin' up here. Why, I was just talkin' to an office manager the other day, and she said ..."

"Officer, I appreciate what you're saying. But I haven't got much time. Was wondering if you ever solved that case?"

"You get it off VICAP?"

"Yeah. Ran it yesterday."

"We're not like you big city guys. Here we have to do a lot of stuff by hand. Don't have the big staff like you."

"I understand. Really. But like I said, I don't have a lot of time."

"Big case, huh? I had one in Eugene a number of years back. Old lady gets hammered to death. She's a widow, so we can't get her husband." He laughed at his little joke like he was on Comedy Central. "You know – husband is always the perp when the wife goes down." Like I didn't get it. "You know who we finally nabbed?"

I didn't want to encourage him, but couldn't think of anything to say without being rude. He was waiting for me to reply. I guess he doesn't get to show off much to us *big city* cops. But I could tell if I didn't answer, he'd just let the pause linger. Waiting me out. "Nope," I finally said.

"Pool guy, by God. Last place most folks would look. But I had a hunch. You guys down there probably don't play your hunches very often, seein' as how you got all them computers and things to do your thinkin' for you." I looked at the IBM 486 on my desk. If you only knew, you stupid shit, I thought but didn't say.

"But hunches, by God, have solved more crimes than all the computers in the world. Know what I mean?" This guy was really getting on my nerves.

"Big staff."

"What?"

"Big staff." I think I could tell where he was finally going to end up and I wanted to short circuit the process. "You said we have a big staff, but you don't."

"That's right. We have to do a lot by hand. That's why I didn't get around yet to takin' my case off

127

VICAP. Arrested and already got a conviction on the creep. That's somethin' else again. We don't have to wait around while all those lefty lawyers you got down there file motion after motion. Delay things. Tellin' the judge that the perp was abused or somethin' when he was a year old. Anything to get him off. Nope. Here we arrest 'em, try 'em and then send 'em to jail. Pronto. No messin' around."

Good old-fashioned country justice. No worries about guilt or innocence or degree of culpability. Black and white. Easy way to live. "What are you telling me here? Is the case closed?" Irvine was waiting impatiently for me to get off the phone. He had something. I winked at him and held up my finger to indicate this would take only a few seconds longer.

"Solved and closed."

"Wasn't the pool man, was it?"

He paused. Not sure if I was yanking his chain. Making fun of him. Guess he decided I was because his tone became decidedly less friendly. "No. It *wasn't* the pool man. Some drifter. Took her jewelry and credit cards. Used the cards. That's how we got him. Guess I forgot to mention the jewelry and credit cards in VICAP, huh? Well, just goes to show you."

"Thanks for your help, Officer. I gotta go." I hung up. "Son-of-a-bitch," I said to no one in particular.

"Who the hell was *that*?" Irvine asked.

"That was Billings. Scratch Gilligan. What did you get?"

"I talked to my guy in Orlando. He pulled the Monroe file. Somebody did her on May 25th. This year. No suspects. Same as we got here. No forced entry, so they did the usual – ex-husband, boyfriends, co-workers. Anybody who knew her. They came up with zip. I asked him if there was anything else in her background that could establish motive. Anything out of the ordinary, and ..."

My phone rang and I held up my hand to Irvine to hold off a minute. "Might be Bill O'Keefe ... my guy in New York calling back." It was.

After a bit of small talk, I told him about our case here and when I pulled the VICAP, it looked like he had a similar. Rebecca Steele. He remembered her and put me on hold while he retrieved the file. "It'll be just a minute," I said to an obviously impatient Irvine.

O'Keefe came back and started to fill me in, reading from the file. Rebecca Steele was a financial analyst in Flushing. Lived in a good neighborhood. Married. Her third. No children. Lived an upstanding middle-class life. No priors except some notations from the FBI while she was in college. Her husband found her. No forced entry. Single gunshot wound to the head with a .22 caliber long-rifle hollow point. Husband had an ironclad alibi. As did the two exes. As did everybody else in the case. The ropes baffled them. He guessed that's why I was calling. He thought the ropes might be a diversion but couldn't find any motive.

I asked about the FBI notation in her file. What was that all about? The answer stunned me, though I knew in my heart where this case was going. Irvine saw my shoulders slump as I ceased taking notes and leaned forward over my desk. He knew I was being told what he had already found out from Orlando PD.

The only blemish on an otherwise ordinary life had been that Rebecca Steele, at age twenty, made a trip to North Vietnam during the war. The FBI had a flag on her file with the notation "security risk." I thanked him and hung up.

"Looks like we got our connection, huh?" Irvine said, guessing at what I'd been told. I grimaced and nodded, head down, eyes closed. "And I'll bet when we ask about Jennifer Tower, we'll get the same answer. Wanna bet?"

"I knew her, you know."

"Knew who? Jennifer Tower?" he asked.

"No. Ruth Wasserman. Well, I didn't know her personally. But I knew she'd been in North Vietnam in those years, and knew she'd been big-time in the anti-war shit. If for no other reason than only those with juice got to travel in the North.

"Every time some American or group of Americans came through, it was another excuse to make our lives a little more miserable. I can't describe the feeling I had when you told me Saturday morning it was Wasserman that got whacked. I was glad. I know I shouldn't have been. Let bygones-be-bygones. But I was. And you know what? I'm still glad."

Irvine wheeled his chair over next to my desk. "I know this is hard for you ..."

"You'll never know."

"I know that, too. That's why I've never asked. In all the years I've known you. Been your partner. I've never asked. I figured let the dead bury the dead. But it might help if you get it out. Help you personally – *and* help us get this guy."

I sat back in my chair and looked out the window at the San Francisco skyline. Ghostly buildings silhouetted against a dull leaden sky. An overwhelming sadness enveloped me as I struggled to tell Mike the story, so long buried in the black hole of my soul.

Where do I start?

22

"We were the best-and-brightest of our generation. Or so we thought. Warriors! Asked to defend our country in time of war. We never questioned what we were asked to do. We never thought we'd be shot down. We were *invincible*. But when we *were* shot down, we had our Oath to uphold. Even through the torture. It's hard for me to think about even now. After all this time. The utter brutality of what they did to us. Inhuman is the only word I could think of then, and the only word I can think of now. Some guys wrote books about their experiences as a prisoner of war. Maybe a way to come to grips with the sheer terror of those years. I never could. I have never, ever uttered a word about it to anyone. Even when I was married. To my wife. My son. Not only because I didn't want to suffer anyone's pity, but also because the memory itself was too painful.

"Well – you know about the torture. The ropes. You saw it at Wasserman's. They tied you up and then hung you on a meat hook. Pop your shoulder right out of its socket."

I stopped. I could tell I was about to lose it. Irvine sat silently. Respectful of my feelings. When I composed myself, I continued.

"But I can live with all that now. What I can't live with, Mike, is that I broke. I thought I was a tough son-of-a-bitch. I was the personification of tough. I could survive anything they threw at me. Or so I thought. But I couldn't, Mike. I broke. Know how long it took them? A fucking day-and-a-half. They tied and hung me for a day and a half, and I broke like a baby. Spilled my guts out, Mike. Signed everything they wanted me to sign. Bomb hospitals? You bet. Target women and children? Absolutely. Those were my orders. I was a traitor to my country, Mike, as much a traitor as Wasserman was, maybe more. I'd taken the Oath to defend my country, not betray it. And I did betray it. In a day-and-a-half, Mike. In a god-damned day-and-a-half."

I lost it then. Tears leaking from my eyes. I clenched my teeth together, willing myself to stop. Didn't help. The memories of my failures were just too powerful. In my utter despair, I started to sob uncontrollably. Mike came around behind me and placed his big hands on my shoulders.

Leaning close to my ear, he whispered, "You can't beat yourself up, Mac. No one could have withstood what you went through. And you know it. Everybody cracked. I've read at least that much."

"I tried to kill myself, Mike," I managed to get out between sobs. "I beat my head against the wall of my cell. Tried to fracture my skull. I even failed at that." I gave a half-hearted laugh. Mike was still behind me, talking soothingly to me as I slowly regained composure. I took out my handkerchief and daubed my eyes, already fat from crying.

"See why I didn't want this to happen? I don't know if I can do this, Mike. If it is a POW, I probably knew him. Those guys were, and are, like brothers to me. Closer than brothers. What we went through together. What we came through together. For five, six, seven years, Mike, we suffered together, cried together, held each others' hands. Shared a bond few people ever share. Mike, tell me, what the hell am I supposed to do?"

"Mac. I understand. I really do. You want me to ask Bristow to take you off the case? I will. No one will ever be the wiser. Even if they did know, no one could blame you." He patted my shoulder paternally and went back to his chair.

"No. But thanks, Mike. I've got a job to do, dammit, and I'm going to do it. Took an oath, remember?" I snorted derisively. Irvine just looked at me, nodded once, and said, "Then let's get to it."

Over the next hour we made lists of questions. Next to them, we listed where the likely answers were and then divided them between us. We knew now for sure what tied these particular women together. What we didn't know was were there others? Of all the Americans in the Sixties who visited North Vietnam, why had only these four been picked out? I asked Mike to go over to the Chronicle personally and pick up the bio and any other information on Wasserman that Cummins dug up.

While Mike called the paper to make sure the guy was going to be there, I called information for the number of the Bureau of Veteran Affairs in Washington. I got through on the third ring, told the receptionist what I wanted, and left 850's main number for someone to call me back. It actually saved time going through our switchboard in cases like this because I knew they'd be asking me for some identification. Being connected to the main SFPD switchboard would prove I was legit. I looked at Irvine opposite me. "They'll be back to me whenever," I said. "Nothing to do now but wait."

I wanted to call Michele but didn't particularly want Irvine hanging all over my conversation. I didn't have to worry. It was lunchtime, and Irvine never missed a meal.

"I'm on my way over to the Chronicle. Want me to pick you up something to eat? My treat."

"Maybe a banana."

"Banana?"

"I'm on a diet."

"Shit. See you in an hour or so." He left shaking his head.

23

"Hi. Remember me?"

"Remember you? How could I forget?" Her voice was different on the phone. The pitch lower. More intimate. Sexy. If someone had been in the room with her they'd know she was talking to a lover. "Is this the man who made me so sore this morning that I can hardly walk?"

"Hmmm." I settled back in my chair. Good thing no one was in the squad room. My voice was different, too. Images of her in various stages of our lovemaking slotted across the vortex of my brain. Even the hairs on my chest itched. "What an image," I murmured to her. It was all I could think of saying. Silence followed as we both relived memories we took away from our coupling. Finally I said, "We still on for tonight?"

"We'd better be. I went to the store after leaving your house this morning. Walked bowlegged, too. Cashier asked if I'd been horseback riding." She laughed softly. "I told her yes and it was the best ride ever." She laughed again. "Got stuff for dinner. You better know how special you are, McGuire. I haven't cooked for a man in years."

"I'll be hungry," I said, pausing just long enough for emphasis, then said, "For you."

The light on my other line lit up. "I gotta call coming through, babe. What time tonight?"

"Is seven-ish okay?"

"Perfect."

"And dress?"

"Don't wear much." She laughed again. "But remember I may keep you overnight so bring those clothes with you. Just in case."

"I love it when you talk dirty," I said. "Gotta go. See you at seven."

I punched the flickering light. "McGuire."

"Inspector McGuire? This is Jeff Wright at the Bureau of Veteran Affairs. I'm glad I got you before lunch. The receptionist said you wanted a printout of all Vietnam POWs. Is that right?"

"Right."

"I'm on the computer screen now. Have them in front of me. There were 589 prisoners returned in three increments during February and March of 1973. Your message said you were particularly interested in the prisoners from the Hanoi Hilton."

"Correct," I replied.

"According to our records, 566 of the 589 were imprisoned there. Of those, 43 have since died. These reports are updated every six months, so they may not be completely accurate. The last update was – let's see." He paused, then said, "April of this year. The list I'm looking at shows 523 of the returned Hoa Lo prisoners are still living. I have their service numbers, and date of capture. What else do you need?"

"Do you have current addresses?"

"Not on this screen, but they wouldn't be hard to get. I'll cross-reference on their service number. We should have most of them, though I can't guarantee we have them all. We aren't allowed to make file changes unless someone lets us know – either the veteran himself or the next of kin."

"Do you have any way of checking on service related injuries? Permanent disabilities, things like that?"

"As long as it was reported it will be here. I'm going to guess we have a pretty complete listing because the disabled get a check from us every month."

"Great. Here's what I'd like you to do if you would, please. Could you fax me the names and addresses of all living POWs by state? And a separate list of all who were disabled, either partially or totally?"

"It will take me about an hour. Is that okay?"

"Absolutely."

"Inspector? There's a *Thomas McGuire* on this list. Is that you?"

"I'm afraid so."

"Did one of these men commit a crime?"

"That's what I'm trying to determine."

"I hope not. I was there, too. In 'Nam. 1st Squadron, 9th Cavalry. The *Bullwhip Squadron*. Two tours. '67 through '69. Door gunner on a Huey. Shot down three times. Lucky to be alive, I guess." He paused. "Hope you're wrong about this."

"Me, too."

"There was a time in the Seventies and Eighties when, if a Vietnam veteran got in trouble, the first thing reported was *another Vietnam Vet robs a bank*; or *another Vietnam Vet beats up his wife*; or *another homeless Vietnam Vet* – yada, yada, yada. Made us all look to be a bunch of looney-tunes."

"Yeah, I know what you mean," I said. "Hope I'm wrong about this one, too. Thanks for your help, Jeff. The sooner you can get the information to me, the better."

"It'll be there within a few hours at most. Good hunting."

24

"Long lunch, pardner?" I asked as Irvine waddled over carrying a large box. He put it by the side of my desk.

"Very funny. Next time you want something picked up, pick it up yourself. That son-of-a-bitch at the Chron had me wait over forty-five minutes. I came close to not getting lunch."

"Why don't you cancel your subscription in protest," I said with a laugh. "That'll teach him."

Irvine wasn't in the mood. "Thanks," he said, "but I don't have time to just sit around while some young jerk-off plays like he's God. Look at all this shit. Every frigging article that woman ever wrote." He paused, leafing through the top papers. "I think you ought to read this one though." He passed me six Xeroxed papers. "This is Wasserman's Pulitzer Prize article."

I looked at the title of the piece. "Pawn in the Killing Game." There were three parts to the article. Obviously it ran on successive days. "You read this already?" I asked him.

"Yeah. That Bob somebody who gave me this crap was pretty excited about it. Showed it to me first thing. In his eyes, this put Wasserman right up there with somebody like Mark Twain. Though he probably doesn't know who the hell Mark Twain is, let alone read him. Probably would've thought I was speaking about Shania Twain. Anyway, I'd be interested in what you think. Probably should look into this guy. You'll see why after you read it. Establishes a motive, if you ask me."

I'd just started to peruse the article when Bristow sauntered over with another stack of papers. He looked inquisitively at me as if to ask where I wanted them dumped. "Just what I need," I groaned, "more paper."

"These just came through on the fax for you. From the Bureau of Veteran Affairs. Looks like a list of Vietnam era prisoners-of-war. You order this?" I nodded. "Wanna tell me what's going on?"

"We're just following a few hunches more than anything, Matt. We'll know more in a few hours, I think. We have to go through all this crap first." I waved my hand over the mountain of paper littering my desk. "Maybe we can talk a little later this afternoon?"

"Fair enough. I want you to keep me informed. The press has been hounding my ass these last few days." Of course we both knew that if he wasn't such a glory hound, he could've – in fact should've – shunted the press off to our PR department. But when Bristow smells a headline he wants his name to be featured prominently.

"You'll be the first to know, Matt. I promise." I leafed through the sheets of paper he'd deposited in front of me. True to his word, Wright had the reports in my hands in less than two hours. I took the alphabctized list off the top and put the rest aside. I went down the page, name-by-name. The flood of memories made me light headed. Claustrophobic. Irvine looked at me quizzically. "You all right? You're white as a sheet."

I wasn't all right. Close to hyperventilating. My shirt became damp and clammy. I could even smell myself. Leaning back in my chair I closed my eyes, controlling my breathing until my system calmed down. "It's funny, you know? We were all in prison together. Yet most of these guys I only met one time. On the day we were released. And only a small group was released the same time I was. Yet I feel I know them more intimately than even the closest of lovers. Even if we met in prison, we couldn't speak to one another. To do that meant getting worked over pretty good. Most of us were kept in solitary until the end. The only time we were let out of our cells was to wash or get roped. Our only mode of communication was by tapping on common walls."

"How'd that work?" he asked, putting aside the papers he was reading to give me his full attention.

"We tapped in code. A simple one. Weren't supposed to do that either. Bad shit would happen if you were caught. And we were caught. But we did it anyway. Better to be tortured than to lose your sanity in the silence of your own mind. Sometimes we'd tap away entire nights. You'd be surprised what people reveal about themselves when they faced death on a daily basis. We were friends, priests, rabbis, confidantes and psychologists to one another. I remember this one guy who was in the next cell to mine for about eight months. Quintana. Hell, I can't even remember his first name. I don't see his name here, so I guess he's dead. Anyway, I remember him telling me he got his sister pregnant. He'd never told anyone and here he was telling me ... a complete stranger. His sister moved away so she could have the baby and say someone else fathered it. These were the days when abortion was not an option for most people. He wanted me to know how sorry he was. Begged for forgiveness. You know, Mike, I never met the guy. Never even knew what he looked like. Just taps through the wall." I stopped and looked at the floor. "Sorry. This isn't getting us anywhere. Tell you what. Let me read this article and then we can talk about where to go from here."

"Once you read it, I think you'll know where we should go," he replied.

25

I started the article. Wasserman's thesis was apparent from the get-go. That America was still paranoid about Communism. That the war was McCarthyism under a different name. That America had all these internal problems it was trying to mask by getting involved in a foreign war. I had to admit she was a good writer. If I didn't know better, I might have been persuaded by her prose. She interwove her grand design through an interview with a captured pilot named Walter Morris. Walter was an Air Force captain, twenty-seven years old, from Linden, Alabama. Shot down over Hanoi in '69. He'd been a prisoner for a little over a year when she interviewed him.

I interrupted my reading to look over the list of prisoners Wright sent. Morris was there. Currently living in Riverside in Southern California.

I went back to reading. The questions she asked him were intentionally inflammatory. Did he think America was justified in targeting civilian population centers? And what kind of person would actually carry out such orders? When he denied civilians were targeted, she editorialized about the brainwashing techniques of the American military. What about his government? Did he really think they cared about him? Did he really think they were trying to free him? What about the South where he was from? Weren't they all racists and bigots? The questions were shot-gunned at him. It made no difference what he replied. Another question was ready. But Walter wasn't taking her shit laying down, either. His answers became clipped and sarcastic. He defended his actions and the actions of the country. He was in a no-win situation, and I admired him for standing up. I also felt sorry for him, too, knowing what awaited him after the interview was over. His captors wouldn't look kindly on his argumentative stance.

The last few lines of the article were what really caught my attention. Wasserman was winding up the interview by giving her own spin on Morris' answers. Morris apparently accused her of being a traitor, whereupon Wasserman writes:

I wasn't going to take that from the likes of him. I stood up, signaling the interview was over. Immediately the guards came and took him away. As he neared the door, he turned and said, "If I ever get out of here, bitch, I'll come for you." I dismissed him with a wave of my hand.

His parting words were chilling, but not totally unexpected. It reinforced what a lot of ordinary Americans like me think about the brutality visited upon people when they succumb to the war mentality. Violence begets violence. Hate begets hate. Paranoia begets paranoia. At this time in her history, America must step back from the brink and take a cold, hard look at herself. The capitalistic greed that has permeated the very soul of the country for the past one hundred years, and now motivates all her actions, must be put on notice. A better future for all of us. One that is free from the corruptive influence of money and power. This is what we want. What we deserve. It is what we shall have.

I put the article aside and rubbed the back of my hands over my eyes. "Son-of-a-bitch" was all I could think of saying.

"You thinking what I'm thinking?"

"About Walter Morris? I guess we'd better look into him. If Wasserman is accurately reporting what he said, and I'm not willing to trust her totally, then he certainly threatened her. Also, he is alive. I just checked the list.*"*

"What about the leg? Got any info on that?"

"Good thinking. Let me check." I rummaged through the POW file until I came to the section titled *Disabilities*. It was broken into two categories, *Permanent* and *Partial.* I started with the *Permanent* and scrolled down the list. "Bingo," I said excitedly. "He's here. Listen to this ... 'Walter Morris, Captain USAF, Retired. Both legs broken in captivity. Traumatized area of right femur restricted blood flow forcing bone to shorten, resulting in non-correctable partial abridging of patellar tendon.'"

It went on to list attending physician and date when disability payments were approved.

"Cut through all the crap that's in here and I guess it's telling us he limps," Irvine said.

"Looks like," I answered.

26

I checked my watch as I walked into Bristow's office. Damn, I thought. Already two thirty. And I wanted to get out of here early today. I visualized Michele at my house this morning. "Shut those thoughts down," I whispered to myself. "Work to do."

Bristow's office was sparse, reflecting the man who sat in the chair. His desk sat on the back wall and off to the side as though put there out of indifference. I knew better. Nothing Bristow ever did was out of indifference. It was a large desk of indeterminate wood, completely bare except for a nameplate and empty "In" and "Out" trays. He leaned forward as I took the seat opposite him. Hands folded on his desk, he was the principal waiting for the errant schoolboy. "Got something?"

"Yeah. I think so," I answered.

"Anything I could tell the press? Got a conference scheduled in ten minutes. You're gonna have to make this quick. Heaven forbid we have to make our media friends wait a few," he said cynically, his bushy eyebrows pushing into his forehead. I nodded knowingly. Sharing his exasperation with the press while thinking, Who the hell is he trying to kid? He lives for this shit.

"Well, you know our train of thought. We're focusing on the Vietnam era POW angle because of the way the victim was tied up. Hell of a signature, it seems to me. We ran VICAP and came up with three similar homicide MOs, covering the last year-and-a-half. We don't know for sure what the connection is between the four vics. It looks like they were all in North Vietnam sometime during the war, so that might be it.

"For instance, Wasserman was in North Vietnam during the war. Conducted an interview with a prisoner. Wrote an article about it. Won her a Pulitzer Prize. The highlight of her career, as it turns out. An Air Force Captain named Walter Morris. To tell you the truth, she was pretty obnoxious with him. Questioned his character and motives. Might as well have accused him of planning the war himself just so he could bomb hospitals and children. Well, he didn't take that laying down. Gave it right back to her. Didn't show the proper respect. From firsthand experience I can imagine what they did to the poor bastard after she left. That in and of itself doesn't mean squat. What piqued my interest was the fact that he threatened her." I read Bristow the last paragraph of the article.

"You know I got the list of POWs from the Vets Administration. Walter Morris is alive and lives in Southern California. He also is on permanent disability. Wanna guess what for?" I gave him the opportunity to act like the genius he thought he was, but he flunked. Just sat there looking stupidly at me. Letting me answer my own question.

"Leg problem. Walks with a limp." I let the revelation sit there for a minute while Bristow digested the information. "So, what do you think? Permission to pursue?"

"Go for it," he replied. "Sounds like you have yourself a suspect." He reached under his desk and pulled out a briefcase. Another one of his little affectations. He equated a briefcase with power. Wanted people to think he carried important papers in it. If he could get away with it, I'd bet he'd handcuff the damn thing to his wrist. "I gotta run," he said as he escorted me out of his office. "I'll be back in an hour or so. Talk to me before you leave." With a wave he walked into the hall and disappeared. I knew from the way he hefted the briefcase that the damn thing was empty.

27

"**W**ell, what did Papa Bear have to say?" Irvine asked as I came around his desk. It was getting noisy in the office as Akins and his partner Les Burns were at the desks adjacent to ours and were both on the phone. Next to them Kaufman was interviewing some black dude with what must have been twenty pounds of chains around his bare upper torso. The sum of the spoken words blended into a boiling stew that spattered off the walls and windows of 850's fourth floor Homicide office. I motioned to Irvine to follow me out into the hall so we could converse without shouting. Ramirez and Floyd from Robbery nodded as they passed us with coffee cups in hand.

"Papa Bear said you better start busting your hump on this so a certain Inspector can leave early on account of having a hot date this evening."

Irvine scratched his back on the corner of the wall he was leaning against. "That poor lady. She didn't strike me as that hard up."

We could have spent the next ten minutes shooting barbs at one another. Instead, I asked him who he knew at LAPD. To see if they had anything on our guy Morris. While he did that, I'd call San Bernardino PD with the same query.

The noise level dissipated somewhat as we walked back into the office. I hoped it lasted. It was three twenty by the time the phone connection to Southern California was made. I'd have to hurry if I was to get to Michele's on time.

I told the officer who answered what I needed and was transferred to Records. Reserve Officer Kelly listened politely to my story. I gave him Morris' name and address and heard the clicks of his computer terminal as he typed in the information. "Not in our jurisdiction," he said after a few moments. "The address you gave me is in Riverside. You'll have to check with them. Sorry." He gave me the name of a Deputy West and a phone number. I hung up and dialed again.

In the meantime, Irvine was having an animated conversation with somebody. It must have been fruitful because he was writing furiously in the notebook in front of him.

I contacted West in Riverside and repeated my request. He told me they were having trouble with their computers and could he call me back. As if I had a choice. I thanked him, gave him my number, and hung up.

About five minutes later, Irvine terminated his call. Gently replacing the receiver, he looked up at me with a Cheshire cat grin. I knew he had something.

"Closer and closer said Alice."

"It's *curiouser and curiouser*," I said. "If you're going to quote something, at least get it right."

"I knew that," he replied, "but curiouser and curiouser doesn't fit here. *Closer*, on the other hand, does. We're close, pardner. I think we have something." He flipped back his notebook to the beginning. "I spoke with a friend of mine in the Sheriff's Department in L.A. They have access to all the police records, theirs as well as LAPD's. Turns out our guy Morris had numerous run-ins with our brothers in blue down there. Spent three years in the lockup for B & E. Got out in '88. Stayed out of trouble for about a year and a half, then he's back in jail for a parole violation. Packing! He got out at the beginning of '93, but was sent back in '95 for whacking a homeless guy's head with a baseball bat. Only served six months of the two-year sentence because he got some shrink to say he's suffering post-traumatic stress disorder. She puts him in a halfway house. His wife dies that year, so he moves to an address in Riverside. They have nothing on him until the beginning of this year. He's arrested on a burglary with a *special circumstances* charge. Get this – he breaks into a house. The owner comes home during the break-in. Know what the perp does? Ties the owner to the bed."

He had my attention. "Did you ask him about the way he was tied?"

"She."

"Say what?"

"She. The owner was a female. And yes, I asked. What do you think? I wouldn't ask the most important question? The perp tied her arms behind her and drew the legs up behind. My guy says it looked pretty elaborate, but they didn't make special note of it because of what happened next." He paused, waiting for me to ask.

"Okay, smart ass. What happened next?"

"The perp left, and the woman tried to get herself untied. She struggles and ends up falling off the bed and hitting her head on the nightstand. Opens a big gash and bleeds out before anybody can get to her."

"God. Talk about unlucky. I guess when your number's up ..." Irvine nodded. Cops see this kind of occurrence all the time. Fate is the hunter. No other explanation. "Is our boy in jail? If so, that eliminates him."

"No. Listen to this. The interesting thing is Morris is identified as the perp by the dead woman's neighbor. But he's got an ironclad alibi. My friend says that with the alibi they can't hold him. Then guess what? Three days ago, the alibi collapses. Guy says Morris threatened to harm his family if he didn't supply an alibi for him.

"Seeing as how Morris now lives in Riverside, my guy calls Riverside PD so they can make the collar. The cops go to his address and find ..." He stopped. Being dramatic again. I'm in no mood for this. It's getting late and I want to get out of there. "The house is burnt to the ground. Nothing left. This just happened yesterday. They're still sifting through the rubble. They think he flew the coop and set his house on fire to destroy whatever evidence they might have found there."

"So you think this is our guy?" I said.

"My gut tells me it is. And he's on the run after whacking Wasserman. We've got dates that match up, and we've got motive. What about you?"

"I'm not completely sold on him," I said. "But I see where you're coming from. And it's our only solid lead, so we've got to pursue it. But I think I'll reserve judgment until we find Morris and sweat him a little."

"Dinner?" He asked.

"You're on," I replied.

Sometimes when Irvine and I have differing opinions about a suspect, we bet a dinner on who is right. He must feel pretty confident about this one, I thought. For some reason, I wasn't.

Mike formalized his report for the files and wrote up a "Wanted" profile on Morris. It had to be signed by Bristow, so we couldn't publish it until morning. While he was doing that, I re-called Riverside PD. This time I asked for the officer in charge of the Morris case and was connected with Officer Larsen. Catherine Larsen. She had this husky voice tinged with a New England accent. I made her for a transplanted Bostonian. I was close. Rhode Island. She was pleasant enough but wordy as hell. I'm looking at my watch. It was already four thirty.

She didn't add anything to what Irvine just told me. I thanked her for her help and asked if she could send me a copy of her report along with a picture of Morris. I wanted to say ASAP, but bit my tongue. Sometimes you make that request and end up getting what you asked for a few weeks later. You have to be careful not to ruffle any feathers in this business. Some cops want to feel as if they have the upper hand.

"I'll get it off to you immediately," she said sweetly.

"Bless you Officer Larsen," I said, hanging up the phone.

While I waited, Irvine went to Robbery to check if any items from the Wagner residence turned up. I walked over to Kaufman's desk and shot the shit until the receptionist delivered my report from Riverside. At my desk, I leafed quickly through the material Larsen sent. "Oh, shit," I said to no one in particular as I gazed at the eight-by-ten photo of Walter Morris staring up at me in brilliant 600 dpi resolution. I remembered him from my days in the Hanoi Hilton. I saw him at the latrine daily for over six months. Never talked to him, and hadn't put the face with the name. I went back and looked over the description of the man Michele saw at Wasserman's place, and it confirmed what I was already thinking.

When Irvine returned at four forty-five, I already had my coat on and was heading for the door. "You owe me dinner, pardner," I said, gesturing to the picture of Morris I had placed on my desk. "He's not our perp. Walter Morris is black."

28

First thing I did when I got in my car was turn on the Giants game. Forgot. It was a travel day. They were scheduled to play a day game at Shea Stadium against the Mets tomorrow afternoon. The announcer did have good news, though. Dodgers lost, pushing them three and a half back. Another good day.

And it was about to get even better. After changing at my house and packing an extra pair of clothes for tomorrow, I arrived at Michele's a little after seven. She opened the door before I even reached the top step.

"I'm going to have to get you a key, McGuire. That way I won't have to sit by the window for hours waiting for you."

"Waiting? I thought you said seven. Am I late?"

"Hmmm." She looked at me with smoky eyes. "I guess I just couldn't wait." Her smile lit up the foyer and ignited my libido. I put my arms around her waist and lifted her off the ground. Her legs wrapped around mine and I heard her sandals drop to the floor. I kissed her, our tongues searching each other's mouths, lips, cheeks, eyes. It was five minutes before we came up for air.

We didn't make it to the bedroom. In fact, we barely made it to the couch. Clothes came off in bunches. The only time our bodies separated for the next hour was when she said, "hold that thought," slid out from under me and scampered into the kitchen to turn off the oven. That act clearly shows the difference between men and women. I would've let the damn food burn.

When we were finished, I propped myself into a sitting position, which was none too easy given as how we were pretzeled together. I ran my fingers lightly over her stomach, down her legs, and said. "What's for dinner?" She looked at me through dreamy, half closed lids and squeezed her legs together. She wriggled against me suggestively. "You've already had the main course, but you can stay here for dessert, if you like."

I had the dessert as she suggested. We ended up having dinner fashionably late. It wasn't quite the elegant meal Michele had originally envisioned but a hell of a lot more fun. We ate in her formal dining room, the unlit candles standing as silent sentinels over the unused china and crystal neatly arranged at either end of the small rosewood table. She in her robe and me in my long sleeved shirt and boxers, we picked our way through a Waldorf salad and ham-and-cheese sandwiches. I told her about how far we had come on the Wasserman case and about the POW angle. She perceived my reluctance to talk in-depth about my Vietnam experiences and said, "You don't have to tell me about any of it if you don't want to, but I'll listen any time you want to talk, okay?" She came around the table and sat on my lap. With her head on my shoulder, she said, "Take me to bed, okay? We can deal with Wasserman in the morning."

How could I refuse?

Wednesday, July 7th

The man sat in the bunker looking through the
starlight scope mounted on his old-school
Sterling submachine gun. He quickly swept the field
in front of him. It was 12:35 a.m. Six of them were
just now breaking the tree line. Exactly 20 meters
apart. *Military*, he thought. But sloppy. One was even
smoking. Not expecting any resistance. They were
walking toward the house, each carrying an assault
rifle.

The house the six men were walking toward sat
on a windswept plain overlooking the Pacific Ocean,
on the outskirts of a town called Albion. While
known as a town, it was more of a place – one of the
many hamlets that dotted the Mendocino Coast in
Northern California. Its name came courtesy of
Captain W. A. Richardson, who established the
region's first lumber mill in 1853. The stark beauty of
the coastline reminded Richardson of the high, pale
cliffs of his native England. He christened it Albion,
after its poetic namesake.

The man purchased this property in 1977 after
receiving a small inheritance from an uncle he hardly
knew. He read about Mendocino in an old Sunset
Magazine. After spending a week traveling the

Mendocino coastline from Gualala to Fort Bragg, he decided to buy this fifty-acre parcel situated on a spit of ridgeline just north of the Navarro River. The haunting beauty of the land appealed to him. During his summer off from the high school teaching job he had at the time, he rented a motor home, drove north to Albion, parked the vehicle approximately where the house now stood, took down the chaise lounge strapped to the roof, and sat. Day after day – whether in sunshine, shrouded in fog, or engulfed in mist. It didn't matter. Nothing disturbed his solitude. He only moved indoors when the sun lost its battle with gravity and plunged into the ocean depths. It was his cleansing. His salvation. His rebirth back to sanity. As each confining psychological layer was blasted away by the assaulting elements, it was as if he walked out of a dark cave into the bright sunlight. At first he closed his eyes to avoid being blinded. But slowly, slowly, his eyes adjusted, and he saw the world for the first time. The truth of that revelation burned into the fabric of his being. He knew. He knew what he had to do. And he knew, as through a glass darkly, how he would accomplish it. Ironically, sitting there in the darkness of this night, it was the ambient light from the stars, not the sun, which allowed him to see the beginning-of-the-end of his personal drama.

He met his wife Mary in 1978. On their fourth date he brought her to his private aerie. Hand-in-hand, they walked the high cliffs that formed the western boundary of his property. In the gully where they flushed a doe and her two fawns, they lay down in the soft grass and made love. When they were married, every available minute was spent here building their house. The intensity of their relationship was matched only by the fierceness with which they loved this land.

For the next twenty years his personal demons lay dormant in the dark recesses of his soul. It was only after Mary died that the twin malignancies of cancer and revenge exploded within him. It was now a race against time as to which one was going to be satiated first.

~~~~

Schaeffer was so predictable. He would've already found out that the attempt on the man's life in Riverside failed and frantically marshaled his minions to find the man's whereabouts. Combing through his life and finding Albion wouldn't have been hard. The man knew Schaeffer would look here. Sending his "professionals" to finish it once-and-for-all.

The bunker in which he now sat was one of two carefully constructed on weekends over the past six months. They'd been built at either end of a thirty-foot trench he carved out of the hill to the east of the house with his backhoe. They both commanded a one hundred eighty-degree field of fire. Perfectly camouflaged with scrub oak, the hunters would have a difficult time fixing his position. Once the would-be assassins left the tree line, they'd have to traverse one hundred twenty yards of open field to the house. They were already fifty yards through it. Time to rock and roll.

The L34A1 Sterling submachine gun he now held in his hands was purchased three months prior at a Soldier of Fortune convention in Las Vegas. Even though he could've bought a kit to convert the Sterling from its legal semi-automatic mode to an illegal fully automatic, he didn't think the risk of drawing attention to himself by making such a purchase would be worth it. He was perfectly content with its semi-automatic configuration. He knew he'd be squeezing off single rounds rather than spraying a wide area. What sold him on the L34A1 was its integral silencer. The barrel of the Sterling featured seventy-two small holes that dispersed some of the propellant gases into a diffuser tube. This had the double effect of slowing the bullet and reducing the muzzle report. The silencer itself extended forward from the end of the barrel. At the distance the men were from him now, they wouldn't recognize the sound of the weapon firing until it was too late.

The men crept out of the tree line in a rough semi circle, the two on the flanks leading. No need for a point. This would be a piece of cake. A man alone. Probably asleep in his house. Unsuspecting. Against six highly trained professionals. A piece of cake.

They were in effective range as soon as they left the shelter of the trees, but the man held his fire until they couldn't easily retreat back into the brush. He was at a 30-degree angle from their line of advance, making the guy at the deepest part of the semi circle about seventy-five yards from his position. This was to be his first target. Since he was the furthest back in formation, it wouldn't be immediately noticed when he fell. The man sighted the cross hair of his night scope on the gunman's ear. Taking a deep breath, he slowly exhaled and squeezed off his first round. He saw the head on his target explode like a ripe cantaloupe. By the time the body hit the ground, he had the second gunman in his cross hairs. As he fired, the target turned into the bullet and caught the round full in the face. The four survivors were sprayed by bits of blood and bone and instinctively hit the ground, frantically searching through their scopes for the shooter.

The man didn't have time to admire their discipline under fire. He sighted again and squeezed off another round. Three down. In a crouch, he sprinted through the trench to the second bunker. He gave the men credit. Even though they were caught out in the open, there was no panic in their response. They calmly hand-signaled to each other where they thought the shots were coming from. But they were firing blindly. Spraying the whole hill, hoping to suppress fire. Hoping to get lucky. Not tonight. The man sighted and fired again. He was proud of himself. Four shots, four kills. The remaining two men decided to try to get back to the safety of the trees. One would stay prone and fire while the other retreated. Leapfrogging one another. The man fired a fifth time, and dropped the one closest to the trees. The remaining gunman knew his only hope was to make an all-out sprint to the tree line. Trying to outrun death. Not a chance. The man's sixth shot shattered the sprinter's spine. He twitched for a few seconds and then lay still.

The man surveyed the field through his night scope, lingering over each body. Watching for any signs of life before he broke cover. He was drenched in sweat despite the coolness of the early morning. Five minutes passed before he raised himself from the bunker. Carefully he made his way toward the bodies. One-by-one he checked for a pulse and then pulled each corpse to the edge of the cliff before rummaging through their clothes for identification. He didn't expect to find any and was not disappointed. Clean. Sanitized. Professional.

He pulled his field knife from the scabbard on his left hip and methodically cut off the right index finger of all but one of the bodies and placed them in a Ziploc baggie he retrieved from his front pocket. Evidence. If he ever got the chance, he would give them to McGuire to run prints.

Finishing his grisly work, he pushed the de-fingered corpses off the cliff and into the churning waters of the Pacific Ocean below. Their weapons soon followed. Two of them had full clips. They were first to die, he noted with grim satisfaction. If he had the time or energy he would've combed the ground for spent shell casings. But that would be a task better done in daylight, and by daylight he needed to be well clear of the area. His watch read 1:15 a.m. He had much to do in the next four hours. Behind the house was the backhoe – his bunker and the connecting trench had to be obliterated. He wasn't a fool. He knew upon inspection his trench line would be found and recognized for what it was, but he hoped the planned diversion would fool the locals long enough so they wouldn't look too hard for other explanations. At least right away.

By half-past three, he'd re-parked the backhoe and was carrying the sixth body into the garage. He dumped the corpse into an overstuffed chair that he dragged from the house. Carefully putting newspapers around the chair, he rolled the lawnmower over on top of them. Removing the cover and spark plug to make it look like someone was working on the machine, he sprinkled gasoline around the mower and the chair. Next, he placed the half empty container of gasoline within easy reach of the body he'd positioned sitting upright in the chair. He went into the house, left his car keys on the kitchen counter top, and took down a bottle of Jim Beam from the shelf above the sink. He carried it back into the garage and placed it on the floor beside the chair. With any luck, the local fire chief would read the scene as some city guy, getting himself stinking drunk, deciding to fix his mower in the dead of night and passing out with a lit cigarette in his hand. The cigarette dropped on the paper. The paper caught fire. The flames spread to the gas can. The gas can exploded and sprayed flaming gasoline all over the garage causing such a conflagration that the empty propane tank at the back of the garage exploded and incinerated the stupid shit beyond recognition.

Leaving the car here was a nice touch, he thought. Along with the keys on the kitchen counter top. Added just another layer of believability to the story. They would eventually trace the car back to his neighbors in Southern California, but by that time this whole drama would be finished.

It was close to five by the time the man finished preparing the place. He'd thrown the Sterling into the ocean and hurriedly stripped off his bloody clothes, laying them in a pile at the corpse's feet. He dug fresh clothes out of the bike's saddlebags. The last thing he took from the house was a picture of Mary and himself on the deck three weeks before her death. He lovingly wrapped the picture in a blanket and packed it in the saddlebags. Next he placed the saddlebags over the rack above the back tire and tied them off. The bicycle was a brilliant idea he'd conceived months ago. If they did catch on to his charade they would be looking for a stolen car or a hitchhiker. They would never guess he would pedal all the way to San Francisco to kill Schaeffer.

Walking back into the garage, he sprinkled more gasoline around the chair and on his hastily deposited clothing. Positioning the body one more time, he lit the cigarette and dropped it below the chair's arm. Jumping back from the sudden rush of flames, he slid the garage door closed, mounted his TREK 2000 mountain bike and pedaled down the dirt path leading to Highway 1.

The man had just turned into the KOA campground five miles away at the foot of the Navarro Ridge when the first fire truck screamed past.

30

How I made love to her yet again, I'll never know. Usually, once a night and I'm done. Recently – when there had been a "recently" – once a night and I was done for the next *three* nights. Tonight was different. Maybe this was what love did. At least at the beginning. But love was not a word I was willing to use just yet. And I was sure neither was Michele. We were both old enough to know it wasn't a word to be taken lightly. When I was young I threw the word around with abandon, hoping it would get me laid. But as I got older I knew to use it with caution. Knew the obligations you assumed in its telling. Another person to consider and protect. A mutual ownership. I didn't know if I was ready for that.

Michele snuggled up to my back and whispered in my ear. "McGuire, with stamina like yours, what the heck happened to your marriage?"

I laid there in silence, not quite knowing how to answer. Not sure I even wanted to answer it. Finally I said, "It wasn't just about sex." Then I thought better of it. "I take that back. Yes, it was. It was about sex. Isn't everything?"

This intrigued her, I could tell. She burrowed in closer. A relationship story in the offing. Danielle Steele in real life.

"You don't have to tell me if you don't want to." Her way of saying, "you'd better tell me, or else." Her fingers traced the curve of my spine. Her breath hot on my shoulder. No choice now. She was settling in.

"Paula was a good lady," I prefaced. I felt strange even talking about her. Like it was behind her back or something. Like she wasn't there to defend herself. With all that taken into consideration, I simply added. "We just weren't at all alike."

"You didn't realize that until it was too late?" It was the right question. One I asked myself a hundred times in the intervening years.

"You know how it is – you have hints, here and there. But they're all so hidden in the beginning. In the first blush of love. Hell, that masks everything." Her fingernails across my back were getting more insistent. Driving me crazy. "You're going to have to stop that or I'll never be able to finish my story." She stopped. The story interested her more than sex.

"Well, I'm a real touchy-feely person, as you might've guessed by now. I believe that's how you communicate best. Through touch. My dad told me right after the birth of my first child to be sure to touch him. That's how he'll know you love him. I remembered that. And tried to follow that advice."

"But?"

"But Paula was never like that. In fact, she abhorred touching."

"Abhorred?"

"Maybe that's too strong a word. But safe to say, she didn't like it. I guess it was the way she was brought up. I don't know. Except in bed. She was okay in bed – when she was in the mood. But otherwise, it was *keep your distance*."

"How sad," Michele said. And I could tell she meant it. A good sign, too, because I was telling her who I was. My emotional make-up. If she couldn't handle it, she should sign off right now before it went any further.

"She didn't want to hold hands when we walked down the street. Or have me put my arm around her. When we kissed, she arched her body away from me, like you do with strangers. No full-body contact for her. No, sir! I used to envy the lovers I saw – all over each other. Showing the world how they felt, while at the same time oblivious to the world around them. That's how I wanted to be.

"Paula and I got into this fight one night. I mean, a real nasty one. I playfully reached up under her skirt as we were walking up the steps to our house. There was nobody around. I grabbed her ass. She got real pissed at that. Then I got pissed that she got pissed. She told me that night something I guessed at but never wanted to admit – that she hated any public display of affection. It was wrong. It was ugly. It was disgusting. It was obscene. God, she went on and on."

"Sounds like she had a real problem, poor thing. But she was okay in the bedroom?"

"Like I said, when she was in the mood. But this much was true for her – affection was only to be displayed behind closed doors. No other place.

169

Anyway, her expressing that out loud was the beginning of the end of the marriage."

"I like it when you hold me," she said. "You can reach under my skirt anytime. I don't care who is watching."

"Tell me that two years from now and I'll believe you."

"I'd love to have the chance." And with that, she rolled me over on my back and climbed aboard.

I can't remember the number of times since my divorce that I've awakened in a strange bed. It hadn't been many. That I *do* know. I was momentarily disoriented but then felt Michele's foot touching my leg. I felt weak, like all of my precious bodily fluids had been drained out of me – which they had. I smiled at the memory. I started to think about whom I could tell. I'd be the envy of the entire squad room. But no one would believe me, and, what the hell, I wouldn't want to tell them anyway.

It was seven o'clock. I'd only been asleep for four hours, but my internal clock awakened me. Time to get dressed and go to work.

Michele stirred beside me. She slid over and spooned herself around me, fingers playing over my chest.

"No," I cried in mock horror, grabbing her hands. "I can't. Don't even think about it." I snuggled back into her, feeling the warmth of her body conform to mine.

"Why do I get mixed up with *older* guys," she sighed into my back. "A girl needs a little loving early in the morning and their guy can't even get it up."

I grabbed the covers off her and gave her a playful slap on the butt. "Nice ass."

"Yours is kind of cute, too," she giggled, snatching the blankets back and covering herself. I wiggled it at her as I padded back to take a shower.

When I returned, Michele was sitting against pillows propped up on the bed, modestly covered by the sheet, and smoking. When she saw my disapproving look, she said, "This is all your fault, McGuire. I vowed I was going to quit. At least not smoke in front of you. Carry a pack of gum to mask my breath." The smoke curled up in front of her and drifted toward the ceiling, making little shadows in the sunlight streaming through her bedroom windows. "But you walk through my bedroom naked and then deny me." Her mouth formed into a little pout. "My only relief, it seems, is my cigarettes." She stubbed out the cigarette in the ashtray on her lap and stretched like a jungle cat.

"You are so incredibly sexy, baby. I know you've heard the old saying 'the spirit is willing, but the flesh is weak.' Well that just about says it all for me right now. And besides, I've got to get back to 850. Some of us do work for a living."

31

"Well that's a shit-eating grin if I ever saw one," Irvine said to me as I plopped my weary body into the chair opposite him. It was a little after nine fifteen. I was feeling pretty high and guessed it showed. "Must've been a great night, huh?" Irvine said. He leaned forward and in a conspiratorial whisper said, "Tell your old partner all the juicy details."

Mimicking him, I leaned forward in my chair, looking side-to-side as if I didn't want anyone else to hear, and whispered back, "Had dinner, a drink, and was in bed by ten. My bed."

"Bullshit!" he roared, causing Kaufman and Wilkins to stop their conversation and look over at us. "Come on, Mac ..." back to his whisper again. "You come in here walking funny and with that *I just got laid* look, and you expect me to believe you went home a virgin? Did you ever get home?"

"Mike, I'm not walking funny." I pulled at my crotch, wiggling around as if I had to straighten myself. "I'm just a naturally happy guy. I'm always like this." I sat back, cupped my hands behind my head, and started humming. "See, just a happy guy."

"Contented is more like it. But if you don't want to talk about it ..." He shrugged his shoulders in a "that's okay, screw you" manner and flipped over a FedEx envelope. "This came for you about half an hour ago."

I checked the return address and saw it had been mailed from the FedEx office over on Montgomery Street on Monday. No name of sender. I pulled the tab across the front and looked inside. A note and a key down at the bottom. I reached in my desk and pulled out a pair of plastic gloves. I motioned for Irvine to do the same. I laid the contents of the envelope carefully on my desktop. The key was obviously from a safety deposit box somewhere. I unfolded the note and read it. Irvine, who was looking at me the whole time, must've seen the change in my demeanor. "Got something?" he asked, quickly coming around to my side of my desk. I passed him the note. "Son-of-a-bitch," he exclaimed as he read it.

Dear Tom, go to the B of A at Fifth and Market. Key opens Box 2379. You'll find contents interesting. Wasserman confession enclosed. You'll then understand. An old friend.

I reread the note, folded it carefully and put it in the plastic baggie I'd retrieved from my bottom drawer. "Probably should take this to the lab," I said to Irvine, handing him the container. I picked up the key, turned it over several times, and pocketed it. "Guess I should go see what my 'old friend' left me, huh?" The euphoria of last night with Michele dissipated in a heartbeat, replaced by what was becoming an all-too-familiar foreboding. I knew now for certain that I was tracking someone I knew – someone who was bringing me personally into a world I'd been trying to forget. I wasn't a happy camper.

"Well, it looks like we were right about the POW angle, just fingered the wrong guy," Irvine observed, taking the baggie from me and returning to his desk. He looked over his shoulder and said, "Sorry, Mac." He waited a beat and continued. "How do you want to play this?"

"I'll go down and get whatever it is he left and call you. It'll take me about half-an-hour. Why don't you take the letter down to the lab. Have the guys do a complete workup, starting with prints. I don't think they're going to find anything useful but it's worth a try. And let Bristow know, okay? By the way, did you happen to hear how the press conference went?"

"Pure Bristow. Mostly bullshit, but it sounded like the perp was all but caught. Didn't mention the Vietnam angle at all. It was on the tube last night. About a thirty second clip. Thought if you'd gotten home as early as you said, you might've seen it." He was trying to inject a little levity in the situation for my benefit, and I appreciated it, but wasn't in the mood.

"Nice try. Thanks." I patted him on the shoulder and walked out the door.

I was having trouble concentrating as I negotiated City traffic trying to get to the corner of Montgomery and Market. My body was sore, my stomach was growling from not having any breakfast, and my eyes felt as if someone dumped a bucket of sand in them. *The wages of sin*, I thought to myself. And damned proud of it, too!

I double-parked outside the bank, put my "SFPD Official Business" placard on the dash, and ran inside. The cacophony of horns blasting confirmed the number of motorists I'd succeeded in pissing off. Putting on my plastic gloves, I retrieved a small cardboard carton from the safety deposit box. Walking quickly back to the car, I put the box on the passenger seat and pulled out into traffic. Two blocks down Montgomery Street I pulled into a vacant bus stop. Carefully undoing the cellophane tape, I looked inside. Four audiocassettes, each one neatly identified in large block letters. *Wasserman, July 2. Tower, March 11. Munro, June 5. Steele, May 14.* Underneath was a sealed envelope, cryptically addressed *Thomas McGuire, Lt(jg), USN (ret).*

With a mixture of excitement and dread, I tore it open. My heart skipped several beats, and I began to feel lightheaded as I read the note. It was a quote from Cicero. The killer was pulling me back to another time and another place.

.

32

I became more and more anxious as I fought my way home through the downtown traffic. Who was this guy? He obviously knew me – but why was he trying to personally involve me in Wasserman's murder? The cop in me was trying to put all this together. The man in me was thinking about the quote. The goddamned *quote*!

It was from a class I took at the Naval Academy. Taught by Professor Springer. No one who took that class would ever forget him, nor forgive him for that matter. It was a quasi-philosophy class. The subject was an officer's duty to resist an immoral order given him by a superior. The class was popular. Those who got in considered themselves lucky. I was one of those.

The subject matter was extraordinarily complex. As a military officer you're trained from day one that obedience to superiors is the glue that holds the military apparatus together. Without it discipline would break down, and without discipline, the military would cease to be an effective fighting force. That was why the Academy held out so long on outlawing hazing. No matter what demeaning or stupid things you were asked to do, you obeyed. It was good training.

At the same time, however, you were told you must resist an immoral order. The dilemma, of course, is the meaning of "immoral." I remember in high school the priests telling us that the Catholic Church taught we were bound by God to follow our conscience. Hey, I could live with that. But then they inserted the caveat that you could only follow a "rightly formed" conscience. What the hell did that mean? How would you ever know your actions or decisions were the result of a "rightly formed" conscience instead of just an ordinary conscience? I figured I would let greater minds than mine wrestle with that distinction. For me? Just tell me what to do and I'll do it.

Professor Springer's class opened up the same territory. What constituted an "immoral" order? It's easy when you're talking about putting people in ovens. You didn't have to be Saint Francis of Assisi, or Mother Teresa, or Gandhi to see you were morally bound to resist an order like that. A no-brainer! But what about more subtle issues? Like, is it immoral to send troops to capture an objective when you know the objective can't be taken with the force you send? That the attack would result in the wholesale slaughter of troops? And what if you happened to be one of the troops being sent to that slaughter – or even worse, been ordered by your commanding officer to order your troops to go? Was that command immoral? Could you be sure? Was your conscience *rightly formed*? Could your questioning of the order simply be evidence of cowardice on your part?

Knowing you probably wouldn't come back alive? To classify such an order as immoral you'd have to be privy to the tactical reason the objective was chosen, and, therefore, how it fit into the overall strategic battle plan. Reasons that in the normal course of events you never would've been given. Is your conscience *rightly formed*?

I was in the Hanoi Hilton when the My Lai Massacre occurred, but we heard about it. They made damn sure we heard about it. At the time, I was glad they wasted the bastards. But now, in hindsight, there's no doubt in my mind that Lt. Calley issued an immoral order, and the troops should've resisted. After all – if mowing down defenseless women and children doesn't fit right up there on the immorality chart, I don't know what does. Shit, it's so easy to see thirty-some years later, when you're safely home tucked into your own bed. But when you're sloshing through the rice paddies day after endless day and see your buddies maimed and killed by fire from villages just like My Lai – and when you know there are women and children in those villages pulling those triggers, or planting those mines – what do you do? I'll tell you what you do. You get on your knees and thank the good Lord that you weren't one of Calley's troopers.

And then there was the question about what *we* did. Naval aviators. Hell, we were bombing civilian population centers. Hanoi. Haiphong. And while we took every precaution not to hit civilian areas, even at the expense of our own safety, we knew our bombs weren't all that accurate. Some of them were bound to hit noncombatants. Collateral damage, it was called.

Was that "immoral"? Were our consciences *rightly formed*?

And speaking of bombs, the Professor waited until the last day to drop the biggest one of them all. The question he left us with was debated among ourselves long after graduation. He started by reminding us that in a few weeks we would graduate from the Academy and be sworn in as officers in the United States Navy. At that time we would take our sacred Oath – to uphold the Constitution against all enemies, foreign or domestic. He said the "foreign" part was easy – but what if we faced a domestic threat? Someone, say, who'd been duly elected as president of the United States but little by little started to dismantle the freedoms guaranteed us in the Constitution. "What should be our response in such a case?" he asked. "Were we honor-bound by our Oath to resist and to take up arms against him?" The same scenario played out in Germany in 1934, he pointed out. Hitler succeeded Hindenburg after Hindenburg died. First thing he did was to consolidate power, suppressing all resistance and naming himself Fuhrer. And the German military? They chose to stay on the sidelines, and, as a consequence, the world was plunged into war where millions of people died. What would you've done in those circumstances, he asked? Honor your Oath, or sit on the sidelines?

Professor Springer timed the class perfectly. Just as we started to debate the issue, class ended. He kept us there for a few minutes and then dramatically wrote on the board in big block letters a quote from Cicero: *Grecian nations give the honors of the gods to those who slay tyrants* "Have a good day," he said, as we filed out of class for the last time.

I hadn't thought about that shit in years. That was all about to change.

33

The first thing I did when I got home was phone Irvine. I told him about the quote and briefly what it signified. I asked him to call Wright at the VA and have him call the Academy to get the name of every person in Professor Springer's *Honors* class from 1958 through 1973. Once we got those names, we could cross-reference them with the names of anyone who'd done a stint in the Hanoi Hilton. I told Mike to tell Wright that we needed that information today. I also asked Irvine to go through every article Wasserman had written. No matter how long it took. The killer's identity was in one of them. I was sure of it.

I walked into the living room, ejected a Guns N' Roses tape from my cassette recorder and inserted the one labeled "Wasserman." Before hitting the play button, I turned on the Giants game. Curious. It hadn't started yet. Rain delay. I listened to a few minutes of the announcers talking to the Giants manager. He was saying how important this series was. How every game in July counts just as much as the ones in September, blah, blah, blah. He was right, of course. I made a note to check in later.

I settled back in my recliner, took out a notepad and pushed the play button on the remote. A few seconds later my senses were assaulted by the metallic voice of my prey coming at me from all six surround-sound speakers.

"Just to set the scene," the voice said, "I am here with Ruth Wasserman." There were indecipherable noises in the background. "In San Francisco. It's July 2nd at ..." a pause ..." at twenty-three minutes past eight in the evening. Say hello, Ruth."

"Hello." Her voice further away from the microphone.

"Ruth and I are here to discuss things past and present. Isn't that right, Ruth?" God, the guy was about to murder this woman and was talking to her like he was some game show host.

"Yes." I tried to picture the scene in the house that Friday evening. They must've sat at the kitchen table. Did he have a gun on her? Her voice didn't seem to register fear. She wasn't crying. Had they rehearsed? Did she know the danger she was in, that she wouldn't be getting any older than midnight?

"You know who I am, right?"

"Yes."

I clicked the stop button on the remote. "She knows the killer," I wrote in the notebook on my lap. *Met him before*. In Vietnam, most likely. I knew in my heart that I was still trying to dismiss the POW scenario. But I was stuck. There was just no other way of interpreting this. I wrote *POW?* in my notes. Now I had to hope Irvine would find the relevant article that would reveal our killer or the person who'd taken Springer's class. I hit the play button again.

"I've already talked to Heidi, Rebecca and Jennifer," the man's voice said. Wasserman made some kind of noise in the background that I couldn't make out. "I've a pretty good idea of what your group was about. How it was formed. How you got to Vietnam. That sort of thing. What I'd like you to supply is the *why*."

"You promised if I told you that you wouldn't hurt me, right?"

"I won't hurt you, Ruth. I promised you that, and I will keep my promise." I guess the guy thought since he was going to shoot her in the head, death would be instantaneous. Technically, then, she wouldn't be hurt. Shit. This guy was something else. "I don't even have a gun on you now, do I?"

"No, but you've got one. I saw it. And you brought these awful ropes."

"But you're not tied up, are you?"

"No." Her voice louder because the microphone was now closer. "Where do you want me to start?"

"Let's start with your relationship with Governor Schaeffer." There was a long pause. "Ruth?"

"Why do you want to know about him?" Her words clipped. Petulant.

"Why don't you start by telling me how you first met?"

"Well ..." another pause. I sat there expectantly. Wanting her to be cooperative. Knowing that it wouldn't make a damn bit of difference to her fate. "I think it was my junior year in college. I was a journalism major with an English minor. At

Columbia. I thought myself a great writer. The female Ginsberg. I read my poetry down in the Village. In coffee houses, you know? That was the *hip* thing to do in those years. Schaeffer just showed up one night. In those days he had a ponytail and this monstrous beard. He had done some writing, too. We'd all take turns reading our work. Hoping our own personal Ferlinghetti would be in the audience. Afterward, we'd do a few joints and talk politics. I grew up in what would be called a *progressive* home. In the Bronx. In our circle Vietnam came up quite a bit. Most people in the country had never even heard of Vietnam in those years, let alone know where it was. But we knew. Our group knew." Her voice changed again. Defiant. Proud.

"What year, or years, are we talking about here?"

"I don't know. Let me see – probably '59 or '60. I graduated from college in 1961, so it must've been, yeah, probably 1960. Why?"

"I was just wondering. It seems odd to me that Vietnam would even be a topic of conversation in 1960. Doesn't that seem odd to you? We weren't even involved there yet."

"Your ignorance is showing." Her voice now scolding. "The United States never left Vietnam. It had a military presence there since the Geneva Accords were signed in '54. You're reading the history books the government prints. You're like all the rest. The herd.

"Thinking *America* ..." she spit out the word "... was this wonderful peace loving country, when in fact its imperialistic claws were in countries all over the world. Iran. Lebanon. All over South America. Just like today." Her voice was hard. Commanding. Sure of herself.

The man snorted. "So, what did your little group have to say about Vietnam?"

"It wasn't just Vietnam. We knew America was subverting legitimate governments all over the world. How we were using the CIA to make the world safe for *corporate* America." She again spat the words out. I gave her credit. She no doubt knew the danger she was in, but she didn't back down. Maybe she didn't care anymore. Probably sensed she wasn't going to get out of this alive. Might as well let it all hang out. I've seen this before. In interrogations. Where the suspect knows you've made him. He thinks *fuck it,* and while he's at it he thinks *fuck you*, too. False bravado.

"Did your little *clique* – all what – all eleven or twelve of you? Did you think you could change things? Make a difference?" The man's voice took on an edge now. You could hear the anger in his voice.

"We did change things. In case you've forgotten, America lost that war. Your rotten little dirty war fought for the oil companies. We did change things – my little *clique*."

"He hung you out to dry, didn't he?" The change in the conversation was so sudden it was jarring. There was a long silence. I smiled inwardly knowing the trick of a good interrogator. Keep 'em off balance. Especially if you felt things getting away from you. Get back in control by changing the subject.

When Wasserman didn't answer, the man continued. "You did all that work for him. Believed in him. Slept with him. The *cause*. The *revolution*.

And you were just becoming famous in your own right, too. A great journalist. Well known. And then he dropped you. Turned you in for a younger model. Isn't that what happened?" His metallic voice alternating between challenging and sympathetic.

"No. That's *not* what happened," Wasserman responded. Her voice not as strong now. Unsure of where this was headed.

"Come on, Ruth. You got fired from the Village Voice. Schaeffer orchestrated that. We both know it. He got you the job there and then when you got too big – bigger than him – he got you fired. That's really what happened, isn't it? Did you think he was your *comrade* then?"

"Go to hell," Wasserman said, recovering some composure. Trying to get back on the offensive. "I didn't get fired. I ... I quit."

The man's laugh mocked her. He must've stood up then and moved. You could hear the chair scrape on the floor and then his voice from further away. From the sound getting alternately closer and then further away, I guessed he was pacing. I could see him in my mind just as clearly as if I were in the room with him.

"Where did he get the money, Ruth?" He was changing directions again. Keeping her off balance.

"Money?" There was confusion her voice.

"Come on, Ruth." His voice stronger now. Closer to the machine. "Money. He didn't work, did he? That you knew of, anyway." No answer. "He traveled all over the country. Sent your pathetic little group to Vietnam. There was even talk of him being in Cuba part of the time, if I remember correctly. Where'd he get the money, Ruth?"

"I ..."

"Pass around the hat at the coffee houses?"

"You …" A ringing in the distance drowned out the next few words. I was disoriented for a moment until I realized it was my phone. I pressed the stop button and hurried across the room. It was Irvine.

"Sorry to bother you, Mac. I think I've got something. I've been going over Wasserman's columns. She spent more time in Vietnam than you did." He chuckled at his little joke. "I'm up to the summer of 1970. She'd been there at least three times by then. Each time she did an interview with a prisoner. I broke them into three groups. In the first she didn't mention any names. Used them as foils to further her point of view. The second and third groups totaled twelve prisoners – seven in the second group and five in the third. She interviewed each guy and actually devoted a column to each one.

"Good thing you're not reading these columns. Pretty damn inflammatory. Calls you guys things like 'racists' and 'imperialistic monsters.' Things like that."

"Journalistic impartiality at its finest, huh? Hey – it was a long time ago. What names you got?"

"In the second group, a Kevin Atwater, Peter Regan, Lewis Small, Robert Carlton, Bill McKinney, Joe Stanko, and a Richard Carter."

"All of them Navy?" I asked, hoping to cull down the list.

"No. Let's see. Atwater, Stanko, and Carter were Air Force. Lewis Small was Army. Did the Army fly airplanes, Mac?"

"No. The Army guys were all picked up in the South and brought north. They were the lucky ones. Most of the trooper types they caught in the South they either killed outright or worked them to death. Held them in those tiger cages, remember?"

"Oh, yeah."

"Scratch the guys you just mentioned. The guy we want is definitely Navy."

"You sure?"

"Yeah. Springer. Cicero. The Oath, remember?"

"You're right. Sorry. Of the five persons in Group Three, let's see … four are Navy. I've got a Richard Gomez, Matt Riordan, Maurice Birnbaum and James Appel. You know any of these guys?"

"Out of both groups? A few. Carlton and Appel were in my class. McKinney was a year ahead of me. Good football player. That's why I remember him. The rest? Some of the names are familiar. I probably met them at some time or other. But it doesn't make any difference whether I knew them or not."

"Except you said the killer knows you," Irvine responded.

"Yeah. That's a factor but shouldn't prevent us from looking at all these guys. Did you talk to Wright?"

"Just after you called. He said he'd do what he could. He'd try to get back to me this afternoon."

"Good. When you get his report, cross-reference the names on your list with Springer's classes. Also, look at the disability list Wright sent yesterday. See if any of your names filed for disability for a bad leg."

"Will do. How's it going on your end?"

"Interesting, but ghoulish. A conversation from the grave. It's an interview with Wasserman. He's asking her all kinds of questions about her motives. And then he's got this whole thing about Schaeffer."

"The Governor?"

"Yeah. Strange. I don't know where he's going with it, but he *is* going somewhere. I can feel it."

"How'd Wasserman sound?"

"Dead," I answered.

I brewed some coffee and rewound the cassette so I could pick up the thread again. Before I pushed Play, I quickly checked the Giants game. Top of the second. Four to one for the good guys. Sweet!

34

While McGuire was on the phone to Irvine, the man crested the hill on the outskirts of Yorkville and stopped to admire the sweeping expanse of the Alexander Valley laid out before him.

It was 11:05 a.m. He'd been on the road since eight and just completed the most strenuous part of his journey. The past twenty-six miles had been mostly uphill as he biked through the coastal mountain range that lay between Albion and the Pacific Ocean to the west and the winegrowing valleys of California's interior valleys to the east.

He was tired. Besides getting just a few hours sleep, the cancer eating away at him sapped his endurance. Knowing this would be the case, he'd allowed two days for his ride to San Francisco. The saddlebags mounted on the frame over his back tire contained plenty of water, some food, spare bicycle parts in case of unforeseen mechanical failure, light camping equipment, and a 9 mm Beretta. The sniper rifle was broken down and carefully wrapped inside a three-foot tube strapped diagonally across his back. He planned to reach San Rafael by four and find a deserted schoolyard to spend the night. From there it would be a short twenty miles to the City.

He took another drink of water. In the distance he could make out Highway 101 as it meandered its way through the vineyards of Asti and Healdsburg. His journey's end, and most probably his life's end, awaited him some eighty miles south down that highway.

35

I rewound the tape to where I'd left off. The man was making fun of Wasserman's group. Talking about passing the hat around the coffee houses. What followed so surprised me that I replayed it again just to make sure I didn't misunderstand what I heard.

Wasserman's voice. "You're so naive. You and the rest of your kind. Middle America. God, I pity all of you. I know what you want me to say – that we got our funds from the Russians. The KGB. But we didn't. Not a penny, at least that I know of. We didn't need their money. There were plenty of wealthy people right here in America who were fed up. We are at war. Don't you understand? You think you do, but you don't. You were a soldier in a small part of a small war. In an inconsequential part of the world. Your war was nothing. The war I'm talking about is the global war."

Her voice took on the tone of a preacher. "The one we will always be in until America learns its lesson. Look at what has gone on in the name of ..." here anger in her voice "... in the name of democracy. Oppression of the poor. Oppression of your own people. Raping the world's natural resources as if they were yours exclusively. The rich getting richer on the backs of the poor. I hate this ..." Wasserman's voice was drowned out in a spasm of coughing. Violent, lung-ripping coughing. "Are you all right?" The concern in Wasserman's voice sounded genuine, but was lost in an even more furious round of gasping and wheezing. "I'll get you some water." You could hear the chair pushed back, and a raspy, hollow voice commanding her to stay still. The next few minutes were filled with panting moans as the man tried to regain composure. "You should see somebody about that," she said. "You sound like you're dying."

"I am." His voice asthmatic. Sucking in air loudly. "We all are." A pause. "Soon." I couldn't tell whether Wasserman caught the reference.

A few minutes went by, and then the man said, "You were telling me how much you hated America. Continue."

His seizure seemed to take the virulence from Wasserman's oratory. In a softer voice she continued. "I was saying how ashamed I am to be an American. Go ahead and kill me. I don't care." Her tone was one of resignation. Like she was tired of trying to teach this unteachable pupil. "You believe that just because Communism failed in Russia the war is over? Guess again. The Russians were idiots. A group of power-hungry old white men stuck in a time warp. The Chinese have it right. This vile system of yours will be destroyed. They'll kill us economically, and then all the oppressed peoples of this earth will unite and finally be free. A new world built on the ashes of a corrupt Western Civilization. I may not be alive to see it. In fact, I'm sure I won't. But I'm secure going to my fate knowing that my side will win. That I'm on the right side of history. You aren't. People like you impede the sweep of history. We're going to win. You're going to lose. Now, shoot me or get the hell out of my house and be damned."

There was no talking on the tape for a long while. I knew it was still running because I could hear sounds. Footfalls. What sounded like a faucet running. Coughs. Then the man said, "I spoke with the other women who were with you. None of them said anything like this. None corroborated your story."

"None of them knew. They were fools, too. Like you. Nice middle-class college girls. Caught up in the war. Oh, they could talk the talk. Thought they were smart. Doing something *radical*, you know? Hating America was in vogue. Chic! It was all crap. We used them in their naiveté. It helped serve our purposes. But they weren't true believers. When the war ended, they went back to their middle-class existence. Got married. Had kids. Moved to the 'burbs. Probably sat around their country clubs and bragged to their girlfriends about how they were big war protesters back in the day. How they got arrested for the cause. How they went to Vietnam. Put their bodies on the line. Changed the world." She laughed. "God help us all." There was a long pause. A chair scraping the floor.

"I know what you're thinking. About how you're going to publish this. *Once-famous journalist comes clean. Admits to being a commie. Funded by the KGB.* If you think that, you're an even bigger fool than I thought. Who's going to believe any of this? You break in here with the gun and those awful ropes and expect people to think you didn't coerce me into saying these things? Give me a break. Hey – all of you listening to my voice." Wasserman was now yelling into the microphone. Almost hysterically. "Not a word of this is true. He's forcing me to say this." She laughed. "How's that? You think the press will touch this? You're so naive. So full of shit. You're all so full of shit."

"Why did the Voice fire you?" He was again changing direction.

"I told you. I didn't get fired, I quit." Wasserman now sounded tired. Absolutely exhausted. As if her confession sucked the soul out of her.

"Ruth, I talked to Heidi. That's not what she told me."

"Heidi. Cute little blonde Aryan Heidi. How is that bitch?"

"Schaeffer didn't think she was a bitch, did he. Heidi said you thought Schaeffer was yours. But he was sleeping with everyone. And that made you go crazy. You were out of control. That's what she told me."

"I can just picture Heidi saying that. She was jealous. Could see there was something special between Schaeffer and me. Something she wanted. Something she had no right to. Something she hadn't earned. So she conspired with some of the others. They ganged up on me, made up things that weren't true. Remember that I was older than all of them. Much more sophisticated. Wired. They thought they *knew*, but they didn't. They were idiots, the whole bunch of them. Heidi was the worst. But she was the pretty one so she got away with it."

"Will you outlaw beauty in your new world order?" The man was no dummy. He'd found a weakness and was going for the jugular.

"Men are so gullible. So frustrating. Led around by their gonads. But we women are learning. Not acting like sheep being led to the slaughter anymore. Look around, will you? The Heidi types of the world are losing."

"Not according to Schaeffer. He left you for Heidi." Boring in.

"She was such a little bitch. And Schaeffer fell for her act. Betrayed me. I wrote an article about him. Suggesting that he betrayed the cause. One lousy article. How he'd lost the fire. It was my way of getting back at him. But he got furious. Either he or some of his friends got to my editor. Asked me to print a retraction. Said they were afraid of a lawsuit. I knew it was bullshit, and they knew it. I quit."

"I read the news reports on that. Made a big splash. For about a day. That must've made you feel good, huh? Thinking you're important. Finding out you're not. That you're expendable. As expendable as Heidi or Jennifer or the others."

"You forget – Schaeffer had powerful friends. Still does, for that matter. Friends in the media. Friends in high places. I had to pay for what I did to him. And I did."

"You certainly did. Your next job was four months later in Buffalo. That's a big fall." Was there sympathy in the man's voice? It was hard to tell.

"Some shitty little two-bit rag in Buffalo." She laughed miserably into the microphone. "They kept me from getting a job just to let me know who had the power. After that I got better jobs, but ..." She let the rest of the sentence hang there. It wasn't hard to complete. She never again attained the prominence she once enjoyed. The price she paid for jealousy. For love. For being *bourgeois*. I wondered if the man had any remorse for what he was about to do.

There was a pause, then Wasserman again. "The irony, of course, was that he used my article to get where he is today. Once Reagan got elected, and it was clear that the mood of the country was changing, Schaeffer reinvented himself. Three piece suits, button-down shirts, wing tips – the works. He used my article to show he wasn't the radical that his enemies accused him of being. Just a patriotic young man trying to keep America true to her core principles. Keeping her out of that unjust war. Just like thousands of other young men of his generation."

"But we know better, don't we Ruth?"

Another long silence. Then Wasserman again. "The gullibility of the American people. It's amazing. They actually believe him. That he has changed. Maybe he has. I wouldn't know for sure. Haven't talked to him for decades. But knowing him back in the day, I'll bet not. He was a true believer. I was surprised when the people in Los Angeles elected him mayor. Twice, for God's sake. Then he was elected governor. And who knows – now maybe even president. Wouldn't that be irony of ironies? And who paved the way for him? Me. My article."

It was hard to get a read on what Wasserman was feeling at that moment. Her voice was calm. Neutral in the face of what must've been the ultimate irony. My gut told me she'd thought about this for a long time, for so many years, that she could relate it to a complete stranger in tones that would remind you of someone reading the Sunday funnies aloud.

She gave a little laugh. "You know, they contacted me recently." She didn't go on.

The man, like me, waited for her. Nothing more.

"Go on," he finally said. Closer to the microphone again. Chairs scraping. Probably re-seating himself.

"He wanted my help in his presidential campaign. Well, not him. I mean he didn't contact me directly. One of his staffers. Asked me to write an article about him. For the Chronicle. How he'd changed from the early days. You know what I told them?" Her voice quavered. Then with dignity, "I told them he could kiss my ass." She laughed softly. Even through all these years, cause or no cause, *hell hath no fury...* Victory was sweet.

The tape kept running. It was quiet in the room. I pictured them both sitting across from each other. The silence communicating their thoughts. Exhausted. I've seen both cops and bad guys sleep for twenty hours after a particularly grueling interrogation. This one was over. I could tell from the tone of their voices during the last exchange.

"Is this where you kill me?" She was remarkably calm in the face of death.

"I'm afraid so." Movement. The man positioning himself. I could just barely make out Wasserman sobbing. I felt sorry for her. I knew how it was to face death.

"I want you to know, Ruth, that I'm going to get Schaeffer, too. For what he did to me. For what he did to you. For what he's done to the country. Within a week, we can all meet up in hell."

The sobbing continued until I heard the muffled gunshot. Then nothing else.

36

"Governor's Office. Please hold." The phone went dead in my hand. God, I hated that. Didn't even give me a chance to respond. Could be a god-damned nuclear attack I was calling about. Or a million-dollar campaign contribution. On second thought, the people with the million dollars would no doubt have his private number. *Whatever*! The point was they didn't care. Just cut your ass off.

The first thing I did when the recording ended was get the phone number for Schaeffer's office. Time had become a factor. The man said within a week it would all be finished. I did the math. Wasserman was killed on Friday night. Today was Wednesday. Two days. Schaeffer had two days to beef-up his security and call off all scheduled public meetings. Come up with a good spin. Wouldn't do to say he cancelled appointments because some crazy vet thought he was a traitor to his country and was stalking him.

"Please hang up and try your call again." Son-of-a-bitch. Now the bastards cut me off. I slammed the receiver down. Incompetence! The world was full of incompetence. I often wondered how anything actually got done in this country.

Willing myself to calm down, I redialed the number. This time a man's voice answered. Multiple lines, I thought. Unless they just fired the incompetent bitch who hung up on me. Serves her right!

I asked to speak to the Governor. They must get calls like this all the time. Some guy wanting to tell the Governor what he thought of him, or how he should spend millions on pre-kindergarten. In a practiced voice the man replied, "I'm sorry. The Governor is out of the office. May someone else help you?"

A canned answer, but a good one. Showed concern. Taking the voter seriously.

I told the guy who I was and that this was an emergency situation. An official call. I emphasized the word "official."

I was put on hold again but this time was not cut off. A woman answered who identified herself as Alice something-or-other and that she was the Governor's legislative assistant. How could she help me? I went through my spiel again about how it was official police business and how I needed to talk to the Governor in person. Whoever Alice was, she was an officious son-of-a-bitch. In a syrupy voice she told me she would relay any message I cared to give her to the Governor personally. Just give her all the pertinent information. Like she was some shrink or something and I was the god-damned patient. I was getting really annoyed by this time.

"Look, Ms. ..."

"Turner."

"Turner. Tell the Governor, in case he doesn't know, that an old acquaintance of his, a Ruth

Wasserman, was found murdered last Friday night in San Francisco. We've reason to believe that the person responsible for the killing is now after the Governor. I am the inspector on the case. There's also some information of a highly personal nature that has come to my attention that I doubt he'd like broadcast all over hell-and-gone. But the most important thing is that his life is in danger."

"From whom did you receive information about his life being in danger?" asked Ms. Turner.

She got me more than annoyed. "The killer." I left it like that, hoping it had an effect.

There was a pause on her side as she digested the information. "Please give me a number where you can be reached and I'll speak to the Governor about it. If he thinks it is of sufficient importance, he might be able to slot you in today. His calendar is full, as you might imagine."

I gave her my home phone number. "He's got two days to live."

"Pardon me?"

"He's got two days to live. Tell him that. Two days."

I hung up and dialed Irvine.

37

"The son-of-a-bitch is going to kill Schaeffer," I blurted to Irvine without introduction.

There was silence on his end. I knew he was digesting what he just heard and putting it together with my voice. Not an instantaneous progression.

"Mac?" He'd recognized my voice at least. "Kill Schaeffer? The Governor?" It was a cross between a statement and a question. "Who's going to kill him? Our perp?"

"Yeah. I just heard it on the tape. Right before he popped Wasserman. He told her he was going to do Schaeffer, too."

"Couldn't have been futzing with her, could he?"

"No reason to play around with her at that point," I said. "Five minutes later he shot her. You've got to hear it to understand. He said they'll all be in hell before the week is out."

"*This* week? Jesus, Mac. Doesn't give us a hell of a lot of time, does it."

"No. I called the Governor's office. The dumb son-of-a-bitch is there, but you've got to go through layers of bureaucrats to talk to him. I'm waiting for a callback now. I'm going to meet him in person."

"Why in person? Why not just put out an APB on the guy and call the FBI?"

"Normally I would. But, Jesus, Mike, you should hear this tape. A shit-load of first-hand information on Schaeffer. In his early radical years. None of it good. I don't think he would appreciate us making it public. At the least I'd want to give him the opportunity to keep it under wraps. It'll be up to him. If he won't see me, we'll do what we have to at this end. By the way, did Wright ..."

Just then my call waiting beeped. "Hold on, Mike. I've got another call coming in. Might be him." I clicked to the other line.

"Inspector McGuire?" A female voice. "The Governor said he would see you at 2:00 p.m. sharp. Please be on time. He has a number of appointments scheduled and he can't spend a lot of time with you."

"Thank you," I said looking at my watch. It was close to noon. I had to get rolling if I was going to make it up there on time. Sacramento is two hours from the City.

I clicked back to Irvine. "Okay. That was his office. I'm seeing him at two o'clock. Tell Bristow everything. We don't want to be accused of going behind his back on this. Especially where politicos are involved. Did Wright ever call back?"

"About half-an-hour ago. Said he'd have an answer for us sometime later today. Didn't say when. He said trying to deal with Annapolis is worse than dealing with the Pentagon. But he'll get what he can and fax it out ASAP."

"Good. When you get it, call me on the cell. We'll talk, okay?"

"Got it. Tell Schaeffer I said hello."

"You bet," I snorted. Hanging up, I called Michele.

38

"Hi, baby. I've got to take a trip to Sacramento. Thought if you weren't doing anything, you'd like to hitch a ride."

"Absolutely," she replied with no hesitation.

"Great. I'll pick you up in fifteen minutes."

I knew this was a Department no-no. Taking a civilian along on police business was a quick way of getting yourself suspended for a few weeks. But I thought, What the hell. I was taking my own car. If I had to drive to Sacramento, I might as well enjoy the scenery. And besides, if anybody found out, I could always plead her as a witness to a crime related to why I needed to see the governor.

I decided to take the scenic route to Sacramento, so after crossing the Bay Bridge, I headed east on Highway 24 through Oakland toward the Caldecott Tunnel. While it wasn't a windshield-wiper foggy day like in the City, the cloud cover over Oakland was still low enough that I kept my headlights on.

The Caldecott Tunnel ran through the Oakland hills. About a mile in length. Took about four minutes to drive through. But weather-wise, that four minutes took you from black-and-white Kansas to the colorized land of Oz. It was an amazing phenomenon.

On most days there was at *least* a 20-degree temperature difference between one side of that tunnel and the other. And so it was today.

I pulled off the freeway at Orinda and put the top down. Now this is what life is all about, I thought. Rolling down the highway on a warm sunny day, in a convertible with the top down and a pretty woman in the passenger seat. The only thing missing was the Giants game, which I quickly remedied. After switching on the radio, I reached over and put my hand on her thigh, feeling the warmth of the sun on her skin. She put both of her hands over mine and squeezed.

In my simple mind, the mark of a good woman is one who knows when to talk and when not to. If you're listening to a Giants game, for example, a good woman would know not to talk. Games only take two or three hours. That gives you at least nine hours the rest of the day to talk your little hearts out. And if there are important matters to discuss? Hell, that's what commercials are for. Used to drive me nuts with Paula. She talked through the games. It was hard concentrating through her chitter-chatter. Michele? She remained silent. Smart woman. I could get used to her. While I'm listening, however, she did finish two cigarettes. I'm sure it was her way of saying, "I'm putting up with your little idiosyncrasies, so you'll have to put up with mine." Okay, okay, so she wasn't perfect. But damn near.

By the time we crossed the Benicia Bridge twenty minutes later, the game was over. Shawn Estes went eight and gave up only three runs, two unearned. Giants scored four in the first, two in the seventh, and one in the ninth to get the win. It wasn't even the All-Star break and they were in first place by four games. Didn't mean jack, but it kept your hopes up.

Michele and I talked about the case the rest of the way to Sacramento. I told her what I'd heard on the tapes, and that the perp was probably an ex-POW and knew me. I told her, without getting too gruesome, a little about what we'd gone through as prisoners and how this guy apparently thought I'd be sympathetic to what he was doing. That I would understand.

"Do you?" Michele asked me. "Understand?"

"Hard to say," I said. "I've chewed on that all day. God, baby, it was so long ago. Was there a time I would've welcomed revenge? Hell, yes. I was bitter. About a lot of things. But I'm a cop. It's as big a part of my life now as being a prisoner in Vietnam was then. Actually bigger. I put killers in jail now. Maybe I can say I understand where he is coming from, but I don't sympathize."

"So tell me about Schaeffer. Why does this man want to kill him?"

"Well, for a couple of reasons, it seems. The main one, I think, is because he's the guy who sent those women to Vietnam. The mastermind, so to speak. But something else is going on here, too. This guy thinks Schaeffer hasn't reformed himself. That he is still a snake, but only in a different skin. And you know what? Wasserman didn't contradict him. I told you, didn't I, about the note this guy left me?"

She shook her head.

"Well, it was really interesting. It was about a class many of us took at the Academy. The subject was whether it was right – hell, not only *right*, but a *duty* – to kill a traitor. The quote itself doesn't actually use the word *traitor*. Rather, it uses *tyrant*. But the way this guy talked on the tape, a traitor in high places – let's say *high* like in President of the United States – could or would move easily to being a tyrant."

"And that's what he thinks he's going to do?" she asked. "Kill a traitor slash tyrant?"

"That's exactly what I think. If the hypothetical traitor becomes president."

"That's a big *if*," she said.

The conversation went on like this the rest of the way to Sacramento. Michele was a bright lady and asked good questions. Made the right distinctions. Explored the possibilities with me. Made me look at the situation in a number of different ways. There was one problem she couldn't help me with, though, and that was the name of the damn killer. I knew I had to find that out quickly if I was going to save Schaeffer.

I parked in the underground garage at the State Capitol. Michele said she would wander around the area. We agreed to meet at the car at 3 p.m. I knew she was waiting for me to offer her the use of the Mustang, but I still didn't know her well enough to trust her with my most prized possession. We'd have to be damn near married before I'd do that. Even then, maybe not. Depends.

I checked in at the security desk at one fifty. The guard called up to confirm my appointment and told me someone would escort me to Schaeffer's office. I took the Heckler & Koch P7 out of my holster, gave it to the guard along with my badge, and stepped through the X-ray machine. Not a peep. The guard gave my badge back but put my gun in his top drawer. No weapons in the building, he explained.

About five minutes later a surly young guy with a silk suit and slicked back hair came for me. Introduced himself as Chris Riley, the Governor's private aide. He smelled of garlic and shoe polish.

I'm personally not much into politics, but I've been around a number of politicians. Where do they get guys like Riley, I wondered as I followed him up the long, curved stairway. They're all so cookie-cutter. Like the job description said you had to look and act like a punk and be completely obnoxious.

"The Governor is running late," he said as we came to the top of the stairs. "Asked me to interview you myself."

I shook my head. "I don't think you can handle it," I said in the sincerest voice I could muster. I didn't drive all this way to talk to *this* son-of-a-bitch.

We reached an anteroom, and he sat down at the far desk. He looked up at me with a sneer, telling me silently that he didn't appreciate my challenging his authority. "Urgent business for the Governor's ears only," I said trying to be friendly. Like out of some damn spy movie. The corners of his mouth twitched and he began wrapping his knuckles lightly on the desk. I'm thinking of telling him that I've got a lot of important things to do today, and lippin' with him wasn't one of 'em. But I held my tongue. Didn't want to piss him off even more. He sat there looking at me for what seemed like an eternity. A standoff. Then he got up and disappeared into the corridor that ran off to the left behind his desk.

He returned three minutes later and motioned me with his head to follow him. We walked in silence down a long hallway, at the end of which I could see was a large mahogany door with the seal of the State of California emblazoned on. Garlic breath knocked once, opened it, and stood aside so I could enter.

39

The Governor sat in a high-backed leather chair behind an ornate mahogany desk. He didn't rise as I entered the room, merely motioned for me to come in and, with a wave of his hand, gestured to where I should sit.

The room was paneled in walnut. Along the walls were gilt-framed paintings of every governor in California's one hundred forty-nine-year history. The vastness of the room contrasted with the smallness of the man now holding the office. He rested, toad-like, behind the desk, his long, smooth fingers intertwined beneath his chin. His beady eyes were embedded in a pockmarked face and devoured everything they gazed upon. He was not an appealing looking individual, but I had to admit there was aura of power emanating from him that filled the space between us. A formidable opponent, I casually thought as I measured him. But not invincible.

"Inspector McGuire, I presume," he greeted me in a voice that came up from the depths of him, attempting to make up in its powerful sound what his body could not represent in its stunning lack of physicality.

I find it hard to talk to guys like this. Celebrities. You see them on television all the time. Being interviewed or giving a speech somewhere. Looking right at the camera. Looking right at you. Talking in earnest only to *you*. A one-way conversation, to be sure, but you still felt they were talking just to *you*. So when you were in their presence, what do you say? It's a problem. Like now. Schaeffer's "Inspector McGuire, I presume*"* greeting was intended to break down any barriers between us. Inviting me to say something clever back, like "Governor Schaeffer? I'm thankful to be here." My playing Livingstone to his Stanley. And then we'd both laugh at our little historical inside joke and bond.

I was having none of it. I've learned over the years that when talking police business, especially with someone in the *celebrity* class, never get too chummy. The Governor fit that category.

"Inspector Thomas McGuire, SFPD," I replied formally. "Thank you for seeing me."

"My aide said – and oh by the way, I apologize if he was rude to you. He is young and still thinks that rudeness equates to power. He'll learn as he matures. Like us." He paused, waiting for me to reply. He was still trying to bond. I stared at him impassively. He shrugged and went on.

"He said I'm the subject of a murder investigation."

"You are not the *subject*, Sir. You are the *object*."

"I don't understand."

"I've reason to believe your life may be in danger. There was a murder in San Francisco last week. A woman you know."

"Ah, yes. Ruth Wasserman."

"Yes, sir. You've heard about it." I said it as a statement rather than a question.

"Of course I've heard. Ruth and I knew each other in our past lives. I even spoke to your Lt. Bristow about it."

That took me completely by surprise. It obviously registered on my face because he smiled and continued "You seem surprised, Inspector. You didn't know? Well, actually it was just this morning. Right after you called. I've known Matt Bristow a number of years. A fine, professional police officer."

A whimpering, ass-licking bureaucrat, I thought but didn't say. Instead, I just smiled and shook my head like we were in complete agreement.

"He told me of your suspicion that Ruth was killed by an ex-POW bent on revenge. Is that what you think, Inspector?"

"The investigation points in that direction, Sir. Four women in a group calling themselves *Women Against Imperialistic War* were murdered. You had some affiliation with that group at one time."

"Long ago, Inspector," he said.

"Long ago," I echoed. "The killer recorded the conversation he had with Ruth right before he shot her. I just finished listening to it this morning. I called you immediately. He stated unequivocally that he's going to kill you. The guy has a great track record so far. He's four for four. I'd take him seriously if I were you."

"Four for four against defenseless women, Inspector. What do you think – this maniac is going to come into the Capitol Building with guns blazing?"

"No, sir, I don't. I think he'll wait until you're outside at some public event and get close enough to shoot you. Someone did it to President Reagan. They can do it to you."

"Frankly, Inspector, I think you're reading too much into this. I appreciate your concern. I can tell you are a good, thorough policeman. Maybe I can find a place on my staff for you. I'm in need of competent, conscientious professionals." He let it hang in the air for a moment.

The son-of-a-bitch is trying to bribe me, I thought, but said, "Thank you. I appreciate the offer, but I'm happy with what I'm doing."

"Whatever. As you know, Inspector, I am at the beginning of exploratory talks about a possible run for the presidency. What I don't need now is a bunch of hysteria created by a rather wild idea that an echo from my past is out to do me in."

"I don't think it's a wild idea at all, Sir. I heard him say just that."

"Did you listen to all the tapes?" he asked.

The man was full of surprises. "*All* the tapes? Did I mention there was more than one?" I was trying to think if I mentioned there was more than one to Irvine who might've told Bristow. I might've said *tapes* plural, but I wouldn't have said I listened to more than one. There were four of them in that box. I only listened to the Wasserman's. I don't know why I would've mentioned more than one.

There was a slight catch in his voice and his eyes registered an instant of doubt. "Uh ... I don't know. Maybe. If it wasn't you, it must've been Lt. Bristow. At this point, who cares?" He was trying to recover.

"Can you tell me what else was on the tape you listened to?" His demeanor changed imperceptibly. He was wary now. Edgy.

"I can't tell you in detail, Sir. It's an ongoing investigation. You understand, I'm sure." Standard cop line. "But I *can* tell you that you were the topic of much of the conversation." What the hell, I thought. I might as well let the asshole sweat a little. His precious reputation was on the line.

"Am I a suspect in this case, Inspector?" he chuckled. Trying to bond with me again. How could anyone vote for this little shit?

"No, Sir." I played it straight. Like I didn't get his joke. "I was merely stating what I heard on the tape." I emphasized *tape* – singular, just to let him know I recognized his *faux pas*.

He nodded and closed his eyes. When he reopened them there was a blankness there that was truly scary. As if in a trance. Like staring into the eyes of a dead person. "I trust, Inspector, that none of what was contained in that tape – or any of them if there *was* more than one – will see the light of day." It was more of a warning than a statement. He stood up abruptly and punched a button on his phone. "Inspector McGuire will be leaving now," he said into the receiver. "Can you come and fetch him?"

I was being dismissed. As I stood he said to me, "I simply think you're barking up the wrong tree and would appreciate it if you not pursue this any further." He paused, looking directly into my eyes. "Why would someone go to such extremes to kill me? Because I took certain positions on the Vietnam War?

More than thirty-five years ago? Doesn't this sound a wee bit far-fetched even to you?"

"I was there."

"Pardon me?"

"I was there, Sir. In Vietnam. A prisoner in the North for close to seven years. You were the leader of the resistance on the home front. I don't want to get into the morality issue with you, but I do know that your opposition, and the way you chose to carry it out ..." I heard the door open behind me "... was the cause of a lot of good people being tortured and killed."

"Ridiculous, Inspector. You've no proof of that outrageous accusation."

"I was there, Governor. I saw it with my own eyes. I survived. One of the lucky ones. I can imagine, though, that there might be a lot of veterans, especially POWs, that wouldn't care a whole lot if this guy was successful."

"And that includes you, Inspector?"

"I didn't say that."

"You didn't have to," he said. "Chris," he motioned to the man at the door, "show the Inspector out."

40

Michele was at the car by the time I returned. As we drove, I recounted my conversation with Schaeffer. She and I shared the same feeling – something was not adding up, and she actually voiced what was swimming around in my head. "I wonder what he knows and when he knew it?" she said, paraphrasing the question that hounded President Nixon from office.

About a half an hour out of Sacramento, my cell phone rang. It was Irvine.

"Mac, we identified the guy. His name is Robert Carlton."

"Carlton? Are you sure? How'd you finger him?" My heart was racing, partly because I remembered Bob Carlton and didn't want to believe it, and partly because I could smell the prey. The hunt was on.

"Wright called back. You were correct. Of our original seven guys on the list, only five took that class. McKinney, Carlton, Riordan, Birnbaum and Appel. He did some checking for us. Two of the guys, Riordan and Appel, are dead. McKinney's been in jail for the past five years. Some kind of white-collar crime. Birnbaum has shoulder problems, but nothing regarding his legs. Carlton's name rises to the top because of his disability. His leg was broken in Vietnam. Didn't get immediate attention, so the bone never set right. After he returned to the States, there was some conversation with the VA that maybe they could re-break his leg and reset it. That didn't work out, unfortunately, because there was something about bone-density and blood supply. Whatever! The bottom line is that his right leg is two inches shorter than his left. He walks with a pronounced limp."

"Okay. Let's start the process on him. Get him in the system. Do we know where he lives?"

"As a matter of fact, we do. Guess where? Riverside. Same place as that Morris guy. What are the odds of that? Small world, huh?"

"I guess. Have you alerted Riverside PD yet? I'll be back in the office in an hour, maybe hour and-a-half. "

"Already done, Mac. They're checking it out as we speak. Oh – and Bristow wants to see you."

"Damn! What about?" I knew whatever it was couldn't be good.

"I don't know, Mac. He just came over to me about ten minutes ago and said that if I talked to you to tell you to come in and see him today. I know he left the same message at the desk in case you called in."

"Okay. Tell him I'm on my way. I've got to take ..." I stopped in time. No use telling anyone that Michele was with me, even my partner. "Never mind, tell him I'll be in later."

Michele listened excitedly to my conversation. "They got the guy, right? Who is he? Do you know him?"

"We know who he is, but we haven't apprehended him yet. He lives down in Riverside. The police department there will pick him up for us. And, yeah, I knew him."

I pictured Robert Carlton in my mind. He was in my class at the Academy. Close to my height. About five-feet-ten or -eleven. Sandy blonde hair. Glasses? Not that I remembered.

"I got shot down in the summer of '66, two months or so before Carlton was hit. But I didn't arrive in Hanoi until March of '67, a few months after Carlton. They'd moved some of us from prison to prison – that's why I showed up later. A few got their ticket punched directly to the Hilton. *Do Not Pass Go, Do Not Collect $200.* Carlton was one of them. By the time I arrived he already had a reputation for being a tough guy. Took some incredible beatings before he broke. No shame in that. We all broke – but Carlton held out a long time. A long time in that house of horrors meant two, maybe three, days. And he paid dearly for his patriotism. I remember his leg was broken. Pigeye did a number on that leg. I remember our gracious hosts – when they wanted him to sign some propaganda bullshit they would truss him up like a pig and then take turns kicking and jumping on his broken leg. Nice guys, huh?"

Michele winced and put her head on my shoulder. "I'm sorry," she said. I accepted it for what it was worth. She was trying to comfort me. Not much more she could say.

"To be that brave you had to be a little bit crazy," I said. "We were cellmates for a time. He told me about the time he killed a rat in his cell. Now you have to understand, you've never seen rats like they've got in Vietnam."

"Oh, Mac, do you have to tell me this?" She shivered.

"I'm sorry, baby. But it will give you an idea of what kind of guy we're dealing with. And, besides, it's a good story." I chuckled at the memory. "Those rats – they were as big as jackrabbits. Mean, ugly-looking bastards. They used to come into our cells through the drainage hole. In the early days, when we were all in solitary and going through torture every day, we'd be shackled to our beds at night. We couldn't move. Those rats would come in and crawl over us. Attracted by our blood and wastes. If you didn't yell at them they actually gnawed at your wounds. You couldn't sleep, because if you did they'd eat you alive. Carlton told me he got so pissed one night that he managed to bite one of those bastards as it was walking across his face. Got it right by the throat. The rat fought like hell but Carlton wouldn't let go. When the guards came in the next morning, he still held that rat in his mouth. Blood all over the place. Here he was, legs manacled to the bed, arms stitched up behind his back, and this rat in his mouth. Carlton told me he put on a real crazy look. The Vietnamese thought he'd lost it. Gone 'round the bend. So they left him alone for a couple of months. We laughed like hell over that story."

"Ick! That's a terrible story." Her right hand caressed my chest. "I'm sorry," she said again.

"Yeah, well – that's how it was. I'm sorry it's Carlton. He was a brave guy. I liked him."

"Did you see him after? I mean after you came home?"

"No. In fact, I was moved to another part of the prison after the first of that year. There was neither rhyme nor reason as to how they moved us around. For the next two years I changed cells and cellmates about once every four months. The peace agreements were signed in Paris on January 27th, 1973. During February and March, they sent us home. In three increments. I was in the first group. Carlton wasn't. I never saw or heard from him again. Until now."

41

We got back to the City a little before five. The clouds we'd left that morning still hung sullenly over the hills like lead netting. I dropped Michele off, promising I'd be back by seven for dinner, and headed downtown to 850.

I walked into the office and saw Irvine roll his eyes and nod toward Bristow's office. The door was open and I could see him hunched over his desk doing some paperwork. Might as well get this over with, I thought. I could tell by Irvine's body language that whatever it was he wanted to see me about wasn't going to be pleasant.

"Lieutenant?" I said, poking my head through the doorway.

"Oh, hi, Mac. Come on in. And close the door, will you?" While his voice was friendly enough, his hooded eyes had the look of a cobra ready to strike. "Sit down."

"You wanted to see me?"

"Yeah." And here the friendly banter stopped. "What the hell were you doing in Sacramento today? You never got permission from me to see the Governor," he said. "Christ, Mac. He called down here and chewed the Chief's ass off. And then the

Chief called me and chewed my ass off. A little later the Governor called me personally and chewed on my ass a little more. I don't need this. Your career can go down in flames, but you aren't taking me with you." His voice raised a few decibels. Loud enough, I was sure, that the guys in the squad room could hear the conversation if they wanted. "What the hell did you tell him? He says you were rude and abrasive. You actually accused him of having something to do with Wasserman's murder?"

"That's bullshit."

"And then you tell him that someone is out to cap him? No proof, no nothing?" He was just getting warmed up. The cords in his neck bulged like a weightlifter doing a clean-and-jerk. "And ..."

"He's full of bullshit, Matt. I don't care what he told you. I went up there to warn him that I personally heard a guy threaten his life."

"What guy? This *Carlton*? The guy who recorded all this shit?"

I was somewhat taken aback by his using Carlton's name. I don't know why. There was no reason for Irvine not to tell him. "Why didn't you just call him?" Bristow continued. "Or, better yet, follow procedure and call the Chief and have *him* call Schaeffer."

"Christ, Matt. I thought I was doing the son-of-a-bitch a favor. First of all, he wouldn't even take my call, so telling him on the phone would've been impossible. I had to go through some puke aide of his."

Bristow smiled at my reference. He must've dealt with the guy at some point, too.

"There was a lot of sensitive information on that tape. About Schaeffer. I thought he'd appreciate it if I kept it to myself and told him about it in person. Now all I'm getting is grief from the guy. That's crap."

"You should've gone through channels, Mac. You know that." He was softening now. Fatherly. Talking to his wayward, chastised son. Forgiving me. But letting me know it wouldn't be tolerated again.

"Matt, this guy Carlton said he was going to whack the Governor within the next two days. I didn't have a lot of time to send this up through channels and hope it got to Schaeffer in time to save his fucking life." Now, I was getting mad.

Bristow steepled his fingers under his chin and looked at me, not saying a word. Finally, coming out of his trance, he said, "Well, no harm, no foul, I guess. Your trip up there was for naught anyway. Carlton's dead. Case closed."

I couldn't have been more stunned if you told me the Pope just turned Mormon. "Wait – how do you know that?"

"Anonymous tip," he said. "About an hour ago, somebody called the desk downstairs and said – well, hell, he recorded it. You can listen for yourself." He pushed the button on his cassette player.

"SFPD." I recognized Sergeant Carney's voice. "How can I help you?" There was a pause, like a person on the other end was deciding whether to talk or not. Then a voice, obviously disguised but sounding faintly Oriental said, "The man you're looking for in the Wasserman murder is named Robert Carlton. He lives in Riverside. He was killed in an explosion at his house on Monday."

"Excuse me, sir?" It was Carney's voice. "Could I have your name, sir?" Silence. "Can I ask how you came by this information?" Again silence. The tape spun on, making several revolutions before the voice came on again. "He's dead," was all that was said before the phone disconnected.

Bristow pushed the stop button, fished out the tape and returned it to his desk drawer. "Irvine checked with the Riverside Police Department. In fact, there was an explosion and fire that destroyed the house of one Robert Carlton, former Vietnam POW. On Monday morning. A fatality was logged." He looked pleased with himself, like he alone just solved a crime.

"A *fatality*? What does that mean? Was it Carlton?"

"They haven't made a positive ID yet. But who else could it be? You can ask Irvine. He has the particulars. But from what he said they told him, the explosion was enough to knock Carlton's body, or what was left of it, into the next area code."

"How'd the guy who called know all this?" I asked, nodding toward the cassette player.

"I've no idea. You heard it. He doesn't say. Maybe he was an accomplice. Who knows? *Who cares*? The bottom line is the case is solved and therefore closed. Chalk one up for the good guys. Another murder case solved and off the books. Good for statistics when we ask the Board of Supervisors for more money in next year's budget." He smiled at me and lifted his bulk out of his chair. I could tell I was being dismissed. This was getting annoying. First Schaeffer, now Bristow.

But I wasn't ready to go. "Come on, Matt. Doesn't this sound a little fishy to you? Out of the blue a guy calls and has this kind of information? How many times does *that* happen?"

"It happens," he replied. "Ours is not to reason why, ours is but ..." he left the rest for me to fill in. Ours is but to take it up the ass just because the Governor said bend over, I finished in my mind.

"I don't like it, Matt. When did that call come in?"

"About an hour ago," he answered.

"Before or after you talked to Schaeffer?"

"Don't even go there, McGuire," he warned. "I tried to be nice to you. I didn't say anything about the woman who was with you in Sacramento. That in-and-of-itself was a breach of Department regulations. You know that."

Holy shit, I thought. Somebody's been shadowing me. That's the only way Bristow could've known that Michele was with me. I sat there dumbly. Not knowing what to say. Caught with my hand in the cookie jar.

Bristow could tell by my silence that he had me. He pressed his advantage. "And not going through channels in a homicide investigation. That's another violation. What do I have here, a rogue cop? That's what the Governor wanted to know. And what could I tell him? Come on, Mac, he had me in a sling." Bristow was playing good cop, bad cop with me. Schaeffer was the bad cop, Bristow the good. Unfortunately, the bad cop was going to win this little exercise. I could see it coming.

"What could I say to him, Mac? You tell me. No, wait. I'll tell you. There was nothing I could say. I told him I would relieve you of your duties for the next few days. Disciplinary leave."

I was dumbfounded. My back ached and goose pimples assaulted my neck and shoulders.

He wasn't looking at me now. Pacing behind his desk, head down. Pondering my fate. "But Schaeffer said that would be too severe. He said you were essentially a good cop, trying to do your duty. A little rambunctious, but still dedicated. Asked me to give you the next few days off. Until, say, Monday. Like a vacation. Clear your head of all this foolishness. No notes to your file. Full pay. I'll tell you, McGuire ..." He stopped pacing and looked me full in the face. "He's doing you a big favor. It could've gone really badly for you. If I took this upstairs – well, there's no telling what would've happened. They might've thrown the book at you. You've Schaeffer to thank personally that you're not up before Internal Affairs."

"A vacation," I said dryly.

"Until Monday. With pay. Look at the bright side. You can take that honey you were with today and ride up the coast. Have fun. Hell, I've got to be here all weekend." He paused. "And I don't want to see your ass in here. Understood?"

"It still doesn't make sense, Matt."

"God-dammit, McGuire. Get your ass out of my office and out of the building before I have you escorted out. The Wasserman case is officially closed. I'm meeting the press tomorrow and issuing a statement. Closed! Finished! Over! Got that? Now, please leave. I have work to do."

"One thing, Matt," I said as I was walking toward the door. "When you spoke to Schaeffer this morning, did you happen to mention how many tapes were in our possession?"

"Not that I can recall. Why?"

"Just curious," I said. "Want me to shut the door?"

Irvine was waiting for me by my desk. "So, what was that all about? You look none too pleased."

"He's closed the case, Mike. On a fucking anonymous tip. I can't believe it. And then he has the balls to suspend me."

"*Suspend* you?"

"Well, a leave of absence. Until Monday. He doesn't want me on this case. Doesn't want anybody on this case. Why?"

"Not to stick up for him or anything – but for one thing, Carlton is dead. The tip was genuine, Mac. I checked it out myself."

I sat down at my desk, Irvine standing over me. "Monday," I said. "Blown up Monday. Hell, Mike, it doesn't fit. The tapes were in the box Monday night."

"Must've been a friend or something, then. Maybe the guy who called, for all we know. My guy in Riverside says Carlton was blown to shit. In his house. Big explosion. They're still looking into the cause, but they're pretty sure it was a gas leak. That's what they think. They got body parts, Mac. And his car was in the garage."

"They get a positive ID?"

"Not yet. Not much left of the poor bastard. They're still collecting. Bagging everything. Should have something by tomorrow, I imagine."

"Mike ... you're sure about this? The guy you talked to down there – you know him? He's a cop, right?"

"Yeah, he's a cop. He says it's a coincidence that the guy we're looking for in a murder case blows himself up. Maybe a suicide is what they think."

"Too much of a coincidence, Mike. You know that. There are never any coincidences." Irvine moved back to his desk, unconvinced. "Will you do me a favor? I'll be home tomorrow most likely. I now have four days off, after all."

"Lucky you."

"Yeah. Lucky me," I said sarcastically. "Anyway, if you get a call from Riverside PD with an ID, will you call me? I'd feel a lot better about this."

"Sure, Mac."

Just then Bristow walked out of his office. "You've got the tapes at your house?" he yelled to me.

I waved in the affirmative, thinking the whole time what a complete asshole he was.

42

As I waited for the elevator, Lynn Carter came down the hall and joined me. She was a pretty, thirty-something blonde, with the most luminous blue eyes I'd ever seen. You could literally drown in them. I had.

"What was all the shouting about? God, I could hear you and Bristow going at it through the walls."

Lynn was one of only two female inspectors in Robbery. She'd worked her way up from Patrol. No affirmative action hire at work here. Lynn was a smart, tough lady. We'd dated a while after my divorce. Had been separated from her husband for a few months when we first went out. It was an ego thing on both our parts. Confirming that we were still attractive. Still desirable. We both knew it, too. Our romance was short-lived, but we remained friends. She subsequently got a divorce and married a lawyer in the District Attorney's office. I, on the other hand, went home every night alone.

"Bristow has delusions of adequacy," I said, shaking my head. "Want to change units? Tell you what, Lynn. You wanted to be in Homicide. Trade you straight up."

She looked over at me. "Gee, what a friend. That bad, huh?"

"Worse."

"Okay. To a lighter subject. Who was that lady you had lunch with yesterday?"

"Michele? How'd you hear about her?"

"Come on, Mac. You know you can't keep a secret around this place. So, who was she? Guy who told me – I could have stepped on his tongue it was hanging out so far. Serious?"

"Just someone I met in the course of an investigation," I said, sidestepping the question. The elevator door opened. "Going down to One?"

"Yeah. Well, Mac, she seriously turned some heads is all I know," Carter said, trying to keep the conversation alive. Trying to find out.

"The people around here have got to get a life." She could tell I wanted to drop the subject. And she did. Lynn was a good lady.

"So, back to Bristow. What's going on?"

"It's a long story, Lynn." The elevator clanked to a stop on One. We exited into a crowd of handcuffed prisoners being escorted up to the seventh floor lock-up. I turned right toward the parking lot. Lynn followed.

"The trouble with Bristow," I said as I opened the outside door for her, "is that he's completely unspoiled by failure."

She laughed. "Well, thanks for the offer to switch, but I think I'll stay put. And speaking of failures, who are those two dudes hanging around your car?"

I looked over and saw two black guys doing a slow shuffle around my Mustang. The 850 parking lot was theoretically secure but it's been known to have a car or two jacked on occasion. I wasn't about to let mine be one of them. "I'd better go see. Have a nice weekend. Say *hi* to what's-his-face for me."

"Peter," she said with a smile. "Come on, Mac, you know his name."

"I vowed never to speak it in public when he took you away from me," I said, a pout on my face.

She gave me a little shove. "Don't give me *that little boy lost* expression. I fell for it once, but not again." She laughed. "I'll tell him you said hello. And say *hi* to your new squeeze for me. Tell her I'm jealous."

I watched her walk to her car, admiring the way her ass twitched as she walked. Remembering how it looked without that damn uniform on.

43

"**N**ice car, huh?" I said, walking toward the two men admiring my 'Stang. "It's mine, and it's not going anywhere."

"Hey, man, we was jus' lookin'," the taller one said. Both men wore matching black, calf-length leather jackets and enough gold chains to open their own pawn shop. The guy who answered me never even looked up, just kept running his hand down the fender of the car. Caressing it, like you would a woman. He knows I'm a cop, I thought. He knows I'm white, and he knows he doesn't like me.

"Hey, Truck. How you been doin' man? This yo' car? Nice!"

I recognized the speaker. Edvent Walters. "Don't get any ideas, Eddie." Eddie Walters is known on the street as Slow Eddie. This was to distinguish him from Fast Eddie Walters, a dope dealer over in Hunters Point. Slow Eddie picked up his moniker because an old lady, whose purse he snatched while making a run up Mason Street late one night, ran his ass down. After catching him she proceeded to whack the shit out of him with her shoe. Truth was, Eddie was high on something-or-other, tripped over the curb after the snatch and fell, hitting his head on a newspaper stand and knocking himself out cold. By the time he came to, the lady was straddling him, skirt hiked up around her thighs and hitting him with her shoe. A high heel that was doing some real damage to Eddie's skull – along with his ego. He was yelling "Hey, mamma! Hey, mamma!" with each blow. I heard the story from the arresting officers, both of whom laughed like hell describing it to me. Eddie did four months for that little caper, and by the time he gets out he's known as *Slow Eddie*.

"You comin' or goin', Eddie?" I asked as we bumped fists and did all the cool handshakes.

"Hey, man, I'm just here visitin'. Got relatives on Five."

Fifth floor. Cells for robbery and drug suspects. "You gotta find better relatives, Eddie. How you been doin'?"

"Hey, Truck. Want you to meet a brutha. Turnel Townsend." I nodded at him. He looked up at me with murderous eyes. Got an attitude, does Turnel. I'd be seeing him again, I knew. "Turnel, this be ho-mo-cide inspector Thomas McGuire. Don't you evah be liftin' his car or nuffin'. Truck and me go back a long way. Ain't that right, Truck?" Him calling me "Truck" comes from my nickname "Mac", which he coupled with "truck", as in Mack Truck. That's my take, anyway. With Slow Eddie, you never knew. "What?" he said to me. "Ten years? Sumpin' like that. You be on what, Vice?" I nodded. "I did git myself in some trouble down in Bayview. Not my fault."

"It's never your fault, Eddie," I said.

"True that, Truck. So true. Anyways," he turned back to Turnel, "I've got this dude pointin' a piece at me. Sayin' I was screwin' his little girl. I knows I'm history. This dude is pissed and is going to off me right there. But then Truck here rides to my rescue. He's just cruzin' the hood when he sees this commotion. Draws his piece and persuades this other dude to put his down. I owes him my life."

This wasn't quite how it happened, but hell, who am I to spoil a good story? Didn't have much effect on ol' Turnel, though. He fixed me with a sullen stare and wouldn't let go. On another day I would have taken the challenge. But not today. I knew I'd be seeing him again. You can just tell with some guys.

"You living the same place, Eddie?"

"Same place. Over on Copper. I've been settlin' down. Got me a *good* woman. Lookin' for a job. Legit job. Why? You got somethin' for me?"

"You never know. I might. Just wanted to be sure in case I had to look you up. You got a phone?"

"Got me a cell, Truck. You want that number? In case you needs me?" I knew if I ever called he'd shit in his pants. I wrote it down.

"And say *hi* to all your relatives on Five. Don't want to be seeing *you* up there."

"Not me, Truck. I be livin' clean, Dog.''

"Keep it that way. And keep better company, okay? "I gestured toward Turnel. "He's trouble, Eddie. You got too much going for you to be hangin' with trash like this."

If looks could kill, Turnel would've had me splattered all over the parking lot. I smiled to myself as I started the 'Stang. Small victories!

44

Robert Carlton wearily pedaled the final block to the schoolyard he'd picked to spend what might be his last night on earth. The day had been tougher on him physically than he expected. His age and illness combined to sap him of strength, the kind of strength he had ten years ago when this sixty-seven-mile bike ride would've been a piece of cake. All he wanted to do now was crawl under the big tree at the far end of the schoolyard and drift into a dreamless sleep. He needed his body to be completely rested for tomorrow's final act.

He'd found Saint Catherine's School in the phone book. He'd picked out four private schools and canvassed them all before deciding on this one. It was in an upscale neighborhood and was just far enough out of the way for him not to have to worry about druggies or homeless people bothering him.

As he unpacked his saddlebags he heard the car enter the school's parking lot. He didn't turn around. Instead, he fumbled through his pack until he found the reassuring grip of the Beretta and thumbed off the safety. Fixing a smile on his face, he turned to see a young San Rafael police officer getting out of his squad car.

Carlton nodded his head and said, "Good evening, Officer. I just stopped here to rest. It's all right, isn't it?"

The baby-faced officer looked him over and then the bicycle. Motioning to the saddlebags, he said, "Going on a trip?"

"Been on one," Carlton answered. "Started in Seattle a week ago Monday. Going to San Diego. If I make it." He was conscious of making his voice sound wearier than he felt. It was an attempt to distract the cop from asking the wrong questions. Wanting him to be thinking "old man." It worked.

"I don't know how you guys do it," the officer said. "Just last weekend my girlfriend and I – she's an avid cyclist – biked the Silverado Trail in Napa." He gestured with his thumb over his right shoulder. "We only go about twenty miles and I'm bushed. And I think of myself as in pretty good shape."

"Well, like anything else," Carlton replied, "you have to train for it. I've been doing this since I was thirty-five. Nineteen years ago." Getting the age factor clearly established.

"All I can say is I hope I'm in as good a shape when I'm your age," the cop replied. "Planning on spending the night here?"

This is where he had to be careful. "If it's okay. Schools have been my home- away-from-home, so to speak, since I started this ride. I try to stay two nights camping, and the third night I break down and get a cheap hotel room. So I can shower and shave. It gets a little itchy," he said, rubbing his chin. Distraction. "They all let me stay. I'm out by first light. Even before the custodians get here. If it's all right?"

Playing just the regular guy. Asking permission. Harmless.

"I don't see anything wrong with it, tell you the truth. As long as you're out of here before the kids show up. That's about seven thirty."

"I'll be an hour down the road by then," Carlton said. And he would be, too.

"I'm on 'til seven tomorrow morning. I'll be by before I head into the office. I don't want to see you here, okay?"

"You won't. You have my word."

"All right. I guess I should check your identification while I'm here – just run a quick check. Make sure you're not a child molester or anything." He laughed as he said it.

Carlton handed him his driver's license. This was the critical time. He didn't know what was out there on him. He figured his two diversions would take time to sort out, but you never knew. He set his pack on the ground and sat behind it, facing the officer. His fingers curled over the butt of the Beretta. Carlton didn't want to shoot the guy, but he would if he had to. He was so close. Nothing was going to stop him now.

The policeman was in his car speaking into the radio. Carlton tensed as he opened the door but then relaxed. He could tell by the cop's face that nothing had been reported.

He stood as the officer gave back his license. "You're one of the good guys," he smiled. "Good luck on the rest of your journey. I don't know how you do it. But remember, you have to be out of here by six thirty or seven. I'll be back to check. Okay?"

"I promise," Carlton said again. "And thanks for letting me stay. I'll send you my press clippings when I reach San Diego."

He laughed and shook Carlton's hand. "You do that."

45

Since I didn't have to go to work tomorrow, I went home to change and grab some clothes to bring with me to Michele's. I expected to stay tonight.

"My, aren't we casual," she said seeing me in my gray cords, white golf shirt with Big C Athletic Club emblazoned above my left breast, and Timberlands. Nodding at the gym bag in my right hand, she teasingly asked, "Planning on staying the night?"

"I was hoping," I replied as I took her in my arms and kissed her. "I got a few days off."

She kicked the door closed with her foot and melded her body into mine. We stayed like that for several minutes, the spell broken by my dropping the gym bag to floor.

Taking my hand, she led me into the kitchen. "No burnt dinner tonight, okay? I want to impress you with my culinary prowess." Whatever she had cooking, it smelled wonderful. I pulled out a chair from the small table and sat down facing her as she fussed around the oven. She was wearing a copper-colored sleeveless mock turtleneck. The black leather pants hugged her ass in the most provocative way. Eye candy. She must have felt my eyes all over her because she looked over her shoulder and ask coquettishly, "Liking what you're seeing?"

"Incredible," I replied with a leer.

She wiggled her butt and said, "We're eating dinner first tonight. Just so you know. Before you get any ideas. Because of you, I am rediscovering my cooking talents. It's been a while since I've spent this much time in the kitchen. I want to impress you with some of the other things I do well. Not just good in bed."

"The hell with cooking," I teased. "Just as long as you're good in the sack. I can always take you out to eat."

"Yeah – and you could always go out for sex, too."

"It's just not the same. And definitely a hell of a lot cheaper here."

"Keep talking like that McGuire and I'll cut your ass off."

"Just as long as it's only my ass," I answered back.

She laughed. "If I cut the other thing off, how would you be able to think?"

She came around and sat on my lap, her forehead touching mine, eyes so close it was hard to focus on them. "I'm serious," she said. "I want to cook you dinner. Have you like me for something besides sex." I couldn't tell if she was kidding or not. "And after dinner, I want to have a glass of wine and sit by the fire and talk to you."

"You don't have a fireplace," I said.

She stood up, leaned over, kissed me on the cheek and said, "Okay. I guess we'll have to drink the wine first and make our own fire afterward."

She may have been out of practice, but you couldn't tell it by the dinner she served. She gave me a blow-by-blow description of what we were eating. I was impressed. A salad of Bibb lettuce with slices of papaya and avocado (which I gingerly picked out) and ceviche – which she explained were raw scallops that had been marinating all day in lime juice. The main course was Cornish hens served with little red potatoes. Sounding like a waitress articulating the specials of the evening, she proudly told me the potatoes were oven-baked with parsley and rosemary and freshly grated Parmesan cheese. I honestly didn't care – but I knew she did, so I made a big deal of it. Besides, it was really good. Not something I would have found in the freezer section where I shop. For dessert she served Irish coffee in stemmed glasses. With real whipped cream on top, I was informed, and little grated orange rinds sprinkled around. Her concern with the meal was so decidedly *female*. Whatever it was that attracted me to this woman, it was first and foremost that she was "*decidedly female*."

She was genuinely pleased when I complimented her dinner. And I was pleased that she was pleased – that she valued what I thought of her. During dinner I told her about being pulled off the Wasserman case. About the all-too-convenient demise of our prime suspect. About how the damn system was becoming so politicized. About how I thought Schaeffer might be dirty. Michele listened politely and then summed up the conversation by saying, "Why not just forget about it? If Schaeffer gets himself assassinated it's his own damn fault. You did the best you could. And besides, he gave me four whole days with you. For that alone I'll vote for him."

I helped clear the dishes from the table and put them in the dishwasher. For being such a routine action, it seemed somehow very intimate. Proprietary. Like you were married or something. She poured two glasses of wine and led me into the living room. "Let's talk for a minute."

"Oh, oh. Sounds serious to me," I joked.

"Come on," she said. "I *am* serious." And she was. The tone in which she said it was not lost on me. I didn't respond, waiting for her to continue. She was silent for a minute. I was getting nervous. "So ... what's going on with us?"

"Uhhh ..." I fumbled, not knowing quite how to answer.

"Okay. I didn't mean to put you on the spot like that. Forgive me. I just ..." she stopped and took a sip of wine, the silence in the room claustrophobic. "Dammit, Mac, I just don't do this sort of thing. Do you know how long it's been since I cooked *dinner* for a man? Since I've invited one to my *bed*? To stay *overnight*?" The questions just hung there, like wisps of smoke drifting through a hazy light. "And I enjoyed it. So, tell me, what's happened, or happening, to me?"

She was asking me to put flesh and blood on the skeleton she'd just constructed. She didn't want to be the first to say it. To be out there. To be vulnerable. I knew exactly how she felt.

I could think of a hundred smart-ass things to say. To deflect the intent of her questions. Something like, *I get the feeling that if I don't answer right, I'm not going to get laid tonight.* But just as you know not to go near a snarling dog, I knew not to make light of her questions. She was serious. You didn't have to be a clairvoyant to see that we were at a crossroads. It was being left up to me. I could take us down either fork in the road. One led somewhere – one was a dead-end.

"Baby," I said, wanting to tell her, but still being cautious. "I like you. You know that, don't you?" Her head bobbed on my shoulder, her face buried in my neck. I couldn't get a read by seeing her eyes. Trying to artfully craft my words, I continued. "I like you a lot. But I'm really careful about using the *L* word. Partly because it's used so freely nowadays. Lost some of its meaning. Like antibiotics. You take too much of the stuff when you're not sick, then they don't work when you really need them." I was trying to lighten up the conversation a little. She wanted no part of it.

"Be serious," was all she said.

"I want us to go down the road together. To see where it leads. Can I see a future for us? Yes, I can. But it's been less than a week that we've known each other ..."

"I've known you all my life."

"Yeah. I know. Mike's baby sister ..."

"That's not what I meant. But forget it. Go on."

"I've wanted to say it."

"What?"

"That I love you. But would you believe me? Would you think that my saying it was just a cheap way of getting you into bed? That's what's held me back. How you would react."

"Okay. That's all I want to know. I don't want to be hurt, that's all. I don't want to give my heart away and have it handed back on a platter. And it's starting to be given. I can feel it – and there's nothing I can do about it. As long as there's a chance with you, I'm willing to risk it."

"There's more than a chance, Michele."

"That's all I need to know." She took the glass from my hand and led me to the bedroom.

We made love only once that night. Slow and caring. Not the frantic, rip-off-your-clothes, needy sex we had the night before. Something had definitely changed in our interaction with one another and reflected itself in the way we touched and caressed and explored. The sex was not just sex. It was making love. Putting into action the weaving together of two hearts. I hadn't experienced this in a long time. Satisfying, but definitely scary.

Afterward, we just held each other closely and talked about things that had long been left hidden in the recesses of our souls. She about Mike's death and her mother's Alzheimer's, me about LT and what the divorce did to them.

It was after two when we finally whispered goodnight, both of us looking forward to a sleep that promised a peace neither of us had known for years.

46

Thursday, July 8th
6:40 a.m.

McGuire and Michele weren't the only ones who slept peacefully that night. Carlton awakened refreshed, the tired achiness of the previous evening replaced by a nervous excitement that grew by the minute. He recognized the adrenalin rush and knew enough to calm it or by one o'clock he'd be too tired to do anything.

He pedaled into a McDonald's and bought two Egg McMuffins, orange juice and coffee. He hadn't eaten much the day before and found himself ravenously hungry. He chuckled, remembering the number of times he'd warned friends that eating at McDonald's was probably the worst thing they could do to their health. It didn't make any difference to him now. The cancer in his stomach didn't mind if he filled it with every fat and cholesterol molecule imaginable. Bring it on! Just a different kind of food to satisfy its deadly appetite.

He lingered in the booth until the sun cleared the Sonoma hills to the east. The Marin sky turned sapphire blue as it greeted the morning sun. Walking out of the restaurant, Carlton turned his face into the wind that came off the ocean – its coolness carrying the scent of hay and newly mowed lawn from the nearby hills. He smiled to himself, got on his bike, and started the final leg of his journey. It was a good day to die.

47

I woke up with a monumental ache in my left shoulder. I discovered the cause when I tried to move my arm – Michele's head was resting in the crook of my elbow, exactly where it was when we drifted off to sleep. I obviously hadn't moved all night, and my arm and shoulder were complaining about the inactivity. I faced a dilemma – if I moved, I would probably awaken her. If I stayed still, my arm would fall off. No contest. I pulled my arm from under her.

I did awaken her. Sort of. She put a pillow over her head and burrowed under the white eyelet comforter. I would have to say something about the color scheme here – I loved her femininity, but there were limits. A white eyelet covering was appropriately feminine for her bed. But not for *our* bed. I'd be afraid to show any of my friends around the house. I'd never hear the end of it.

While I was rotating my shoulder, trying to get the feeling back into it, Michele came to life. She stretched sensuously, turned over and propped the pillow behind her head. The comforter fell carelessly around her breast. She didn't seem to notice. I sure as hell did.

I was still in awe of her beauty. Probably always will be. Her face, unmarred by the passage of time, was still flush from the warmth of sleep. She watched me exercising my arm.

"Something you didn't tell me? A deformity, perhaps?" she asked bemusedly, rubbing the sleep from her eyes.

"Your head was on my shoulder all night. Now I have these little pins being stuck through it. I guess I'm not used to having a woman in bed with me."

"I'm sorry. If you never want to sleep with me again, I'll understand." She rolled over, exposing the flare of her hip, the comforter tucked between her legs.

"I think I can handle it," I replied, and jumped on the bed, my face inches from hers. She held me as my tongue outlined the curve of her lips.

"I think we should get dressed," I whispered. "I want to take you to this really neat place for breakfast."

She pulled me on top of her. "Let's eat in."

We surfaced an hour later and lay there as daylight filled the room. "I was serious about taking you to breakfast. There's a little café down by the beach that I go to a lot. I want you to know all about my little peculiarities. In case you want to change your mind about this relationship." I slapped her bottom and got out of bed. "Come on. She'll be closed if we don't get moving."

I took her to a real old-fashioned Sunset District establishment called Ida's Café. It was on the corner of Fulton and 48th Avenue, a stone's throw from where the old Playland at the Beach used to be. Ida's had been here for over twenty years. I first discovered it when I worked Robbery. We had a stakeout going up the street, and each morning my partner and I would have breakfast there. I'd been back at least once a week ever since.

There actually *was* an Ida. She was a delightful sixty-nine-year-old lady who wore her white hair piled high atop her hairnet-covered head. You never found one of *her* hairs in your scrambled eggs, by God. Something she never missed telling new customers to her eatery.

Ida escaped from Hungary in 1948, just as the Communists were consolidating power over the Eastern Bloc. As a young woman of twenty, her parents put her in the care of a group of Catholic priests who were fleeing the country. Her tale, which she told me one day over a milkshake, was harrowing to say the least. Hiding in abandoned barns during the day, it took twenty-six days to make the journey from Nyul on the outskirts of Gyor to the Austrian border, a distance of only thirty-one miles. When they got to the border they found it teeming with Russian soldiers and dogs. After two days of hiding and scouting out a safe corridor, they made a mad dash to freedom under a hail of gunfire. One of the priests was hit and subsequently died in the hospital in Salzburg. She never saw her parents again, hearing from friends that they were both killed by Russian troops in the Hungarian Revolution of 1956.

I guided Michele to one of the back booths – all red and yellow Formica. A real slice of old-time Americana. I sat down and caught Ida sizing-up

Michele and arching a quizzical eyebrow in my direction.

"And who is this charming lady you have brought to me, eh, McGuire?" Ida had been in the country since 1953, but could still put on the Hungarian Gypsy fortune-teller accent when need be.

"Ida, I'd like you to meet a friend of mine. Michele. Michele, meet Ida, the owner of this fine establishment." I sat in silence as they both exchanged pleasantries. But I could tell Ida was measuring her up against whatever standards she'd set for me. I expected it was high. Ida treated me like her son.

"Ida, please tell Michele today's specials, okay?"

"Today's specials," she announced proudly, "are bacon and eggs, ham and eggs, sausage and eggs. Same as they are everyday. But for you," she said with a toss of her white head, "because you're a friend of McGuire's – you can have your choice of toast. White or wheat."

"Do I take you to nice places, or what?" I said as I grabbed Ida by the waist and gave her a noisy, smacking kiss on her arm. "Ida likes me because the first time I came in here I noticed the menu said *two eggs – any style*. I told her I wanted one fried and one scrambled."

"And then tell her what I did," Ida said.

"You laughed."

"And then?"

"And then she poured a whole pitcher of ice water on my lap."

"I fix wise guys," she said. "You let them get away with their little jokes and they never stop. So

252

my advice to you, sweetie, is never let him get away with the funny little jokes. Pour ice water on him. Also helps for other things, eh? You know what I mean, eh?" They both shared a good yuk on that one. Female humor.

We were about halfway through our meal when Michele said, "I have a question for you."

I put my fork down and leaned over the table and kissed her. "No, I'm not that good every night. But close."

"Come on," she laughed, pushing me away while looking around to see if anybody could hear us. "Be serious for a minute, will you?"

"I am being serious. I am that good."

"Come on. I want to ask you something I thought of last night. If Carlton didn't die in that explosion in Riverside, who did? They found a body, didn't they?"

"Parts of a body, yes."

"So, who was it?"

"That's the sixty-four-thousand-dollar question. Could have been a Seventh Day Adventist trying to leave a Watch Tower magazine. Picked the wrong house. Just bad luck. Or a salesperson. Or a newspaper boy. Could have been anybody. There's something that doesn't make sense in that scenario, though. According to the guy Irvine talked to in Riverside, the person was killed at the back door. Not too many sales people I know go to the back door to do business, do you?"

"So what do you think happened?"

"I wish I knew. The one thing I *do* know is that Carlton is still alive. Did he set this up? Lure some poor, unsuspecting person to his back door and remotely blow him up? To tell you the truth, it doesn't sound like the Carlton I heard on the tape. Not his M.O."

"But you don't think it was accidental?"

"I like the way you think. What you say we go find out, huh? Let's go over to my place and I'll call Irvine and get the latest."

"But I thought you said you've been taken off the case."

"Hey, nothing wrong with just checking in."

Michele waited by the door while I paid the bill. Ida leaned over conspiratorially and whispered in my ear, "Good choice, McGuire. Don't let her get away." I breathed a sigh of relief. Michele passed the "Ida" test.

48

I was about to put the key in the front door when I noticed the curtain. Something not right. It was parted about two inches. I close the curtain tight. *Always*! Alarm bells started exploding in my head. I reached back for my gun, but realized it was in the damn house. I'd left it there when I went to Michele's. As nonchalantly as I could, I turned around and took Michele by the arm and said, "I just remembered. I left my laundry over at Mrs. Callahan's across the street. Come on. Let's get it. I want her to meet you anyway."

Michele started to protest as I turned her around and marched down the stairs. But she did notice I was agitated – that and the vice grip I had on her arm.

"What's going on, McGuire? What's wrong?" she whispered as we crossed the street.

"Just keep walking like it's the most normal thing in the world. Don't look back. Somebody's been in the house. Could still be there." I let go of her arm and reached for her hand. Two lovers going to the neighbor's house.

I rang the bell. Mrs. Callahan's door had a peephole in it but set too high in the door for her to see through. Her strong voice asked, "Who's there?"

"It's Tom McGuire from across the street, Mrs. Callahan." I answered. The sound of the chain being pulled and two deadbolts being released noisily announced that she was going to admit us.

"Thomas," she wheezed in greeting. "It's so nice to see you." Mrs. Callahan was nearly eighty years old. She'd lived in this house close to fifty years. Her husband died twelve years ago, and from the sound of her emphysema, I didn't think it would be long before she joined him.

"Mrs. Callahan, I want to introduce you to a friend of mine. This is Michele. Can we come in?"

"Of course you can, dear." She shuffled out of the way to let us pass. "Go into the living room. Can I get you something? Some coffee? Perhaps some tea for you ..."

"Michele."

"... for you, Michele?"

"No, Mrs. Callahan," I replied for both of us as we seated ourselves on old-fashioned, high-backed upholstered chairs. They were the most uncomfortable damn things but would probably bring a fortune at an estate sale. From where we were sitting we could see my house across the street. "By the way, did you happen to see anyone going into my house today?" I knew if anybody had gone through my front door, Mrs. Callahan would have seen them. Most of her day was spent in one of these chairs staring out the front window. Getting old is a bitch.

"You mean the cleaning service? Yes, they were here early this morning. About eight thirty. Carried all their mops and brushes with them. They looked professional."

She'd picked the right word, I thought to myself. Professional!

"Times sure are different," she continued. "Used to be only women cleaned homes. These were two men. Had a van. Parked right over there." She pointed to the curb between my house and the house next door. "Are they expensive? I've been thinking of having someone help me out, too. At my age, it's all I can do to just dust the place."

"What did the van say?" When I saw the quizzical expression on her face, I said, "You know. What service? What company? On the side of the van. What did it say?"

"Well, now, that was the strange thing. I remember thinking about it when I saw them go to your door. There was just a small sign on the side. I could hardly read it. *Bill's Cleaning Service*. But you'd have to have binoculars to read the phone number. It was so small. Not a good way to advertise, I'd say. And another thing, Thomas – I hope you're not paying them a lot of money. They only stayed about twenty minutes. Couldn't have done a thorough job in twenty minutes."

Thorough enough, I thought to myself. "Now you have me wondering, too, Mrs. Callahan. I think I should go over and see what kind of job they did. Do you mind?" It was a lame excuse, but I couldn't think of anything else to say without alarming her. "Do you think you could entertain Michele for a few minutes? Maybe give her some tea, after all? I won't be long."

"Tea would be nice," said Michele, following my lead.

"Of course, Thomas, of course. I'd be happy to."

I let myself out the front door and walked casually over to the Mustang. I didn't expect anyone to be in the house, but I'd be damned if I was going to go in there unarmed. Opening the driver's side door, I reached under the dashboard and undid the small latch by the steering wheel and slipped out my CS40. The CS stands for "Chief's Special", a name it got because Smith and Wesson, in a fit of marketing genius, introduced this line at the International Association of Chiefs of Police in 1952. Since then it's gone through a number of incarnations, the latest of which I now held in my hand. Small, lightweight and chambered for the S&W .40 cartridge, the semi-auto CS40 wasn't going to win a long-distance shootout, but as a small, close-in personal safety weapon, it was lethal. The Department frowned on its officers carrying hideouts, but we all did. It made us feel marginally safer.

I didn't expect any prints but still took out my handkerchief, wrapped it around the doorknob, took a deep breath, and let myself in. This was the moment of truth. If I were going to get shot, it would be here. There was a reason cops called the doorframes of homes "vertical coffins." More police officers are killed walking through the front door than anywhere else. It makes sense. You're walking into a house where you have some reason to believe bad guys lurk. All you could count on in a situation like this was the bad guys had either left or were negotiators, not killers. With all those thoughts swimming through my brain, I was relieved to find no one waiting for me.

I walked room-to-room just to make sure no one was still in the house. Then I went through the house again more slowly, looking for whatever it was they were looking for. This was a professional job, no doubt about it. Hardly anything was disturbed. A drawer left slightly ajar. The stereo moved inches forward in its cabinet. One of the cushions on the sofa replaced with the zipper side out. Little things. Things you wouldn't ordinarily notice if you weren't looking for them.

What the *hell* were they after? The only thing I could think of was the recordings. But why would they want them badly enough to B&E my house in broad daylight? I couldn't get my mind around that concept. Have to figure it out later. Right now, I wanted the crime lab guys down here dusting for latents, not that I expected they would find any, but you just never knew. Even the best still made mistakes. I picked up the phone and called Irvine.

"Mike, we've got some funny shit going on. My ..."

"You've got funny shit? You should hear what is going down on my end."

"Hold on, Mike. Someone just broke into my house. I want the crime lab boys down here now."

"God-damn, Mac. I'm sorry. Are you all right?"

"Yeah."

"When did it happen?"

"Sometime this morning. I was over ..." I hesitated. Not sure I wanted him to know I spent the night with Michele. I decided I didn't. "... I was gone. When I got back, I discovered the burglary. Professionals, Mike."

"Professionals? Are you sure? What would professionals be looking for at your place?"

"You tell me. It's got to have something to do with the Carlton thing."

"Maybe it was Carlton that did it."

"Sure. Carlton's dead, remember? Ask Bristow. Ask Schaeffer. Hell, even you think so."

"Well, that's the funny thing, Mac. About nine this morning I got a call from a cop named Marcy in Riverside. He'd seen that we flagged the Carlton explosion, so he called up with the latest." Irvine paused, obviously trying to pique my interest even more. He was successful.

"Come on, Mike. What?"

"Looks like we've got two vics in that explosion. I probably should say, *at least* two." He paused for effect.

"Say that again. I don't understand."

"We've got at least *two* victims. They found the bottom half of a leg with a shoe still on it. Nike cross-trainer. A 'Turf-Marauder,' I think Marcy told me." Irvine found that amusing.

"What size?" I asked excitedly.

"Hold on. Hold on. Let me finish first. They also found another shoe about 100 yards from the back of the house. A boot, actually. You know, one of those hiking boots so popular now. Well, they wouldn't have paid much attention to it except that there was a foot in it, also. So, unless this guy Carlton was in the habit of wearing a different shoe on each foot, I'd say we've got two vics."

"Did you get the shoe sizes?" I asked.

"Nike was an 8 medium. The boot was a 9 1/2 medium."

"Do we know Carlton's shoe size?"

"I thought you'd never ask," Irvine said, obviously pleased with himself. "I called Wright back. The guy from the Veterans Administration? He looked it up. Carlton wore a size 11."

"God, Mike. You do great work," I said, feeling the adrenalin pumping. We were still in the hunt. "Did you tell Bristow? Are we back on the case?" There was a long pause. I had a feeling I wasn't going to like his answer.

"I went to him at nine thirty this morning with the report. He thanked me and then shut his door. Half an hour later he came out, briefcase in hand, headed for the hall. I'm watching him thinking, *what the hell?* So I run after him. Catch him by the elevator. Ask him straight out. *Are we on or off?* He looks at me with this supercilious grin on his face and says *Off.* He says Carlton's dead. Case closed. Know where he was going?"

"To see ..."

"To give a press conference on how we solved the Wasserman murder. It was on the news about ten minutes ago. I've got it here somewhere – hold on."

I heard papers being shuffled. Irvine came back on and said, "Yeah, here it is. Listen to this. It's his statement to the press."

The San Francisco Police Department announced today that the murder of Chronicle correspondent Ruth Wasserman, killed in her Steiner Street home this past Friday, was solved.

Robert Carlton, a Vietnam veteran and prisoner of war in Hanoi's infamous Han Lo prison, confessed to the crime via audiotapes he mailed to SFPD on

Monday. These tapes were analyzed by the City's crime lab. They contained information only the killer would have known. The tapes also implicated Carlton in three additional murders in Ames, Iowa; Orlando, Florida; and Flushing, New York. The department's Homicide Division is in contact with the police departments in those cities to verify details and help close those cases.

Before the suspect could be apprehended, he committed suicide at his home in Riverside, California. Details of the suicide are still sketchy, but as more information is developed, it will be made available to the press.

No motive for the killing spree was given or any reason why Carlton sent them to the San Francisco Police Department. In consultation with psychologists, especially those dealing with Vietnam veterans, it was their unanimous opinion that Carlton suffered from a repressed post-traumatic stress disorder. Why it chose to manifest itself in this manner may never be known.

"That's it? You told him about the bodies?"

"Yes."

"The ones they just found in Riverside?"

"Yes."

"And them not being Carlton?"

"Yes."

"What's going on, Mike? Why the cover-up? This guy is still alive, and he's going to pop Schaeffer – I know it. And Schaeffer doesn't want to take precautions because he doesn't want to have his past dredged up? Come on! How lame is that? He'd risk getting himself whacked so some people wouldn't be reminded that he protested the Vietnam War, for Christ's sake? That doesn't work, Mike. Something else is going on. Maybe Wasserman was right."

Irvine let that go by. "Maybe Schaeffer thinks he's bluffing."

"This guy killed four people already. He's bluffing? Come on! No. Maybe Schaeffer thinks Carlton is really dead?"

"How could he think that? Bristow knows he is alive. And if Bristow knows, you can bet Schaeffer knows, too."

"Well, we have a different case here now. Bristow can pull us off the Wasserman case, but now we have a B&E on our hands. And, hell, it's got to have something to do with this case, doesn't it? But even if it doesn't, we can say it does. Then we're back in the saddle."

"Mac, I ..."

"Don't say anything, Mike. Just get some lab guys here, pronto. You come, too. Let's talk this thing through. Get going."

I replaced the receiver and did another quick tour of the house.

49

Thursday, July 8th
11:15 a.m.

Carlton concentrated on the pavement directly in front of him as he crested the two-mile grade that brought him to the top of the Marin headlands. Before him was spread the panorama of San Francisco Bay. He felt uncommonly strong after what should have been an exhausting journey. Sitting upright in his saddle, he coasted a few hundred yards to a turnout in the road that served as a place travelers could stop to enjoy the spectacular scenery. The prevailing winds swept the sky over San Francisco clean and left it a cerulean blue. In the distance, wispy white clouds floated over the East Bay hills. Carlton had been here before but still gazed in awe at the sight. He was again reminded why people who lived in San Francisco called it the "City," with a capital C. There was something magical in the atmosphere surrounding it. Even Mother Nature certified its uniqueness by providing its own moat. The provincialism of the inhabitants was demonstrated by the fact bridge tolls were charged only coming into San Francisco. The trip out was free. "Eat, drink and be merry, for tomorrow you may have to move to Oakland" was a popular refrain during the 1906 earthquake and fire. Does pride goeth before the fall? Could be. After all, the '06 cataclysm destroyed more than half the city. Even at that, if God decided to destroy the City with fire and brimstone this instant, Carlton had no doubt most inhabitants would perish singing "I Left My Heart in San Francisco". It was a charming place. Full of itself, but charming nonetheless.

A car drove into the turnout. Sightseers like him. Carlton returned their wave. Time to go, he thought. In an hour he'd be at the rented office space at Fourth and Mission. He'd get something to eat. Maybe even bring some food back. Then he'd spend what was left of the afternoon setting up the shot. And then – well, then it was anyone's guess.

50

I knew it would take Mike and the lab techs about forty-five minutes to get to my house, so I put the CS40 safely back in the Mustang and went to rescue Michele from Mrs. Callahan. I wasn't quite sure what I would tell the old lady – I didn't want to frighten her, and I didn't particularly want to keep up the cleaning van fiction either, because I knew sooner or later she'd find out. It turned out I didn't have to worry. Old Mrs. Callahan figured it out for herself. Michele arched an eyebrow in my direction as Mrs. Callahan lectured me on telling the truth; on concerned citizens; on the police department; the Mayor; the state of the Muni and just about every other thing wrong with the City. I just let her go, nodding my head at the appropriate intervals. I never knew what a monumental pain-in-the ass she could be. When it was finally out of her system, Michele said to me, "She's got a surprise for you."

I looked at Mrs. Callahan expectantly. Like I really cared.

Looking smug, she reached over and produced a small pad of paper on which was written a license plate number.

"You got the license plate number of the van? How did you do that? I thought you said your eyesight wasn't so good."

"It's not," she replied. "But with these I can see the serial number on a dollar bill at 100 yards." Sheepishly she reached under her chair and pulled out a pair of Bausch & Lomb 12-power binoculars.

So this is what old ladies do all day long, I thought to myself. They're the real "neighborhood watch." God bless 'em.

"She's a wonderful lady," said Michele as we walked back to my house. "Did you know she was a little girl when the earthquake hit? Lived Downtown on Jones Street. She remembers it like it was yesterday. Really fascinating."

Michele interpreted my silence as a sign I didn't want to talk about Mrs. Callahan and the 1906 earthquake. She was right. I didn't. "Do you think the license plate number is real?" she asked, changing the topic.

"Oh, it's real," I replied, "but probably stolen. Or the van was stolen. That's the way it usually works. But I'll call it in anyway."

Once inside the house, I went directly to the bedroom. Michele stood in the doorway as I retrieved my P7, a coat into which I dropped an extra magazine, and my shoulder holster. "I don't want to get in the way, you know. I can find my own way home if you want," she said.

I walked over and kissed her lightly on the mouth. "I think it's too late for that, baby. I'm not exactly sure what's going on here, but whoever had the balls to break into my house had to know I wasn't home.

That means they knew I was with you. Which means they know where you live. And whatever it was they were looking for ... shit!" I ran over to the phone and dialed down to 850. "Who is this?" I asked. "Oh, hi, Jack. This is Tom McGuire. I need a favor. I've reason to believe a burglary has taken place, or is taking place, or about to take place. Can you get dispatch to send a car immediately?" I gave them Michele's address. "Tell whoever gets the call to be careful. This may be an *in-progress*, though I doubt it. Have them check the front and back doors. Also check with the neighbors to see if they noticed anything or anyone unusual in the neighborhood. If nothing is shaking, have them wait out front until I get there. In about an hour, I think. I'm waiting for Irvine.

"Yeah. They hit here, too. Nothing was taken as far as I can tell. And, Jack, tell the car who catches this to be heads-up. I don't think the bad guys will still be there, but tell them to be careful anyway. They're pros, and probably shooters, too. Driving a white van identifying them as house cleaners.

"Good, Jack. Yeah, I catch the irony." Michele came up behind me, wrapped her arms around my waist, and put her head on my shoulder. I snuggled back into her. It felt good. "What's going on, Mac?" she whispered into my neck.

"Hold on, Jack." I put my hand over the receiver and pulled her around to face me. Her eyes questioned mine. "Just a minute, baby, okay? We'll talk." I put the phone back to my ear.

"Jack, I want you to run a plate for me. Do it now and get back to me ASAP." I gave them the plate number of the supposed cleaning van. "Got that? Yeah, I'll be here. When did Irvine leave? Good! Thanks, Jack."

I held Michele close as I led her back into the living room. Sitting on the sofa, I said, "I'm sorry to have gotten you into this mess."

"Me, too. I'm not really used to this. I don't think I like it. Is this what it's like? Your job?"

"Not usually. Potentially, I guess. Any time you're working Homicide you are, by definition, working with people who have nothing else to lose. But I don't think this is like that." I said it to reassure her, though I wasn't all that reassured myself.

"When you said 'I don't think this is like that,' what did you mean? What's the 'this' you were referring to?"

"Let's just step it through, okay? We have four women murdered by Robert Carlton. I think we can safely say ..." I heard a car door close in my driveway. "... that must be Irvine. Let's get him in on this, too."

I greeted Mike and the three lab techs at the door. Carrying their paraphernalia, the three of them walked past me and started to set up. Seeing Michele in the living room, Mike took me into the alcove of the entryway.

"We've got to talk," he said. "You're not going to believe what happened. Just as I was getting ready to leave, I received a call from that guy Marcy in Riverside. Seems they found Carlton dead again. This time up in Mendocino County."

"You're kidding. What the hell happened?"

"There was a big fire in a house in Albion. Know where that is?"

I nodded. "Up by Point Arena."

"Exactly. Big fire. Takes out the house and the garage. From the report it looks like a guy had been drinking in the garage. Goes to sleep while smoking. Cigarette falls by an open can of gasoline and poof— he incinerates himself."

"What makes them think it's Carlton?"

"The house. Turns out to be his. The cops ran the tax record. He's owned it for twelve years. Vacation home, I guess."

"So, did they make an ID?"

"Hell, Mac. The body was so badly burned it's impossible. We'll have to wait for dental records, or DNA. Another delay."

"Jesus, Mike. How did the cops up there think to call Riverside PD?"

"Another strange thing – there was a car on the Albion property. First thing they did was run the plates. Belongs to a guy named Robert Elliot in Riverside. The Albion Sheriffs' Department called Riverside PD to report the fire and fatality. They first thought the guy who got burned-up was this Elliot dude. It turns out Elliot lives – guess where?"

"Next-door to Carlton."

"Close. Across the street, actually. So this gets the Riverside cops a little twitchy. Just a few days after Carlton's house explodes, another fatal fire kills a guy who lives on the same block as Carlton?"

"Elliot's car wasn't reported stolen, was it?"

"That's the thing, Mac. No report. So they go over to Elliot's house. Nobody's home. Haven't been home for over a week. The family is in Europe on vacation. They found that out from the neighbors. My guy Marcy tracks the Elliots down in Europe. It turns out they left the car in the care of their good friend, Robert Carlton."

I'm thinking now, trying to piece it together. "So, at least we know how he got from Southern to Northern California. He's in the Elliots' car. No reports of a stolen vehicle because the family is away, and Carlton is supposedly taking care of it for them. He then leaves *his* car in *his* garage in Riverside to make it look like he was killed in that explosion."

"That's what I'm thinking, too," Irvine said. "I could never figure out how he got up here. No rental car. We checked all airplane, rail and bus lines. No stolen vehicle. Nothing. What else was there to do but conclude that he was dead?"

"Okay. You're forgiven. But stay with me here a minute. He delivered the tapes and drove up to his vacation home in Albion. Where no one thinks to check, 'cuz he's dead in Riverside. At least until they identified the bodies there. So he used it as a hideout."

"I'm thinking you're right."

"But somebody knew about Albion."

"I don't follow."

"Somebody knew he was there. Because now we got another body. The one that got fried. Only thing that makes sense is somebody came looking for him in Albion. Carlton killed the dude and then barbecued him."

"Everybody's supposed to think it's Carlton that got himself roasted."

"Who's kidding who here? Bristow can't really believe that all this is a coincidence, can he? That Carlton gets killed twice on virtually consecutive days?"

"Told me so himself."

"Then he's even stupider than I thought. Coincidence factor here is through the roof."

"Well, Bristow might see all that, but the Governor sure doesn't," Irvine said. "At least he's acting like he doesn't. And one other thing of interest I just found out – the Democrats are having a major fund-raising dinner in the City for Schaeffer. Guess when?" I didn't want to hear the answer. "Tonight," he continued. "At the Marriott. Downtown."

"Son-of-a-bitch. That's it. Carlton is gonna whack the Governor tonight. It fits. What time's the dinner?"

"I think he said 7:30."

Michele called to us from the living room. "You guys going to stay out there all day?"

"Just another minute, babe." Irvine looked at me quizzically at my use of the word *babe*.

I didn't have time nor inclination to explain. "We've got to put out an APB on Carlton. Can you do that, Mike?"

"I'll try. Bristow told me again as I was leaving to forget about this case. Besides, what good would an APB do? How do you think he's getting here? Walking? Remember, he's now without a car."

"Walking. Hitchhiking. I don't know. But I do know he's on his way. He's close. Carlton has planned this meticulously so far. I doubt he could've forgotten something as elementary as transportation into the City. And somebody had to have seen him.

272

He had to stop for food. Maybe spent the night somewhere. If he hitchhiked, someone has to remember him. In the meantime, check out any reports of stolen vehicles in that area."

"I'll do it if I can. Seems like a waste of time, though. If he's not dead in that fire in Albion, he's probably already here."

"Probably," I said, "but worth a try. Look, Mike – Michele's in this, too." He frowned and shook his head. "I know. I know. Bad move. But if they've been scouting me, they know about her. And whatever it was they were looking for and didn't find here, they may think it's at Michele's. I called 850 to get a squad car over to her place. In any case, she's involved for better or worse. Don't be afraid to talk in front of her, okay?"

He grunted and walked behind me into the living room.

51

I sat next to Michele on the sofa and put my arm around her. I figured what the hell, it was my house. This show of affection definitely made Irvine uncomfortable. Like a father whose daughter is snuggling up to a date in front of him. Embarrassed. I probably would have felt the same way if the situation were reversed. But it wasn't, so screw it.

We were sharing ideas on how Carlton would try to *off* Schaeffer when the chirping of the house phone broke into our conversation.

"Want me to get that, Inspector?" one of the lab techs yelled from the kitchen.

"Yeah, could you?" I called back. "Take a message."

The muffled conversation from the kitchen stopped and a moment later the lab tech walked into the room. "Got a hit on the van plate, Inspector," he said passing me a scrap of paper with a name and address on it.

"The van belongs to a Chinese restaurant in the three hundred block of Grant Avenue," I said. "*China Village*. Anybody heard of it?"

Both Irvine and Michele shook their heads, but she added, "I don't know if this will help, but while sitting with Mrs. Callahan across the street she mentioned both men in the truck were Asian."

"So what does that tell us?" Irvine asked. We all three shrugged our shoulders. "Exactly. Tells us squat. Probably should check it out, though," he said.

"Let me ask you, Mike. What precisely is my status downtown?"

"Last I heard is what you heard. You're off the Wasserman case for sure, so by definition you are off Carlton, too. This? I'm not sure how they'll view it. A connection? I'm betting they'll deny it."

"They're *all* sons-of-bitches," I yelled at Irvine as if he were part of the conspiracy. I stood up and started to pace. Anything to relieve the pressure I felt. "Sorry, Mike. I know it's not your fault. It's just so damn frustrating. And there's no recourse. No one to go to. Hell, even if there were, it'd probably be too late. Carlton is going to whack this guy tonight. Shit." I sat down. "What about you, Mike? Would you help me on this one? What's your schedule like?"

"Hey, Mac. You know I'll do what I can. But I won't do anything overt. Nothing that can tie me to this if the whole thing goes south."

"Fair enough. Let's piece as much of this together as we can and then figure out what to do. So – me first. I have a question." I turned to Mike. "Remember Bristow's news conference? As you were reading the press release something bothered me. I couldn't put my finger on it, but it just now came to me. Bristow mentioned other tapes. He mentioned stuff that was actually in them." Irvine nodded. "But how did he know what was in them? He couldn't have heard them personally. I have them in my possession. How did he know?"

A deathly silence enveloped the room. It was Michele who finally gave us the answer. "Remember what you told me on the way back from Sacramento, Mac? About your conversation with Schaeffer. About how he seemed to know what Wasserman had said? Well, what if he had copies, too? What if Carlton sent *him* copies? Like he did you?"

Irvine and I had the same thought simultaneously. "Carlton is taunting him," he said. "He sent him the tapes ..."

"So Schaeffer would know who was coming after him," Michele said.

"And what does Schaeffer do? He sends some goons to kill him." It was all coming together.

"In Riverside." said Irvine. "But Carlton anticipates Schaeffer's moves, so he makes plans."

"He wires his house so the bad guys go boom." We were on a roll now. Playing off each other. "When Schaeffer doesn't get a call back from his hit squad in Riverside, he knows Carlton got away. He does some digging and finds out about Carlton's house in Albion. Figures Carlton will use it as a place to hide out, so sends a second team to find him."

"But Carlton is again one step ahead. He's prepared and waiting – and kills whoever was sent."

"And incinerates at least one of the guys. When they don't check back, Schaeffer knows that Carlton's won again."

"You're right. And Carlton knows we'll figure this out when the time sequences don't match. The explosion in Riverside is *before* he delivers the tapes to you. He knows you'll do the same thing Schaeffer did – check tax records to see if he had another home somewhere. A safe house. A place he could hide-out until he was ready."

"You realize what we're saying here?" I said, restating Irvine's voiced objections of a few minutes ago. "The Governor of the State of California has access to hit squads and is not afraid to use them? That's an astonishing accusation – one for which we have absolutely no proof, by the way."

"I have something to say," Michele interrupted. "I was just thinking – what if Schaeffer thought what was mentioned on those recordings was so inflammatory that he wouldn't want it to ever to become public? In fact, didn't he even say that to you, Mac? Or something like that, anyway?" I could see where she was going with this but let her finish. "What if he wanted those tapes so badly, he would hire someone to break into your house?"

"This is getting a little too bizarre for me," said Irvine. "First, we're saying Schaeffer has his own private army. And second, he sent someone here to steal the tapes? It's hard to believe any of this."

"But it makes sense, though, doesn't it Mike? Remember how adamant Bristow was about me getting those tapes back to the office? I thought *that* was a little odd, even for a strange guy like Bristow. We know he knows some of what's on them. If we're right about Schaeffer, then he's feeding Bristow just enough to make him think he's in the Governor's inner circle. And if there's one thing we all know about Matt Bristow, it's that he just loves being close to power. Schaeffer could pull his chain with ease.

277

Schaeffer tells him to pull me off the case because, at that point, he really does think Carlton is dead. That's why he's so confident he won't be assassinated. Because he's assassinated the assassin. Or so he thinks. He also wants me off the case because he doesn't want me nosing around too much. He orders Bristow to get the tapes from me. When they're not back by last night or early this morning, he makes private arrangements to get them back."

"God, I don't know, Mac," said Irvine. "By the way, where are you keeping those damn things?"

"I have them in my car. The irony is I was actually going to turn them in yesterday. I just forgot."

Irvine stood up shaking his head. "I just don't know, Mac, I don't think I want any part of this."

"Do me a favor, Mike. You don't have to believe any of it. Whether you do or don't makes no difference in what we have to do. We know Carlton will try to kill the Governor, and we have to do everything in our power to stop him. We've got to find Carlton. I'll take Michele home. Make sure she's okay. Then I think I'll go to the airport. Schaeffer will probably fly down from Sacramento. I'll scout out possible ambush sites along the route. Maybe stop Carlton that way. In the meantime, could you go over to this *China Village* and check out the story on the van? B&E's still a crime. And it's legitimate that you check it out. If and when you get an answer, call me."

Mike nodded, and I walked him to the front door. He put his beefy paw on my shoulder and squeezed. A gesture that said, I hope everything works out well, but don't count on me too much from here on in.

"You take care. Don't do anything foolish – you hear?"

I assured him I wouldn't. Little did I know that in exactly six and one-half hours, I would put that assurance to the test.

52

After Irvine left I went to my bedroom to use the phone. I didn't want Michele to hear the conversation. Searching through some scraps of paper on my dresser, I found the number.

"Eddie?" I said to the sullen male voice that answered. "This is Inspector Tom McGuire."

I could feel his reaction through the phone line. Even after giving me his number, I'm sure he never expected to hear from me. Especially so soon. I smiled at what must be going through his head. Street hoods were easily spooked. Of course, not many of them had SFPD homicide inspectors calling their cell phone in the middle of the day. Unless, of course, they'd done something. I knew that Eddie was at this very minute searching his memory bank for any shit he might have pulled, and for which he might need an alibi. He must have been clean, because his voice had the sound of a man certain he was in the clear.

"Truck? That you, bro? What chu calling me like this fo'? I ain't done nuffin' and you know it." He chuckled and continued. "And I don't know nuffin' neither, case you be thinkin' I'm gonna rat somebody out." He was having fun with me. Amazing how a clean conscience can all of a sudden make you giddy.

"Eddie, I need a favor. Do this for me and I owe you."

"My man," he replied. "You name it. You know you can count on Eddie." What I really knew was that Eddie was at this very instant counting ways he would be able to call in this chit I was giving him.

"I need somebody to guard my back this afternoon. You got a friend who could ride with you? Just so you know – if you're carrying, I'll be looking the other way. Just this once."

"You be in some trouble, bro?" It probably appealed to him that someone would be gunning for me. Welcome to life on the street, *bro*!

"To tell you the truth, I don't really know. Just a precaution."

"And you tellin' me to carry? And it's just a precaution? Come on, Truck, who you bullshittin'?"

"Meet me at 850 in forty-five minutes. I'll tell you all about it then."

"This doesn't happen to be a *brother* after you, does it? Cause if ..."

"No, Eddie. It's not a brother. Trust me on that! Can you be there?"

"Then I be seein' you in forty-five, Truck." No hesitation. That's what I liked about Eddie. Guys like him. Street guys – if you do them a favor, they'll repay it. That's the code. "And don't bring Turnel."

When we arrived at Michele's house I told her to wait in the car until I checked with the cops parked across the street. They hadn't been in the house, so they couldn't tell if someone had been inside. They also hadn't seen any suspicious vehicles driving around. I thanked them and told them they could go.

Not seeing any sign of forced entry, Michele and I cautiously entered the house. I walked slowly through the house with her and carefully inspected each room. We ended our tour in the bedroom, the mess around the mattress a reminder of what we'd been doing just a few short hours before.

"It doesn't look like anybody was here," I said, trying to sound more positive than I felt. "But that doesn't mean they don't know who you are. I'll tell you what I want you to do. Remember you telling me that every so often, at least a couple times a year anyway, you get a call from some Irish guy asking if you need anything? The boyos looking out for the IRA widow? You still have this guy's number?" She nodded and tapped her finger on the nightstand. "Good. Call him and tell him you need protection. That somebody – you don't know who – but somebody, has threatened you. Ask him to send a few guys over. Just for today, and maybe tomorrow. Can you do that?"

Mechanically, she reached for the phone. You could tell she was not enjoying any of this. Well, I thought, get used to it. It comes with the territory.

I left the room as she started to dial. Better that she be free to say what she wanted.

Five minutes later, she joined me in the kitchen. "Somebody'll be here in fifteen minutes."

"Good," I said. "I'll make some coffee. I want to check these goons out."

53

As McGuire and Michele were checking her house, Carlton turned down Fourth Street from Market. The entrance to the Marriott was on his left. Already barriers were going up, narrowing the sidewalk so that pedestrians had to step into the street to avoid walking into one another. In a few hours the police would have the street completely blocked off to foot traffic. Only people arriving by car could use this entrance.

Carlton slowed and finally stopped in front of a police sergeant directing the placement of the barriers.

"What's all the fuss?" Carlton asked innocently. "Something big happening here?"

"Tonight," the sergeant said, motioning to a policeman to move a barrier a little more to his right. "The Governor's in town. Big fundraiser. Giving a speech here at seven thirty. We're expecting a big crowd." He moved a few feet away and yelled, "No, no. Not there, *idiot*. Another ten feet. Keep going. Keep going. Yeah, *there*." He took a deep breath and shook his head in exasperation. "Sorry – some of these young guys just don't get it." He pursed his lips and shook his head from side to side. "Anyway, yes, the Governor is coming. Have to keep protesters to the side. We always have protesters at these events – that's just San Francisco. Doesn't make any difference who the person is. Politically right. Politically left. Up! Down! Black! White! Chinese! Not a damn bit of difference. Always get some people out here to protest. Must be something in the water in this City."

Carlton chuckled as he knew he was supposed to. "Crazy, huh?"

"Hey, most of the time it's peaceful. But you never know. We keep the protesters on the opposite side of the street. That way they won't block the flow of traffic, preventing the Governor from arriving. But real violence? Nah! Not in all my years on the force, anyway."

Carlton thanked him and remounted his bike. You're in for a big surprise tonight, my man, he thought. A big surprise, indeed.

54

Eddie was waiting for me in the parking lot of 850. He had a kid with him I swear couldn't have been over sixteen. I could tell by his sullen attitude that he didn't like cops. They start young in Eddie's neighborhood.

I wasn't about to tell Eddie what was going on. Only that I was going to drive to the airport and back and make several stops along the way. That I'd probably get out and walk around a few of the stops. He was to follow me at a safe distance. What I wanted to know was if anyone was following me. And if I was being followed, Eddie was to call me on my cell phone and let me know. Make, model, how many people. Nothing else.

He wanted me to know that they were both loaded for bear. If anything went down, they were ready. I told him no violence. Just call me as to who and where they were. To only make their presence known if whomever was following made an overt move against me.

I checked my watch as I left 850. Five hours. I knew there wasn't enough time. Carlton had the benefit of months of planning – I had five measly hours. Hell, here I was, going to scout out places where a sniper could shoot the dumb ass governor on his way from the airport to the City, when, for all I knew, Schaeffer would be driving from Sacramento, not flying. If he and his entourage were driving, there were dozens of spots along that ninety-mile Sacramento to San Francisco corridor where an assassin could hide. The only way Schaeffer could survive that kind of threat would've been to call out the fucking Army. I called Irvine to see if Bristow knew the governor's plans. No luck. Irvine was still in Chinatown tracking down that damned van and hadn't yet talked to Bristow. I comforted myself by knowing I at least tried to save him. If the dumb shit didn't value his own life enough to cancel this damn fundraiser, why the hell was I busting my hump trying to protect his sorry ass? But even then, doing *something* still beat the hell out of sitting at home doing nothing.

Sitting home! I thought about Michele at home with those two IRA guys for baby-sitters. They were both in their mid-to-late forties, but I could tell by the look in their eyes they'd seen a lot of violence in their day. That look also told me they weren't afraid of violence. I felt good about them being with her. One less thing to worry about.

I told Eddie there were two stops I would make along the way to the airport – the first at Candlestick Point where there was a lot of open space next to the northbound freeway that offered both concealment and a clear field of fire. And the second a few miles down that offered a similar terrain.

About two miles from the Candlestick exit my cell phone rang. It was Irvine.

"Mac, I went to *China Village* and talked to the owner, Mr. Chung. He, of course, knew nothing about what I was talking about. Took me out to the employee parking lot. Two vans were supposed to be there. Only one was. What a surprise, huh?"

"So, where is it?" I asked through the static of my supposedly crystal-clear, hear- a-pin-drop, digital phone.

"Told me it must've been stolen. Sometime last night. He said it was there when he closed the place at eleven. Wants to file a report now."

"Does the parking lot lock up at night? Have a gate?"

"Yeah. I asked him about that. He just shrugged his shoulders. Doesn't know how they did it."

"I'll bet. Check him out when you get back to the office, okay Mike? And one more thing – get a picture of Carlton from the VA. Make a hundred copies. If nothing happens before Schaeffer arrives at the Marriott, we can at least pass the picture around the crowd to see if anybody has seen him." He promised me he would. "And be sure to ask Bristow if he knew how the governor was getting down here."

I checked my rearview mirror for any sign of Eddie. Even though the traffic was unusually light for this time of day, I couldn't spot him. Good. That's what a tail is supposed to be – invisible. I shivered at the thought. The bad guys would be invisible, too.

I pulled off at the Candlestick exit and made a series of right turns. That brought me around under the freeway so I was facing the northbound traffic. Ahead of me, in all its faded beauty, was the old warhorse – Candlestick Park. Opened with great fanfare in 1960 as home of the San Francisco Giants, the stadium never lived up to its original hype. For one thing, it was built on a soggy, windblown, god-forsaken piece of land six miles south of the City. Word at the time was the site had been chosen because the builder of the stadium was an old-time San Francisco construction guy with close ties to the mayor's office. The guy owned Candlestick Point and offered to give it to the City in exchange for the contract to build the stadium. A great deal. Besides getting a huge tax write-off for a worthless piece of property, he scored the construction contract. Is this a great country, or what?

For all its problems, though, I liked Candlestick Park. Part of it was, I'm sure, the memories of my youth. My friends and I used to go to the games often. Snuck in whenever we could. There was an unpatrolled section of chain-link fence in those early days – before they put the barbed wire over the top. I was there when Juan Marichal pitched his first major league game. My friends and I not only snuck into the stadium that night, but snuck into a luxury box as well. It was also from a luxury box that I watched Willie McCovey's first game as a Giant. I was also there the night a game actually got called on account of fog. It was so foggy that fly balls, even pop-ups, were lost in the soup roiling over the stadium walls like a huge tidal wave. They had to call the game to protect the players from getting smacked in the face by one of those balls coming down out of the fog. But worst of all was the wind – it whipped through and around the stadium with merciless abandon. The wind-chill factor at times rivaled the temperatures in

Chicago or Minneapolis. Probably even Alaska. But, hey, I was a kid and loved every uncomfortable minute of it.

I parked in one of the many lots adjacent to the stadium and got out of the car. A business park was on my right that a shooter could conceivably use if he had access to the roof. Even if Carlton was an Olympic caliber marksman, it was still a damn far shot. And at a moving target. I doubted he could do it. Behind one of the lots was a hill, dotted with overgrown juniper bushes. Good cover. Clean sight line to the freeway. Iffy because of the distance, but still a possibility. I made a note to have Irvine get somebody here by six to patrol the area. Make up some excuse in case Bristow asked.

I returned to the car and continued my journey south. About a mile down the freeway, my cell phone rang.

"You got a tail." It was Eddie. I reflexively glanced in my rearview mirror. "A green Toyota. Junior here says it's a '96 Camry. He should know. He's jacked a few of them in his time." A laugh rumbled through the receiver. "Can you pick it out?" he asked. "About a half-mile behind you in the middle lane."

I looked in the mirror again, searching. "No, Eddie, I can't spot. What makes you think it's tailing me?"

"Hey, man, what you think? I was born in a white neighborhood? I got plenty of practice at this kind of thing." He sounded pleased with himself. "You turned off at Candlestick. The Toyota turned off. We turned off. You parked in that lot next to the freeway.

Toyota drove past and went three lots over. We pulled into that area where all of them other cars were, between you and the Toyota. Bet you didn't even notice us."

"No, Eddie, I didn't." He wanted me to know how good he was at this. Invisible. I must admit, I felt a grudging admiration for how stealthy he'd been.

"You stayed a few minutes. We waited. Right after you left, here comes that green Toyota. Got the plate if you want it."

"Not right now. Keep it though. I'll run it when I get back."

"Two Chinese guys in the car. Anyway, could be Chinese, Japanese, I can't tell. They're all just slopes to me."

"Eddie, such a racist remark," I chided him.

"Sorry, Truck. If I'd known how sensitive you were ..."

"Yeah, yeah! Listen – stay on the line. I have a plan. I'm going to turn off at the next exit. Let's see if we can have some fun with these guys."

"Good. I'm checking out my piece right now."

"No, Eddie. No violence. I told you, okay? I'm going to turn right. There's a McDonald's about a half-block down on the left. I'll pull in and walk into the restaurant. If they pull in, I'll see them. If they park, you pull up and block 'em, okay?"

"Got it. I've got to speed up a little, though. They be pretty far ahead. See ya."

I pulled into the McDonald's and nonchalantly walked across the parking lot and into the front door. About five minutes later the green Toyota drove in, coming from the opposite direction. It had obviously passed by and come back. I looked out the window and saw Eddie drive in behind them. The Toyota pulled into a parking space and turned off its motor. Eddie's car pulled up right behind and stopped, blocking the car from backing out.

I walked to the driver's side window and knocked on it, making a gesture that he should lower it. It came down slowly. With Eddie and his friend standing by the passenger door, I leaned over and with my nicest smile said, "Welcome to McDonald's. May I take your order?"

The driver was in his early twenties. Asian. Short black hair, flat nose, a serpent-shaped earring dangling from his left ear and a dagger tattoo just peeking out of from the yellow sleeveless tank top. He glared at me with undisguised hatred. "You're a dead man, Mr. Cop," he whispered between his teeth.

"Naughty, naughty, naughty," I said as jauntily as I could. What I really wanted to do was slap the punk silly. "First of all, let's get the hands where I can see them."

The driver's eyes tightened and he looked over at his partner. On the other side of the car, Eddie and Junior had pulled out their guns. Junior even took a step backward so that if anything went down, the two in the front seat would actually have to turn around to fire at him. Seeing they were outgunned and outmaneuvered, the driver and passenger placed their hands on their laps.

"Now, if you don't mind, please exit the vehicle." I stepped back to allow the driver's door to open. By this time a few curious onlookers were gathering by the door of the restaurant. "Have these assholes assume the position, Eddie. Gotta take care of these people first," I said, gesturing over to the customers milling about. "Police Officers." I said, digging out and flashing my badge. Right out of a Hollywood movie. "Everything's under control. Please go about your business." A few continued to stand around but most retreated to the safety of the restaurant. I could see them huddled around the window. Waiting for something to happen. "Now let's see what laws you two assholes have broken," I said, walking back to the Toyota. "Pat them down, Eddie." Except for a switchblade, both guys were clean. I brought them to the back of the car and made them spread their legs and put their hands on the trunk. Eddie and Junior took positions on either side of them. I went to the driver's door of the car and searched. Guys like this put their pieces under the front seat. I wasn't disappointed.

"Well, lookie here," I said, coming out of the car with two Glock 17s. "I hope you boys have permits? If not, I'd say you're in big trouble."

I called the San Mateo Sheriff's Department. Within thirty minutes they'd taken my statement, wrapped and tagged the guns and were driving away with the two punks. I knew they could at least get them on a weapons charge. Probably theft, too, as I would bet the guns were stolen. I asked the officers to call me with any information they got from their interrogation.

"Members of the *Asia Ghosts*," said Eddie. "A Vietnamese gang from the Sunset. Recognized the tattoo. Bad-assed motherfuckers. What did you do to get on their bad side?"

I shrugged, wondering the same thing myself. I thanked Eddie and his friend for their help. Told them their job was finished. They seemed only too happy to comply. With handshakes all around, and a *don't forget you owe me* reminder, they got in their car and sped away. I looked at my watch. It was ten minutes after four.

Thursday, July 8th
4:34 p.m.

Two and a half hours, Carlton thought as he munched on a three-dollar taco from the corner taqueria and looked out the window at the Marriott Hotel entrance a block away. Party starts at seven thirty. Schaeffer will be early. He'll no doubt make a grand entrance. And a grander exit. He smiled at the thought.

It had been an hour since he pulled his bike into the rented fifth floor office space. Leaning it against the far wall, he unhitched the saddlebags and carefully removed the tools needed to assemble the rifle. When they were laid out neatly on the carpet, he unpacked the M40 from the carrying tube and placed it beside the tools. After finishing his meal, he carefully washed his hands with the towelettes he carried just for this purpose, and proceeded to piece the weapon together.

The M40 was the military version of the Remington 700 hunting rifle. Used by snipers in Vietnam, it featured a Mauser-type bolt action and was normally fitted with a 3x9 telescopic sight. For this night, though, Carlton replaced it with the newer Schmidt & Bender 2.5x10 scope. The gun was chambered for the .300 Winchester Magnum and carried the standard 5-shot clip, into which Carlton was going to place a single shell. He wouldn't have time to rack through another round. He knew if he didn't hit his target the first time, there would be no second chance.

After attaching the barrel to the stock he picked up the scope and sighted it on the Marriott's doorman. Even at this distance Carlton could make out the design of the earring the man sported on his left ear.

The effective range of the M40 was just over a thousand yards. When he rented the space Carlton measured off the distance between the hotel entrance and where he now knelt. Eight hundred twenty-seven yards. Well within the weapon's effective range. While waiting for Schaeffer's goons at Albion, he zeroed his scope at that distance, practicing until he was able to place every shot he took within a 3-inch circumference. The only adjustments needed tonight would be allowing for the height from which he would be firing, and the wind. The height would be no problem – but the wind could be. As of an hour ago, though, there was only a slight breeze blowing off the Pacific, not even strong enough to kick up dust-devils on the street corner below.

The retired Marine lieutenant colonel from whom he had purchased the weapon wanted to include a suppressor, but Carlton declined. For one thing, the extra weight it would've added to his trip was unacceptable. For another, any suppressor would alter the cartridge's characteristics as it left the barrel, making it susceptible to whatever adverse meteorological conditions it encountered along the flight path. But in the final analysis, he just really didn't care. Noise or no noise, he doubted whether he would be walking away from this. They knew who he was, and if he wasn't captured or killed tonight, it wouldn't be long before he was.

It was this fatalism that made him so deadly.

56

It was a little after five, and I was just turning onto 19th Avenue from the 280 freeway. It took me a hell of a long time to get back to the City. The seventeen miles from McDonald's cost me an hour. Twenty years ago the traffic patterns were completely different – you could pretty much count on the commute going into the City in the morning and out at night. But then Silicon Valley exploded, and with it the housing prices in the Peninsula. Home prices in the City, which were considered obscenely high, all of a sudden became more attractive, resulting in people moving to San Francisco and driving to their high-tech jobs on the Peninsula. Now there was complete freeway gridlock in both directions during rush hour.

Since Bristow didn't want to see me at 850, I called Irvine and told him to come to my house at five fifteen and bring Carlton's pictures. When I made the call I thought I'd have plenty of time before he came. I hadn't figured on the traffic.

It was five ten when I rolled into my driveway. I reached under the dash and pulled out my CS40, checked the mag and press-checked the chamber. Locked and loaded. Once in the house I went directly to my closet, retrieved my ankle holster from the back of the tie rack, strapped it on and slid the .40 home. I vowed never to go anywhere without a backup after I found myself as negotiator in a hostage situation about six years ago. I was forced to leave my HK P7 at the door. The guy was a real crazy, and I could've taken him down if I'd been carrying a backup. Instead, I was forced to endure five hours of hell. I considered myself lucky to have come out of that one alive. Never again would I go into a dangerous situation unarmed.

I was checking myself in the mirror to see that no bulges showed on my right leg when I heard Irvine knock at the door.

"Got the pictures," he said, handing me a large manila envelope. "Played hell getting them out of the office. Waited until Bristow left. Good thing he's going to Schaeffer's *do* tonight or I'd still be there. Anyway, that's why I'm late."

"I just got here five minutes ago myself. Traffic was a bitch. I spent the afternoon looking at possible ambush sites coming from the airport. I ..."

"Shit," Irvine said, interrupting me. "I forgot you went all the way down there. Too bad, because Schaeffer drove from Sacramento. Bristow told me as he left the office. He's meeting him at City Hall before the banquet tonight."

"Figures," I said. "A wasted afternoon. I'll tell you what, though. I had a tail. I suckered them into a McDonald's parking lot off Airport Boulevard. We had a little chat. They didn't tell me much, but I at least got them on a weapons charge. They belong to the *Asian Ghosts.* A Viet gang in the Sunset. Pretty bad dudes, too, I understand. Ever heard of them?"

"No. But then I'm not up on all the different gangs we've got in this city. But Asian, huh? Another coincidence. Talked to Marcy again from Riverside. They identified one of the bodies from the explosion. Forgot the name, but it was something like Diem or Tiem. Anyway, the guy was one of the top dudes in a Vietnamese gang out of East L.A. Why all of a sudden are we coming up with all these Asian connections do you suppose?"

We both looked at each other, knowing the answer, but not wanting to go there. "Let's at least get through tonight," I said, "and ask those questions tomorrow. What do you say?" He nodded. "Then let's get going. We haven't got a lot of time."

"Nor much hope," he added.

"Nor much hope," I repeated resignedly. "The only thing we've got left is the fund raising dinner itself. These pictures of Carlton will help. Pass them around the crowd tonight. It's still a shot in the dark, but, as I've been telling myself all day, it's a lot better than doing nothing."

"I suppose," Irvine said. "You think he'll be in the crowd? Walk up to Schaeffer and do him like Sirhan did Bobby Kennedy? If that's his plan, it's probably good for us because it gives a defined area to stakeout. If not, he could be anywhere. And I think you better take a look at the pictures I brought. How much help you think they'll be?"

I opened the envelope and groaned. Inside were a hundred 8x10 black and white Xeroxed copies of

Robert Carlton circa 1973, all sparkling smile and unlined face.

"Shit. It didn't even dawn on me that these would be the only pictures of him they'd have. Dammit. Well, it's all we got. Let's get out of here."

~~~~

From his fifth floor perch Carlton watched the crowds gather around the Marriott entrance. Protesters and groupies kept in place behind their respective barricades by a phalanx of police – some on foot, others on horseback. Expensive cars belched out the *crème de la crème* of the City's elite liberal establishment, while behind the barricades an eclectic mix of the religious right, veterans' groups and taxpayers opposed to something-or-other screamed their disapproval and waved their placards in a furious attempt to attract the attention of roving bands of television cameras.

Ah, what people won't do to get on television, thought Carlton, and then admonished himself for his cynicism. Everybody wants to be heard. Even me. The difference, he told himself, was that he *was* going to be heard. Or at least his shot was going to be heard. The *Shot Heard 'Round the World*, he chuckled to himself.

He had no illusions. Most people would think him a common murderer. He wished it could be otherwise but knew that once Schaeffer's friends in the media penned their spin, the weight of public opinion would be heavily against him. He comforted himself by knowing he didn't have a choice. He'd taken the Oath.

He looked at his watch. 6:17 p.m. Little more than an hour to wait.

57

Thursday, July 8th
6:38 p.m.

By the time I parked the car, the atmosphere around the hotel entrance resembled a rock concert. People pushing and shoving each other behind the police barricades to get a better look at the arriving guests. The media was out in full force, the lights from their cameras blinding all as they swept the crowd.

Armed with our pictures of Carlton, Irvine and I fanned out. He took Market Street, I took Fourth. The first thing I did was to seek out the sergeant responsible for crowd control. Seeing him directing one of his crew, I walked over, introduced myself and asked how many patrolmen were on duty tonight.

"Every damn one who wants overtime," he said with a wry smile. "And you and I know that's damn near the whole force." He winked at me. Co-conspirators in budget- busting. "I got twenty-two officers here and another ten inside. Why?"

I took out my stack of photos. "Could you give each of your men a copy of one of these? We're looking for this guy on a homicide charge and have reason to believe he's somewhere in this crowd. Tell your people to keep an eye out for him. We think he is armed and dangerous and has nothing to lose. So tell them not to take any chances – but get him."

"You didn't give us much time," he said resignedly. For him it was just another thing to do. "How come you guys didn't pass these out at the noon briefing?"

"It's a long story, Sergeant. Just give them out, okay? I'd appreciate it."

He took the pictures and I started to leave. "Inspector?" he called to me. "I could be mistaken, but this guy looks familiar." My heart started to pound.

"You saw him? When?" I had to scream to make myself heard above the crowd noise.

"Let me think – I might be mistaken because the guy I saw was a lot older than this, and thinner. Like he was sick or something. But this sure looks like him. I could swear." He looked at the picture again. "Yeah, just a couple of hours ago. Right over there." He pointed to the opposite curb. "This guy rides up on a bicycle. He was really loaded down. Saddlebags on the bike. Had a backpack on his chest of all places, because he's got this big tube strapped to his back. Looked like he was doing some serious long-distance travel."

A bike, I thought. Of course. How simple. We had him walking. Hitchhiking. Taking a bus. Nobody thought of a bike. Except Carlton.

"Anyway, he stopped and asked me what all the fuss was about. I told him. We jawed a few minutes, and he rode off."

"Rode off?" The adrenalin was beginning to pump. The sense of the prey overwhelming. "Where did he ride off to? What direction?"

The sergeant nodded down Fourth Street. I turned and scanned the large buildings looming up on either side of the hotel. I patted the sergeant on the shoulder as I walked by and then started to sprint down the street. Past the barricades. Past the crowds. I stood in the middle of the street, a few latecomers looking at me strangely as they walked past. Frantically I scoured the windows of the buildings facing the Marriott. That was it, I was sure. He was going to shoot from one of these windows, à la Lee Harvey Oswald. But which one? I was looking at possibly a hundred windows, maybe more. As I turned from side to side in mounting frustration something caught my attention. What was it? A movement? The sun glinting off glass? My head jerked around, eyes searching. There! The building on the corner opposite me, a half block away, high up. I counted the floors. 5th floor. A window was being opened. "Holy shit!" I breathed, and started to run.

~~~~

Carlton noticed the man standing in the middle of the street about half-a-block away but didn't pay much attention. It was only after he'd slid the window open about a foot and saw the man running in his direction that he became curious. Picking up the M40, he sighted the running figure through the scope. *Son-of-a-bitch*, he thought with a mixture of both surprise and fear. *Tom McGuire*.

58

I should have kept the god-damn cell phone, I thought as I sprinted down the street. I could have gotten through to Irvine, and he would have diverted Schaeffer to another entrance. I thought about yelling and screaming and pointing in the direction of the open window, but I knew that in San Francisco most people wouldn't have paid any attention. Nothing new! They saw people yelling and screaming and pointing all the time.

I pushed through the glass door and noted the staircase off to my left. Too slow. I was already winded. If I tried to sprint up the stairs, I'd have been dead before I reached the third floor. Thankfully, the elevators were straight down the hall, and fortunately one had just arrived. I patiently waited as two young women got off. One looked at me as I repeatedly punched the *five* button, willing the door to close.

"No use being is such a hurry, Sir," she said over her shoulder. "I think we're the last people in the building. No one wanted to be trapped in the traffic nightmare caused by the big-wigs party at the Marriott tonight." I politely smiled and nodded as the door closed.

When the door finally opened on the fifth floor, I sprinted off, turning right down the corridor. To where I thought the office was. As soon as I heard his voice behind me, however, I knew I'd made a critical error.

"Tom", he said gently. Not a question. Not a threat. A greeting. I froze.

"Bob." A calmness in my voice that belied my fear. I started to turn.

"Don't move a muscle, please." The voice was not so gentle this time. Commanding! The hint of violence implicit. "I don't want to harm you, but I'll shoot you without a second thought if you make me. Everything you do from now on I want you to do in slow motion. Agreed?" I nodded. Didn't have much of a choice as far as I could see. "Hands by your side, please."

I did as I was told. Thinking of hostage negotiations. Hoping Carlton wouldn't pat me down.

"Now, slowly reach under your coat with your left hand and just tickle that pistol of yours out of the holster, butt first. No use being a hero." I did as I was told. "That's it. Now, just let it hang by your side."

In the movies, Clint Eastwood would have said, "Feeling lucky, punk?" Then he would dive to the floor, turn and fire all in one motion. I wasn't feeling that lucky. I was scared and did as I was told. I heard him walk up behind me. Almost tenderly, he took the weapon from my hand. "Okay. Let's go. The second door on the left."

It was a two-room office. Carpeted, but no furniture. A window opposite the doorway looked out at the Marriott. The door on the back wall leading to the second office was open. Out this office's window, I could see what a good job the cops had done of separating the crowd behind the barriers and keeping the street and entrance to the hotel clear. I could also see a knot of police officers standing around waiting for Schaeffer's limo to arrive.

He closed the door behind us. I felt the barrel of his gun at the base of my neck as he fished around my midsection until he found the cuffs. He clamped one on my left wrist and pulled me back toward the door, closing the other cuff around the doorknob. He then settled himself on the floor across from me near the window. Leaning back against the sill, he put the P7 and his own weapon in front of him on the carpet. On the floor to his left lay what looked to me like an ordinary scoped hunting rifle, though I knew better. To the rifle's immediate left was a small, framed picture of a couple smiling at the camera and holding hands. Carlton and his wife in happier times.

"Might as well sit down," he said. "We've got a few minutes yet."

I maneuvered my back against the wall and slid down to a sitting position, my left arm twisted behind me at an uncomfortable angle.

"Well, Tom, it's been a while," Carlton said nonchalantly. Like he was meeting a friend at a bar. Not a care in the world.

I didn't say anything for a minute or so. Just sat there appraising him. Looking for an opening. An edge. This was the hostage situation all over again. Except this time, I was the hostage. This time, I might just be negotiating for *my* life. I kept my right leg bent under me so he wouldn't notice the ankle holster.

"This probably isn't the right time to say this, Bob, given my present circumstances, but you look like shit." I wanted to come at him from an unexpected angle. Shake his confidence.

He smiled sadly at me. "That's because I'm dying, Tom. Pancreatic cancer. Been losing weight like a son-of-a-bitch lately. Of course, all this running around I've been doing hasn't helped. The doc said I had until November. Not a chance. I'll be dead by September or sooner." He cocked his head toward the Marriott. "Depending, of course, on what happens here tonight."

Well, that tactic certainly hadn't worked. No wonder they took me off the hostage negotiation team. I couldn't even get it right when it was *my* ass on the line. I tried again.

"Is this about revenge, Bob? Because if it is, you've already got it. You don't have to go any further. Payback's been accomplished."

"Is that what you think this is about? *Payback*?"

"Well, isn't it?"

"To be honest with you, Tom, that's how it started. After my wife died and I was diagnosed with cancer, I thought *what the hell*? These people deserved it. For what they did to me. For what they did to you. For what they did to our friends who paid the ultimate price because of those pricks. I didn't forget, Tom. I didn't forget *or* forgive. I'd have to die to forget that." He chuckled. "Ironic, huh? I *am* dying. But it's gone beyond that now, Tom. Far beyond that."

"Listen to me," I said in my best fatherly tone. "The war has been over almost thirty years, Bob. A lifetime. Enough killing to last ten lifetimes. For all of us. It's over, Bob. It's over! For you. For me. For Schaeffer."

"You're wrong, my friend. For Schaeffer the war was never over. He's in bed with the bad guys, Tom. He was during the war, and he is now. I've got the proof." A pause. "And so do you, come to think of it. You've got the tapes. Most of it is in there."

"I listened to them, Bob – well, the Wasserman one, anyway. I admit Schaeffer doesn't come off too well. And things've happened where I have questions myself. But you have nothing that would stand up in a court of law."

"Precisely! That's exactly what I told myself, too. And guess what? That's why I'm here – to do the right thing. To do what the justice system fifty years ago would've done to him. Before guys like him helped corrupt it." He was getting worked up. His rhetoric matching his rationale. "I've got other stuff, too, Tom." He said this in a much quieter voice. Willing himself to calm down. "Circumstantial, I'll admit. But you keep piling up those little pebbles on the Scale of Justice, and pretty soon it begins to tilt."

"Did the Scale of Justice tilt for Jennifer, and Heidi, and Rebecca?" I asked.

Carlton looked down at the floor, tracing circles in imaginary dust. "I feel badly about them, Tom. I really do. They were caught up in something way over their heads. But the fact remains – they did betray their country. Let me tell you a story, and then if you think I'm still off base, you can pull that hideout you've got strapped to your ankle and shoot me. I won't resist."

I sat there impassively. Trying not to give in to the panic spreading through me. My leg twitched beneath me.

"That's okay," he said soothingly. "I didn't expect anything different from you." He looked again at his watch and then out the window. "Do you remember guys named Dick Cross, Rick Panetta and Gary Lee?"

Regaining some composure, I replied, "Vaguely. POWs, right? I only remember them because early on we were trying to compile a list of everyone at the Hilton. Their names were tapped through the wall." I paused. "I'm sure you had a reason to ask. Wanna tell me?"

"A year before I got the cleaned, clothed, and fed treatment in preparation for meeting those women, five other prisoners were summoned. Those ladies had been to Vietnam before. Did you know that?"

"Yes. I'd heard that."

"They met with Cross, Panetta, Lee and two other guys – one named Jerry Whalen and the other McClatchy. Never learned his first name. The five devised a plan to get the word out that they were still alive. They didn't know if the North Vietnamese had reported they were prisoners.

"Each of the guys took a scrap of paper on which they wrote their Social Security number, crumpled it up and palmed it. The women went through their standard routine. Asking their inflammatory questions. *Aren't you sorry you bombed babies? Aren't you grateful for the humane treatment of your captors?* Well, these guys thought this was a joke. An act these women were putting on for the North Vietnamese. So while they were shaking the women's hands in front of the cameras, they each palmed off their scrap of paper. Once the cameras were turned off, these women turned to the North Vietnamese officer in charge and handed them those little papers.

"Cross, Panetta and Lee died from the subsequent beatings. That's why you don't know them so well. They didn't make it. Because of those four women. Whalen still can't raise his arms above shoulder level from the beatings he was subjected to. McClatchy was just never heard from again."

I'd heard that story before but didn't connect the four women with it. The cold brutality of their action made me wince – glad it wasn't me they met. And to tell the truth, I began to feel a little sympathy for Carlton. Like ... yeah, good for you. The bitches deserved it.

Not the right attitude for a cop. I felt the .40 pressing itself against my lower calf. A reminder of who I was.

"And Schaeffer was their sponsor," Carlton continued. "So he shared in the murder of those men. But that's not why I'm after him, Tom. Schaeffer's dirty."

"You said that before. But the question is, can you prove it?"

"Maybe not to the satisfaction of the New York Times or Washington Post. No. But I've been collecting stuff for about a year. Have it in a safe deposit box in San Bernardino. The key's in my saddlebag." He nodded toward the pile near where his bike stood. "You can get the whole story after I'm dead and buried. Promise me you'll at least read it."

"I'll read it." That's all I'd commit to. Didn't want to encourage him.

"He's got some real nasty friends, you know." This took me by surprise. Piqued my interest. I had some dealings with Schaeffer's friends recently. "He's tried to kill me twice, now – once in Riverside, and once up in Albion. Has word reached you about those two little episodes?"

"I just heard about them today, as a matter of fact."

"I'll tell you about it. But truth is, I'm surprised he hasn't paid *you* a visit yet." *He has*, I thought, as I remembered the open curtain in my house, and the two Asian Ghost dudes this afternoon. "He's got to know you've heard all the tapes. And I'll tell you, he can't let you live with that knowledge. Just a warning. I've been dealing with the son-of-a-bitch for the past few weeks, and he can get *real* nasty ... *real* quick. I'd be watching my back if I were you."

I just sat in silence, not wanting to give him an opening. I saw the green Toyota with the two Vietnamese dudes. And I thought about Michele. Hoping she was all right. "How do you know all this stuff about Schaeffer," I asked.

"I've got a friend in the FBI. When he found out about my *interest* in Schaeffer, he started feeding me information."

"But if they know so much, why don't they prosecute?"

Carlton toyed with the pistols in front of him. "It just shows you how far down the slippery slope we've come. The whole country has been so politicized. If the FBI went public with this, they'd be ridiculed from now until the next century. It'd be spun as just another vast right-wing conspiracy trying to bring down someone they don't agree with. But this is true with either the Republicans or the Democrats – everyone's just trying to protect his or her own turf. Don't give a good damn about the country. Let it all go to hell as long as their guy wins the next election." He paused, then asked, "Are you political, Tom?"

"I read the papers, if that's what you mean. But I'm not passionate about politics. I'm passionate about catching bad guys. I'm passionate about the Giants, and an occasional golf shot." And now Michele, I realized with certainty.

"During the time Schaeffer's been in office, a lot of questions have been raised about his business dealings with mainland China."

"You mean those high-tech exports? Yeah, I've read about them. But that's all been investigated and nothing's ever been proven as far as I know."

"Nothing public, at least. But some of the facts aren't disputed – that during his tenure as Governor, trade restrictions on the transfer of sensitive technology has been relaxed."

"I've read that. But why isn't that just politics? Why does it have to be something sinister? If you want to blame somebody, blame those greedy bastards who run the tech companies."

"They're at fault, too. No doubt about it. But just listen for a minute. What Schaeffer gave away to the Chinese was unlimited access to our military, civilian and dual-use technology that had been denied them under every other administration in history. Democrat and Republican.

"And what did he get in return? Tons of campaign cash. Funneled through contacts in Taiwan and Hong Kong. Through companies he allowed to do business in California. Since they're now legal California firms, technically no laws were broken. Cute, huh?"

"Your FBI friend again?" I asked somewhat cynically.

He pursed his lips and stared at me. I was evidently disappointing him.

"You know something, Tom?" he said resignedly. "There wouldn't be as many names on that black wall in D.C. if we didn't have so many Schaeffers in this country." He coughed. A deep rasping cough that spasmed his whole body. I felt sorry for him. What a way to check out.

When he'd calmed down, he looked at me with cheerless eyes. "God knows I'm not a brave man, Tom." He held up his hand as I started to protest. "No, I'm serious. I'm afraid of dying. I mean *really* afraid. Shouldn't be, huh? With all we went through. But you get the point. With the certainty of death hovering, you start looking at yourself, asking *what's it all about? Life! What difference have you made?*" He paused, caught his breath, and continued. "I had a good wife." He gestured to the picture on the floor. "She was a good woman. I watched her die. She had cancer, too. But she never complained. A tough lady. S*he* was brave one in this family." He stopped again and looked out the window. "We never had any kids. That was a real sorrow for both of us. Did you have kids, Tom?"

I nodded and held up one finger. "A boy," I mouthed.

"You're a lucky man. I'll bet he's a good kid, too. But that's what I meant by making a difference. See, you've made a difference already. You'll have someone to carry on your spirit, your values – hell, even your life after you've gone. Me? I have nothing. For all the difference I've made, I wonder why I was ever born.

"And that's essentially why I am here. In this room. On this particular day." He paused again, making a sweeping gesture with his hand. "Remember that old prof at the Academy? Stephen Springer – I got to thinking about him a year or so ago. About his class. I sent you the quote he used in class, remember? From Cicero. About how the glory of the gods is given to those who slay tyrants? Remember how he ended that class? By reminding us of the Oath we were about to take as Officers and Gentlemen? To defend the Constitution with our life, if necessary, from all enemies, both foreign and domestic. Both external enemies and internal enemies. A sacred Oath, Tom, in my view."

I just nodded. Wanting him to continue. To play out his anger. But he was right, it was a sacred Oath.

"As military guys, we focused on the external enemy. And why wouldn't we? This country never had any coups. No attempted military takeovers. Things which other countries experienced all the time throughout their history.

"When Mary got sick, I started thinking about those things. Right after she died, it becomes public that Schaeffer was thinking of running for President."

I could see where he wanted to take this. I played along. "You're telling me that Schaeffer is a Marxist? That once he gets in he would just disregard the Constitution? Is that what you're saying?"

"Yeah, something like that."

"But, Bob, this is a democracy. In a democracy the people get to choose what kind of government they want."

"That's a real paradox, don't you think, Tom? You're telling me that in a democracy the people get to choose that they don't want a democracy anymore?"

"I don't know – I never thought about this, but I suppose it's possible that people could vote to abrogate the Constitution."

"Abrogate? Good word. You must've had a good education." He smiled. "But remember your Oath, Tom. You took the Oath to protect and defend that Constitution. Against guys just like this. Who would – your word –*abrogate* the Constitution. If you don't stop him now what chance do you have once he's elected? There will be no more Constitution on which to fight him."

I couldn't think of anything to say. Try as I might to resist, I found myself being drawn in by the argument.

"And the country is already in sorry shape because of people like him," he continued. "The Courts are a mess. The Constitution has been foisted off on us as a 'living document.' What a bunch of crap *that* is. It's a prescription for tyranny. Hell, Tom, how can you have a *rule of law* when the law can be interpreted by those in power any damn way they please? How'd you like to play poker with no rules? I take that back. How would you like to play poker with me under *my* rules? Rules I could change anytime I wanted to depending on my whim at that moment? I'd say *sorry, my two deuces beat your three of a kind.* Want to live in a society like that?"

I glanced out the window. The Marriott was still quiet. Carlton saw me look and checked his watch.

We sat in silence for a while. I thought of the scene from the movie *High Noon.* The hands of the clock inching toward 12. *Tick-tock! Tick-tock!* A countdown to the inevitable. Judgment Day approaching.

"We're still a democracy, Bob," I said. "And in a democracy people get what they deserve." It was an old platitude, but I didn't know what else to say.

"Only if they know the consequences beforehand," he said back. "Do you think the Italians voted for Mussolini because he was a Fascist? Of course not! Italy was in deep shit after the first war. They voted for him because he promised to make the trains run on time. But look what they got.

"And look at our own personal innkeeper, Uncle Ho! How many Vietnamese knew he was a Communist? Hell, how many Vietnamese even knew what a Communist was? No, Uncle Ho was popular because he was a *Nationalist*. And look what he did – loved his country so much he killed a few million Catholics and enslaved the rest of his people. You think they bargained on that? Peasants sent to *re-education camps*? The terrible slaughter in the South that took place in '75 and '76? Are you telling me

317

those people knew what the hell they were getting into? You know better than that."

We heard the commotion simultaneously and both turned toward the window. The anti-Schaeffer faction behind the barriers started yelling and shaking their signs, while the pro-Schaeffer contingent, not to be outdone, was equally boisterous.

"Well, class is almost over," he said with a poignant smile. "One more thing. Those people I blew up in my house in Riverside? They were members of a Vietnamese gang. Schaeffer mobilized them to come after me. What does that say to you? Think about it."

I was thinking of other things. About how Bristow took me off the case. Of how easy that was. One phone call from Sacramento.

"And the guys up in Albion?" he continued.

I looked at him blankly.

"Schaeffer sent guys after me up there, too. Six of them. I'm gonna guess they were ex-Stasi. But you can find out for sure. I brought you a little present." He reached into his shirt pocket and threw me the key to the handcuffs. "Undo yourself and crawl over to the saddlebags. Inside the left pocket is a baggie."

As I was unlocking the cuff Carlton picked up my P7 and pointed it at me. "I don't want you to get too frisky just yet." I wasn't thinking of doing anything rash, and I shook my head in assurance. My arm hurt like hell from being attached to the doorknob. It felt good just to have the damn cuff off.

I picked through his clothes until my hand found the plastic bag. Inside were the tips of five index fingers, all having turned a pale bluish white and already starting to shrivel.

"And what I am I supposed to do with these?" I said, holding the bag at arms' length.

"Pocket them. You won't have a chance to get to them when shit hits the fan here in a minute or two. Get fingerprints from them and find who they belong to. Like I said, I'm guessing Russian or East German ex-military."

"If that's true, there's *no way* I'm going to be able to get a match. They won't release that information."

"Then give them to the FBI. They'll be able to get a match. Now, throw the key back over here and go re-cuff yourself. That's for your own protection, depending on what you decide to do here. But also, I want to put you in a position where you actually have to shoot me if you want to stop me from killing Schaeffer."

As I snapped the cuff back around my wrists, I asked, "And you're convinced that Schaeffer sent those men to your place?"

"Do I have proof that would stand up in court?" he answered. "Probably not."

But those pebbles, I thought to myself. Those damn pebbles. They just kept piling up.

59

I t's all over but the shooting, Carlton thought as he laid the barrel of the M40 on the sill, adjusting the scope to eye-level.

He'd tried his case against Schaeffer and now awaited the jury's verdict – it wouldn't be long. He sensed McGuire squirming behind him and thought he heard the metallic scrape of the hideout gun as it cleared his ankle holster. Can't worry about that now, his conscious mind told him. It's in the hands of a higher authority. Right now, you've got to concentrate on the task at hand.

The 2.5x10 scope brought the Marriott entrance so close he felt he could actually touch the people frantically scurrying around making sure everything was in order.

Schaeffer's black limousine pulled up to the curb. Two men came running from the entrance of the hotel to the car. Carlton followed them in the scope. *Lackeys*, he thought derisively. One reached down to open the rear door of the car – Carlton could read the dial of his watch that peeked out from under the pink shirt.

He felt the beads of perspiration forming on his forehead. He felt one stream toward his eye. With his right hand he quickly flicked it away.

Two men stepped from the back of the car – like moths emerging from a black cocoon. And then a third. Schaeffer! Everyone stepped back, allowing him space. After adjusting his coat and brushing back his hair, Schaeffer slowly turned and waved, acknowledging the crowd.

Carlton pinpointed the crosshairs on a spot an inch above Schaeffer's left ear. He took a deep breath and slowly tightened the pressure on his trigger finger.

"Don't, Bob," the voice behind him said. "Don't. He's not worth it. You have the evidence. Use it. Bring him down that way. Don't do this."

Keeping a steady pressure on the trigger, Carlton replied quietly, "Our Oath, Tom. Remember our Oath."

~~~~

As soon as Carlton peered through his scope I lifted my pant leg and withdrew the .40 from its holster. From the crowd noise I could tell Schaeffer had arrived. *Tick-tock! Tick-tock*! The hands of the clock inching inexorably toward *High Noon*.

From then on, everything happened in slow-motion. I could see a bead of sweat slowly trickle its way down Carlton's forehead. His right arm moved upward and wiped it away. Frame by slow-motion frame.

I brought up the .40 and aimed it at the back of his head.

"Don't, Bob," I pleaded. "Don't. He's not worth it. You have the evidence. Use it. Bring him down that way. Don't do this." The whole of my being focused on his trigger finger as it slowly increased its pressure. My own finger mimicking his.

His quiet voice. "Our Oath, Tom. Remember our Oath."

The concussive explosion of the gunshot in the small room was deafening.

Eight Months Later

Michele was the only person I ever told what really happened in the room that day. And she had it right – if Schaeffer was too damn paranoid to take the necessary precautions, he deserved to get himself killed. And that's exactly what happened.

After firing the shot, Carlton quickly crawled over and released me. "Be a lot of activity around here soon," he said. "Best if you're not here." While I was retrieving my P7, he got the key to his safe deposit box and tossed it to me. "Remember, you promised." I could see the beginning of tears forming in his eyes. Trying unsuccessfully to blink them away, he gave me a hug and whispered in my ear. "There was no other way. Thanks." Just that, and nothing more. I nodded and walked out the door. That was the last time I ever saw him. Exiting the elevator on the first floor, I heard the muffled whump of the pistol shot.

News events have a short shelf life in modern America, and the assassination of Governor Schaeffer was no exception.

For the first month the murder/suicide was the topic of every major talk show on both radio and

television. Schaeffer and Carlton's lives, both pre-
and post-Vietnam, were scrutinized from all angles.
Every psychiatrist and sociologist who hungered for
notoriety was interviewed for his or her "expert"
opinion. But in the end the public simply grew tired
of it all. The sides had been drawn – you either
believed Carlton was a genuine hero and Schaeffer a
scoundrel, or you believed the opposite. And it pretty
much fell along partisan lines, much like Carlton
predicted. Nothing presented now was going to
change any minds, so people just lost interest and
went on to something else.

In mid-August I took a few days off and drove to
San Bernardino. I emptied and closed Carlton's safety
deposit box.

Later that month an FBI agent named John
McGarry visited me. He explained he'd heard Carlton
gave me recordings of interviews conducted with his
victims. If so, would I give them to him? The Feds
were gathering evidence for a case against Schaeffer.
Not only did I give him the tapes and the contents of a
safety deposit box, but from my freezer a baggie
containing five frozen index fingers. I never heard
another word from McGarry or the Feds.

I have no regrets. Schaeffer was probably dirty,
and he paid for it with his life. I kept my promise to
Carlton and my honor intact. Whatever happened
from now on was out of my control.

Michele moved in with me that December. Later
that month I let her drive the Mustang for the first
time – we plan on getting married in the summer and

have been kicking around the date of July 8th in honor of Bob Carlton who brought us together.

The Giants ended the season with ninety wins and seventy-two losses. It was enough to get them into the playoffs. The joy was short-lived, unfortunately, when the Mets eliminated them in the first round of the NLCS. I've just returned from a week in Phoenix watching Spring Training. The weather was warm, the sky blue, and the new grass smelled heavenly. The season opens next week. I really think the Giants have a shot at making the Series this year.

The property stolen in the Wagner murder never hit the streets. The Captain of Investigations announced his retirement effective in September, and the rumor is that Matt Bristow will be promoted. Irvine and I have five murder cases sitting on our desk.

Life goes on!

###

Thank you for purchasing this Pen Books paperback.

Please remember to leave a review at your favorite retailer.

DENNIS KOLLER is author of the popular Tom McGuire suspense series including *The Oath*, *Kissed By The Snow*, and his latest, *The Custer Conspiracy*. Mr. Koller lives in the San Francisco Bay Area.

Learn more about his work at www.DennisKoller.com

Made in the USA
San Bernardino, CA
09 April 2018